THE
BACKPACKING
HOUSEWIFE

Jan... Horton writes contemporary romantic fiction with ... dash of humour and a sense of adventure. In 201... fter her children had left home, Janice and her husb...nd set off to explore the Caribbean. In 2015, they retu...ed to the UK only to sell their material possessio... in favour of travelling around the world.

🐦 @JaniceHorton
📘 www.facebook.com/TheBackpackingHousewife
📷 www.instagram.com/janicehortonwriter/
www.thebackpackinghousewife.com

THE BACKPACKING HOUSEWIFE

JANICE HORTON

A division of HarperCollins Publishers

www.harpercollins.co.uk

Harper*Impulse*
an imprint of HarperCollins*Publishers* Ltd
1 London Bridge Street
London SE1 9GF

www.harpercollins.co.uk

First published in Great Britain by HarperCollins*Publishers*
Ltd 2018

A catalogue copy of this book is available from the British
Library.

ISBN: 9780008302696

Printed and bound by CPI Group (UK) Ltd, Croydon, CR0 4YY

MIX
Paper from
responsible sources
FSC
www.fsc.org   FSC® C007454

To my own real-life hero: Trav

Chapter 1

Bangkok

I've arrived in Bangkok feeling jettisoned and adrift, exhausted, jetlagged, and asking myself – what the hell am I doing here all on my own? In the long line for customs, I stand with everyone else who was on my flight from London. My eyes are fixed on those around me who look so happy and purposeful, so clearly excited to be in the most popular city in the world, while I'm sweltering in my jeans and long-sleeved, far-too-heavy cotton shirt. I've never suffered from a fear of crowds before, but now I do, and I can hardly breathe.

When it's my turn, my passport is scanned, my fingerprints are taken, and I'm given a passing glance together with a thirty-day entry stamp into Thailand. I follow the masses pouring through luggage collection and into the arrivals hall, where behind a barrier, taxi touts push and shove and yell and uniformed chauffeurs wave and shout and people are holding up cards with stranger's names on them. I'm overwhelmed.

Once outside the terminal, it feels like I've walked into a wall of incredible heat and oppressive humidity and an onslaught of noise and voices at fever pitch. Tuk-tuk and taxi drivers beep their horns and jostle aggressively for position at the kerbside. The racket is deafening and the fumes are nauseating. Chatter fills my head – thousands of voices in so many different languages. Odours in the air assault my nose – the unwashed and the over-perfumed smells are so strong that I can taste them on my tongue. Everyone seems so preoccupied with pushing suitcases and gathering children and moving on quickly to wherever they are going that they knock into me without apology or care, as if I'm invisible.

I look around at beggars in rags on pavements with their arms outstretched to well-dressed tourists. I see beautiful and very young Thai girls with long black silky hair and tight dresses, laughing and hanging onto the arms of far older, overweight Western men.

Why couldn't I have run away to somewhere quieter, less smelly, much less scary?

'Lady! Lady! Taxi! Taxi!'

I allow myself to be led to a taxi by an enthusiastic and smiling Thai man and I give him the address of a hotel. I have no idea where it is, or how far, but I'm suddenly too tearful and weary to care. As it is, the smiling taxi driver is a gentleman. He whisks me through the hustle and bustle of the city with the speed and dexterity of a knight in shining armour and delivers me to the safety of my hotel. I drag myself across the sticky vinyl car seat into the hot and humid space that now exists between me and the revolving polished glass doors of the hotel's lobby.

A uniformed doorman immediately rushes to my assistance. I see him hesitate, looking for luggage before realising there is none, then with a smile he ushers me inside. I look round at the opulence – the polished marble, the shiny surfaces, the huge crystal chandeliers, the sparkly water features – which under any other circumstances would have thrilled and impressed me but right now just add to the surreality of my situation.

I walk over to reception feeling completely out of sorts. A very tall, slim, pretty receptionist wearing a body-hugging, green silk dress smiles at me.

I try to smile back, but my lips have so long been set to stoic they don't want to obey me.

'*Sawatdee ka*,' she says, bowing her head graciously.

I repeat the salutation, noting from her name badge that she is called Lola.

'Welcome to Bangkok, madam. Are you checking in?'

I can't help but admire Lola's curiously strong angular

features and her beautiful waist-length long black hair. She is tall and broad-shouldered.

I feel my face softening. 'Yes please. My name is Lorraine Anderson.'

'Ah, yes. I see you have booked one of our Executive Suites, Miss Anderson.'

I would normally have insisted on being addressed as Mrs Anderson, but I didn't bother this time.

I just nod, feeling embarrassed at how red-faced and dishevelled I must look, a fact confirmed to me when I catch sight of myself in a mirrored column.

But why should I even care when nobody knows me here?

And sod the expense of the Executive Suite. It might have been the only room available to me at the time I booked, but right now it's exactly what I need. I'm pretty sure it's going to be a damn sight easier for me to cry myself to sleep in a luxury hotel suite than in a crowded backpacker hostel.

'Just the one night, madam?'

'Yes.' I hand over my credit card and then have a bit of a panic.

I mean, what the hell happens tomorrow?

While fighting tears at check-in at Gatwick, all I'd managed to think about was the here and now. But what happens next? Where I will go? What I will do?

I have absolutely no idea. My life has been turned upside down and I'm in freefall.

It's as if Lola can read my mind. 'I can offer you a complimentary late checkout?'

'Yes, please,' I stammer gratefully.

And Lola's lovely long nails *tap tap tap* on her computer keyboard.

I start shaking and my teeth begin chattering in the chill of the air-conditioned lobby.

She passes me a key card. 'Enjoy your stay Miss Anderson. Your room is on the fifteenth floor. Suite 1507. Do you need any help with your bags?'

The suite is as decadent as I'd hoped. It has a womb-like ambiance and sumptuous carpets and soft lighting across several interconnecting rooms, all with luxurious furniture and fittings. The bathroom is a dream in marble and glass, with soft white fluffy towels, and there is a vast selection of very nice toiletries. I score a bottle of wine from the not-so-mini mini-bar and take it and a goblet-sized wine glass into the bathroom with me while I take a long soak in a deep bubble bath. In the warm water I lie back and close my eyes, feeling safe at last.

A while later, feeling cleaner and calmer and cosseted in a white fluffy robe, I stand at the bedroom's floor-to-ceiling windows looking out at the bright twinkling lights of the busy city below me. I take a long gulp of my wine and then a long and steady deep breath.

On slowly breathing out, I let the feeling of surrealism and distance soothe me.

I tell myself that everything is going to be okay. Here I am, in a city of my dreams, in a country that has always been number one on our travel hitlist. My aching shoulders stiffen when I realise I've used the word 'our' in my thoughts again. Have I been married for so long that it is impossible to think of myself as one single individual person anymore?

Charles and I had always said we'd explore South East Asia together in our retirement, which we intended to take early, while we were still young and healthy and able-bodied.

It was a retirement for which we had saved meticulously and planned relentlessly.

Suddenly, I find it amusing that I'm in Bangkok with no prior planning whatsoever.

I slug back what's left in my glass and start to laugh. Hysterically. Then I crawl into bed, pull the sheet over my head, and cry long shuddering sobs.

How could he do it? How long had it been going on?

What a fool I'd been, thinking we were happily married. Thinking people actually admired our long successful marriage. When in fact, it had all been a lie. A joke. A joke on me.

Not only had I been betrayed, I'd been totally humiliated.

I'm suddenly convinced that everyone except stupid, gullible and trusting me had known that my marriage was a sham – that my husband was an adulterous cheat and my best friend was a lying whore. I hadn't had a freaking clue.

My mind is in a loop replaying the events of yesterday over and over again, in slow motion.

Was it only yesterday?

In hindsight, I realise now that her silver BMW had been parked outside my house.

For heaven's sake – that was a freaking big clue!

I felt so angry, so betrayed. I'd wanted to kill them both violently. But rather than a knife, for some reason I'd grabbed my passport from the kitchen drawer and saved myself all the hacking and bloodshed by calling an Uber to take me straight to the airport.

And at the airport, a strangely calm and rational part of me had stepped up to take control, logged into our savings account via the banking app on my phone and transferred half the money into my account. Then I'd bought a ticket to the furthest away destination listed on the flight departures board. Normally, in planning for such a trip, I'd have certainly travelled economy and I'd have packed meticulously, choosing at leisure which lightweight stylish outfits to pack in my shiny hard-shell suitcase, that came with TSA approved locks and a lifetime guarantee.

But the little voice of calm and rational thought in my head told me I had no choice but to pay for a business class seat because economy was already full, and that buying a rucksack, a couple of sundresses and a sarong in the duty-free while waiting for my gate to be announced would easily suffice on this occasion.

It's November and, just like me, London was cold and dark and miserable. Yet at the other side of the airport, in the departures terminal building at Gatwick, it was like being in a parallel universe of blindingly hot tropical colours and ultra-light fabrics and high-factor sunscreen and designer sunglasses. It was the middle of the afternoon, but the champagne and oyster bar was pulling in the revellers. Wine and cocktails and beers were being knocked back in the faux olde English pub and people were partying in the premium lounges like they were already at their destinations. I felt like a gate-crasher to the party.

I bought a few items of clothing and a squishy travel pillow and a small carry-on size backpack, as I'd come through check-in and security with nothing other than my phone and my handbag.

Then, seeing my gate had already been announced and my plane was boarding, I ran for what must have been half a mile to the gate in such a panic that I hadn't time for reticent thoughts or last-minute misgivings.

On boarding the plane, I'd planned to have just one glass of wine and then, in my extra-large, extra-comfortable, extra-reclining, extra-expensive seat, to sleep for the whole journey. Then I wouldn't have to think about what I was doing, where I was going, and what on earth I would do when I got there. But instead, I drank my welcome glass of champagne with gusto and then continued drinking wine while watching back-to-back movies for twelve hours instead, until it felt like my eyes were falling out my head and we were descending into Bangkok.

Early this morning, I was woken by the light of a brand-new day scorching through a gap in the floor-to-ceiling curtains and across the king-sized bed towards me like a hot laser beam.

I was covered in sweat from a nightmare. It was every married woman's worst nightmare.

In it, I was standing in my bedroom doorway at home with my mouth open but mute and with open eyes that couldn't blink, watching my husband thrusting himself ecstatically into the naked, voluptuous and pendulous flesh of someone I'd previously called my best friend.

It was horrifying. It was disgusting. It was sickening.

On waking, realising where I was and that it had been real and not just a nightmare, I leapt from the bed to rush to the bathroom to throw up. But I could only dry-retch, as I'd eaten nothing since I could remember. Reeling back into the bedroom, I checked my mobile phone and saw that I had lots of 'call me back' messages from my two worried sons.

I also saw my phone was almost out of charge, but I didn't have a two-pin charger.

Instead of calling my sons back, I texted instead.

I'm fine. I'm at the Holiday Inn in Bangkok. Don't worry.

I'd already spoken to my mum and my sons from Gatwick. I'd been in a bit of a state.

Well, that's an understatement, I'd been in a hell of a state.

My mum had been just as distraught and as angry as I was when I told her what Charles had done to me. Josh and Lucas aren't children anymore, they're grown men in their twenties – so although they, too, were upset, they'd also understood my reasons for leaving their father.

'Mum, stay right where you are. I'm coming to get you!' Josh, my eldest, had insisted.

'No. darling, please, I need to get away. I'll call you when I get there.'

'Where is there? Where are you going, Mum?'

'As far away from your father and his whore as I can possibly get!' I'd yelled into my phone.

Now, feeling faint with hunger, I brush my teeth and shower, before slipping into one of the lightweight dresses I'd bought at Gatwick and deciding I'll be brave and go down for breakfast.

I seem to be operating on autopilot. Not so much thinking but functioning. My head hurts from crying, jetlag and dehydration. Downstairs, I manage to buy painkillers, a two-pin plug adapter in the hotel shop, and order coffee and a chocolate chip muffin at the lobby café. It's 1 p.m. local time and so breakfast has apparently been over for quite some time.

The café is busy. I sit at a table next to a couple of middle-aged American ladies who are chatting to each other enthusiastically over a tourist map and planning their afternoon sightseeing. 'I say we go to the Grand Palace and the Emerald Buddha,' says the blonde one.

'Or, we could head over to the temple on the river and save the palace and the Buddha for tomorrow?' suggests the redheaded one.

I listen. These are all places I've dreamed of seeing myself for as long as I can remember.

But now, in such stressful, horrible and lonely circumstances, I doubt I've the confidence or the courage to go out amongst the heaving crowds of strangers to explore alone.

Which makes me question what I'm doing here, if

I'm too scared to even leave the hotel? I could have stayed in London and done the same thing, after all. The two women suddenly stop talking to each other and look directly at me.

I'm tearing my muffin apart into bite sized pieces.

'Which would you recommend, honey? Have you done the palace yet?' asked the blonde.

I falter at being spoken to so unexpectedly. I guess I'm still feeling invisible.

'Oh, erm, I'm sure you must go and see them all.'

'Oh, you're English,' they both say in unison, sounding delighted. 'I love your accent!'

I nod. 'Yes. But I just arrived here last night, so I'm not really the best person to ask.'

'There is so much to see. If you're wondering what to do first, then our advice would be to go to the floating market. It's wonderful. We went last night, didn't we, Marcie?'

Redheaded Marcie nods eagerly. 'Oh, yes, you must. There's wooden boats on the river all piled up with things for sale and local food being cooked right from the boat. It's amazing!'

I smile and nod my head again as if I'm agreeing, but I don't want to go to a floating market. I don't want to go to the palace. I just want to go back up to my room and close the curtains and cry. But I only have another couple of hours or so to decide to either book another night at this hotel or to move on. But to where? I really don't know yet. I don't know what to do. What an odd feeling it is to be so disconnected from normal life.

Here I am; a stranger in a strange land full of strangers.

Yet this feeling of total anonymity has ignited something within me too.

It's a weird feeling. What is it? Excitement? Freedom?

I realise I could start my life anew. I could be someone else entirely, if I wanted.

Because no one knows me here. No one knows anything about me.

Marcie and Joanie continue chattering. They tell me how they've been friends for years but they both now live in different countries. Marcie lives in Australia on the Gold Coast. Joanie lives in Kuala Lumpur, Malaysia. Both their husbands, they tell me, are in banking.

'Boring men who'd rather stay at home than travel!' they chorus gleefully.

'Sounds like my husband,' I agree, wondering why I'd even mentioned him.

'So, we meet up in a different place every year and tick something else off our bucket list,' Joanie tells me. 'Last year, we met up in Hong Kong.'

Marcie roars with laughter. 'Oh, yeah, we had a ball in Hong Kong!'

When we part, the ladies go off laughing and chatting and I go back up to my room. I sit on my bed and plug my phone into its charger, thinking about my own bucket list. I do have one. I've had one for a long time. Only, until now, it's been more of a wish list.

My phone suddenly comes back to life and I see I have two new messages.

One is from Sally, the traitorous whore, and one is from my lying husband.

I can hardly believe their nerve in texting me.

Especially as it's so obviously coordinated.

I open Sally's first. In it, she says she's sorry for the way I'd found out about her and Charles, but apparently, she's not sorry about their affair (which she calls a 'relationship') that has been going on for over a year. *I want you to know Charles and I are in love and that he was planning to leave you.* I feel like her hand has just come right through the phone and slapped my face.

My anger flares up again. Tears of betrayal fill my eyes and pour down my cheeks.

How can this be true? For over a year? How could I not have known about this?

Have there been any tell-tale clues, that I've missed?

Receipts for things I hadn't known about? Meals, hotels, gifts?

Has Charles' behaviour over the past year been an indication?

He'd been a little distant. Uncaring on occasions. Indifferent, certainly.

Should I have been going through his pockets and secretly checking his phone records?

We hadn't been having sex. Was that a factor?

I'd just assumed we were typical of all couples who'd been married a long time.

Charles works long hours for seven days a week, running our business. He often complained of being tired. I understood when he fell asleep in front of the TV at the end of the day. But what kind of wife doesn't have a clue that her husband is fucking another woman?

A busy one? A preoccupied one? A trusting one?

An incredibly stupid one?

I open Charles's message next. It's written in short, sharp sentences, exactly the way he speaks in real life. *Lorraine, I'm divorcing you. We haven't been happy in a long time. Let's keep things amicable. Best of luck. Charles.*

Divorce! Amicable? Luck?!

His reason for having an affair is that we haven't been *happy* in a long time?

On the contrary, it sounds to me like Charles has been very happy indeed.

Going balls deep in Sally behind my back while planning to leave me!

But he's right about one thing. I haven't been happy. I'm not happy.

I've been bloody miserable for as long as I can remember!

It seems clear to me now that I've spent my whole life waiting to be happy on his terms.

Charles is eight years older than me. I was only twenty-two when we met and started dating. We both worked at a travel agency office in town back then. He was the branch manager and I was on the sales desk. It was my dream job and he was my dream boyfriend. He seemed so worldly. Charles and I fell in love over our passionate plans to explore the world together.

During our working day, our job was to plan detailed travel itineraries for our adventurous clients. But in the evenings, sitting in our local pub over two half pints of beer, we would talk endlessly about all the faraway countries that we wanted to visit one day, the interesting places we wanted to see and the incredible experiences we wanted to have when we got there.

We'd plan routes across India, taking in the Golden Triangle of Delhi, Agra, and Jaipur. We'd look at flights to exotic destinations like South East Asia, Japan, Korea and China. We'd investigate travelling by train all the way from Beijing to Hong Kong. We'd even fully researched and planned a three-thousand-mile road trip all the way from the Canadian Rockies to the Mexican Border. Charles used to say to me: 'Don't call it a dream, call it a plan.'

And it seemed that the whole world was ours for the living and for the travelling.

He filled me with wanderlust and inspiration and excitement.

I thought we were soul mates and kindred roaming spirits.

Every summer, on a limited budget, we used up all our holiday leave and money travelling.

We mostly backpacked around Europe: France, Italy, Spain, Portugal, the Greek islands... Charles and I were always talking about and planning and saving up for our next trip. At work, we were surrounded by glossy travel brochures and the spirit of travel and the promise of exotic adventures in lands far away.

Then, a few years later, everything changed. We got married.

Charles and I moved into a flat in town above a shop where we'd decided to set up our very own travel agency. Those were the days before the internet made independent travel possible. Back then, everyone expected to book their holidays through a high street travel shop. We were good at selling the idea of travel and our business boomed. It was the early Nineties and people at that time were starting to look further afield for their holidays. It was a time when those who usually went to Malta and Gibraltar were choosing to go to Turkey and Cyprus instead. Families who would usually opt for the Costas in Spain were starting to consider Florida, for a change.

Then the recession hit, interest rates went through the roof and for the next few years, instead of travelling, holidaymakers stayed at home and we ploughed all our time and money into our now struggling business. Instead of all those inspiring travel quotes, Charles's mantras soon became 'success is a journey, not a destination'.

Well, that's what happens, isn't it? When you get married, your life and priorities change.

Free and single becomes, well, something else, and life gets in the way.

Then our kids came along and the business picked up and life was steady again. I loved being a mother and family life was blissfully happy. But, of course, it was all-consuming when it came to my time and energy. Soon, we needed to move 'up in the world' by selling our little rented flat over the shop to buy a detached townhouse with a garden for our two rambunctious little boys.

We certainly needed the space, even if it was going to be a struggle to afford the mortgage.

When our boys were a little older, we decided to invest in their future and put them both through a very good private school. This was a good decision, which paid dividends in the long run, with both our boys going on to achieve straight As and places at top universities. Everyone said we had it all. And, indeed, it seemed that we did.

A lovely home. A successful business. Two wonderful clever sons who made us proud.

Charles went on to expand the business by investing in the new technology of the time.

Money was tight, so again, we forfeited any holidays or weekends away.

But soon, we not only had the shop in town, we also had an effective and profitable travel website too. I didn't have to work anymore. I was a homemaker. A housewife.

I threw myself into any voluntary work that came my way so that I could feel purposeful.

I did two afternoons a week in a charity shop in town. I helped out at the local hospice and at the homeless shelter and the food bank. At weekends, I worked at an animal shelter.

It made me feel good about myself when I was helping those less fortunate.

I sincerely hoped that I could make a difference in the world.

Then, before we knew it, the boys had both graduated from university and left home.

We suddenly found we were empty-nesters with our mortgage finally paid off.

But instead of taking time out for holidays together or even mini-breaks, like other couples our age seemed to be able to do, we were still scrimping and saving every damned penny.

What for this time, you might ask?

Well, for our retirement and our much-promised trip around the world, of course.

Not as backpackers as we'd always planned, but as 'flashpackers' according to Charles.

He'd decided he didn't want to 'slum it' at his age and he delighted in telling anyone who'd listen all about his considerable and epically adventurous bucket list. When Charles retired he wanted to see the Grand Canyon in Arizona, watch the changing colours of autumn leaves in New England, walk along the Great Wall of China, marvel at the Taj Mahal in India, see the Northern Lights from Iceland, scuba dive on the Great Barrier Reef, trek to Machu Picchu in Peru and climb Kilimanjaro in Tanzania. His list was the subject of every dinner party we attended, and I was getting sick to death of hearing about it and not actually doing it.

My own bucket list was a little different as I really hate being cold and I'm not so keen on heights. But it was still the stuff of dreams. I wanted to walk barefoot along white sand beaches on tiny tropical islands. I wanted to laze about on a hot afternoon in a hammock with a good book. I wanted to sit in the shade of a palm tree and drink a rum cocktail from a coconut shell. I wanted to find hidden waterfalls in the midst of steamy jungles. I wanted to sit in golden temples and experience inner peace and to meditate until I had a quiet mind. I wanted to see the world's most endangered species – not in a zoo, but thriving in the wild. I also wanted to learn to scuba dive in warm seas and to swim through a colourful coral reef garden with turtles and dolphins and whales (I draw the line at sharks) – not in a water park but in the open seas.

And I honestly thought we'd have all the time in the world to tick every single dreamy wish off both our bucket lists, because Charles had always promised me faithfully that he would sell the business and take early retirement when he reached the age of fifty-five.

Well, the bastard will be fifty-five this year – and now he's leaving me!

I scream into my pillow until my throat is sore. Then I stare out of the window again at the sprawling, hot and chaotic city beneath me and I realise that I am in the wrong place to deal with this kind of shit. I need somewhere I can pull myself together.

I need a golden temple to meditate in until I have a quiet mind and can contemplate a future.

I know there are plenty of places in Thailand far more laidback than Bangkok.

I decide for my sanity that I need to go to one of these places until I'm ready to come back here.

So I pick up my phone and book a flight to Chiang Mai in the northern part of Thailand.

I know from all the countless trips to Thailand that I have arranged over the years for our clients, that Chiang Mai is very different to Bangkok. It's known for its slower pace of life. It's an ancient moated city which, thanks to its conservation laws, has mostly stayed intact with it seven-hundred-year-old walls and lack of high-rise buildings. The city is filled with beautiful old buildings, golden temples, sacred shrines, galleries, museums, restaurants and coffee shops.

It's a place that seems like the perfect fit for my current mood.

Chapter 2

Chiang Mai

The flight from Bangkok to Chiang Mai takes a little over an hour. When I arrive, the sun is shining in a clear blue sky and, although it is still boiling hot with temperatures in the high thirties, I immediately find it less humid and polluted than claustrophobic Bangkok.

I take in great gulps of the fresher air and feel my head clearing.

I take a taxi from the airport to the old part of the city and watch the wonders of Chiang Mai unfold in front of my eyes. Here, at last, I can really feel the benefit of time and distance working in my favour. My thoughts this morning are heavily focussed on self-preservation.

It has occurred to me that if I'm going to be alone in future then a positive mindset is going to be my strongest tool for survival. I don't have to be a betrayed wife and a sad empty-nester – I realise I have a choice. I can be the old me, or I can be set free.

It's simply a matter of shifting my perspective.

A small, dirty child runs to my taxi as we wait in traffic in the narrow streets. She bangs her tiny fist insistently on the window where I am sitting. The driver yells something and waves his arms dismissively to scare her away. In her hand, the girl has a small packet of tissues to sell and she waves it at me. Her pretty face is imploring me to buy from her. I wind down the window, much to my driver's irritation, and give her a hundred baht note – the equivalent of around two pounds in sterling. In exchange, she throws me a delighted smile and the tissues and I smile back at her. I don't need the tissues. I suppose I just wanted to do a small act of kindness in the remote hope that karma might smile back on me and provide a little compassion in return.

I feel like I need all the help I can get.

My accommodation of choice is a family-run home-stay. It's ridiculously inexpensive for a three-night stay when I consider what I've just paid for one night in Bangkok. The moment I arrive, climbing out of my taxi in a quiet shady side street just a few minutes' walk from the old square, it's glaringly obvious to me that I'd underestimated how long I should stay here.

The place is simply gorgeous. The house is of a bygone age. Traditionally built in the local thick, honey-coloured stone, it has a first-floor terrace overlooking the street and its long oak balustrade is covered with twisted flowering vines. It looks so weathered by its history and by everything around it, and so reflective of what was once here in the ancient capital city of the Kingdom of Lanna, that I feel immediately enchanted.

I'm welcomed at the kerbside as I get out of the taxi and led into the house by a barefoot old man who insists on carrying my rucksack. I'm assuming he is the grandfather of the family. I slip out of my flip flops and trot along behind him as he shuffles along a cool hallway lined and scented with incense sticks, where the floors are inlaid with beautiful mosaics and where all the doors have big, heavy, wrought iron latches, making the place feel like a safe haven.

At the far end of the hallway, I glimpse a small shaded garden with wrought iron tables and chairs and tropical plants. At the reception area, I meet the mother of the family, whose name is Noon and who speaks very good English. I explain to her straight away how I'd initially booked for three nights but that I might now like to stay longer if that's possible.

She smiles and tells me no problem and just to let her know by tomorrow.

She hands over a heavy iron key that looks like it unlocks a castle gate and bows to me graciously. 'Yours is room seven. Breakfast is served between 7.30 and 10 a.m. in the garden. Enjoy your stay, Miss Anderson.'

And there it is again; the assumption that I'm single and unmarried.

My room is on the upper floor and set back on the terrace that overlooks the street. Inside, it is deliciously cool thanks to a stone tiled floor. I look around to see a double bed and simple bamboo furnishings and a clean and functional bathroom, with a toilet, a vanity sink, and a walk-in shower. It feels strange to be here on my own but I'm not scared.

I'm feeling something else now. *Liberated? Excited?*

I spend the afternoon walking the streets of the old town. I stop for a delicious Pad Thai washed down with a cold local beer at a busy and popular-looking street food stall. I devour the meal. Anyone would think that I hadn't tasted food in weeks. I hadn't realised how hungry I was. The soft noodles and the fish sauce and tamarind and fresh lime flavour is exquisite in my mouth. How can such a basic dish that costs so little taste so good?

With my hunger satisfied, my thirst quenched and my mood lifted, I explore the bustling market, primarily looking for a few more items of clothing and some underwear, but to my dismay, the only undergarments I can find are tiny slips of silk and lace. As my knickers of choice are usually plain cotton from M&S, I flick through all those on offer looking for comfort.

With none to be found, I actually consider buying

26

some men's cotton underpants instead, reasoning that besides the baggy Y-front bit at the front they look like my sort of thing.

You'll be relieved to know I didn't. Instead, I give in and buy several pairs of colourful silk and lacy ones, although I'm convinced they'll be uncomfortable and scratchy.

I am, however, pleased with my other purchases of loose-fitting cotton shorts in lovely bright colours, a pair of elasticated, baggy, hippy-style, elephant-patterned trousers (everyone seems to be wearing them and they look so comfortable), and several floaty cotton dresses and skirts and silk scarfs and sarongs – and all for such ridiculously cheap prices that I can't bring myself to barter for them even a little.

In a second-hand book shop, I browse and manage to pick up a tourist map and a *Lonely Planet: Thailand* guidebook. Then, with my bags of shopping, I wave down a tuk-tuk to take me back to the homestay. I've never ridden in a tuk-tuk before and I'm really looking forward to the experience. It's one of those things that everyone says you must do in Thailand. I suppose it's like a rite of passage. No matter how dangerous and foolhardy it might seem at the time.

I can see there are two distinct types of tuk-tuk whizzing up and down the street at breakneck speeds. All are performing traffic ploys and manoeuvres that would certainly be illegal back in the UK and outrageously dangerous anywhere. The first type of tuk-tuk looks like a small motorbike with a precarious home-made sidecar welded haphazardly onto it. Or, there's the more purpose-built three-wheeler with a domed-cab type that has a bench seat in the back.

The latter looks a little safer of the two, but of course as soon as I raise my hand, the one that screeches to a halt beside me with its engine popping and its driver grinning at me like a maniac is the precarious kind. I climb onboard and we're immediately off, with both the warm evening air and every other vehicle's exhaust fumes blowing in my hot face and through my sweaty hair. I cling onto the rattling open-sided framework, gritting my teeth.

As we enter the main traffic stream of cars and trucks and scooters and other tuk-tuks and open back trucks packed with passengers, we seem to be racing against teams of whole families sitting astride one scooter – Dad is driving and his young son is sitting between his knees, his wife is sitting primly side-saddle with a new baby in her arms, and their tiny daughter is sandwiched on the seat between her mum and dad. No one wears a helmet and all of them are carrying something like a shopping bag or a lunchbox or even a sack of rice.

At the roundabout-of-no-rules, I hold on even tighter and bite down on my lower lip to stop myself squealing in terror as we join the weaving masses, where just one vehicle either slowing or hesitating or wobbling would cause absolute carnage.

We somehow manage to come through unscathed and as we judder to a halt at the next set of traffic lights, I'm distracted from the mayhem of the death-defying junction ahead of us by the sights on either side of me. There is a large monkey sitting quietly in the front basket of a motorbike to my left and of the two men astride a small scooter to my right, one of them is carrying a fridge. It's certainly an interesting and exhilarating way to get around town.

On my first morning in Chiang Mai, I wake early, just as the sun is coming up. I make myself a cup of coffee from the hospitality tray in my room and take it out onto the first-floor terrace that overlooks the street. I had expected the street to be deserted at this time of the day, but the opposite is true. I see lots of people lining the street, all holding bags of food or bowls of fruit and bottles of water, and they all seem to be waiting for something or someone.

Soon, along comes a posse of bald monks wrapped in saffron coloured robes, all carrying bowls. I'd say they were begging bowls, except clearly these monks don't need to beg.

I watch, fascinated, as the monks walk slowly and

purposefully down the street in a single line, oldest first, gracefully and humbly, and mostly barefoot. Then I see Noon, my landlady, standing at the roadside too. I watch her take a step into the path of an approaching monk and lay her offerings onto a cloth on the ground before him. She quickly drops to her knees in front of him with her head lowered and her hands pressed tightly together at her forehead. The monk stops in front of her and picks up the bag of cooked rice and the fruit she has laid down and places them in his bowl before giving her a blessing. His melodic chanting fills the street and floats into the air to reach my ears.

I go back inside feeling like I've just witnessed something very special indeed.

Later, I ask Noon if this procession happens every day or just on special occasions.

She explains that the monks are from a nearby temple and they rely on the people of the town to offer them 'alms' of food, water, and sometimes medicine. 'Every morning, the monks walk along the street to collect what they need for the day. We offer rice, fruit, some steamed vegetables, all to show our love and respect. But, if the giver is a woman, she must never offer her gifts by hand. She must lay down a cloth between them as the monk is forbidden to ever touch a woman.'

'And the chanting? What does that mean?' I ask her.

'That is a Buddhist blessing to honour me with a happy and purposeful life.'

'A happy and purposeful life...' I repeat wistfully.

Her words strike a chord, and I decide right at that moment that all I want in my life is to be happy and purposeful. It doesn't seem such a lot to want or to ask for and yet to be blessed with those two simple ingredients in my life would mean that I have everything to live and to thrive.

'And can anyone get blessed by a monk?' I ask.

Noon laughs and tells me that in Chiang Mai there are over three hundred temples and that in any one of them, should I wish, I can be blessed by a monk.

I immediately tell her that I'd like to stay on here for another two nights.

Then I go out to seek as many temples and as many blessings as I can possibly find.

According to my guidebook, the most significant temple in Chiang Mai is *Wat Doi Suthep*, which is also one of the holiest Buddhist sites in Thailand. It's the one every pilgrim or tourist has at the top of their hitlist. The temple sits on the top of a mountain and it overlooks the city.

I take a '*songthaew*' open back taxi truck with several other Western tourists and we head up the winding mountain road, soon finding ourselves surrounded by dense tropical forest. In the trees, our driver points out

31

colourful birds and small swinging monkeys. I strain my eyes to see them in the wild. I'm captivated by all the monkeys!

As we make our way further up the mountain road, we drive higher and higher past (supposedly haunted) waterfalls that fall dramatically from the cliffs above us and then gather in glistening pools far below us. I feel like I'm on a wild and epic adventure.

When the taxi truck pulls up and we all climb out, it's clear we're not quite there yet, as there is still a towering staircase ahead of us to climb. I brace myself for the ascent but I'm stopped from going any further by a small Thai woman, who I assume is trying to sell me something. I politely decline her several times, but she is ever more insistent, waving a garment at me and shouting 'naughty knees, naughty knees!'

Fortunately, another tourist helps me out. It turns out that I'm being asked to 'rent' one of her long skirts because the hemline of the dress I'm wearing is not below the knee and therefore not respectable enough for visiting the holy temple. Embarrassed, I humbly apologise, pay the small baht fee for the skirt and attach it by its Velcro fastenings around my waist.

Then I huff and puff my way up the three hundred steps or so – but I'm not counting.

I do stop occasionally to take some photos of the views both above and beneath me, and of the incredibly colourful and jewel-like mosaic balustrade of a seven-headed serpent undulating all the way along the staircase. According to my guidebook, this is the longest '*naga*' or 'water serpent' in Thailand. I find the climb as beautiful as it is exhausting.

At the top, although still on the lower terrace, I catch my breath by admiring a life-sized effigy of a white elephant. A plaque explains its significance and its interesting history. In the fourteenth century, a white elephant carrying a relic belonging to Buddha stopped here high on the mountain and after trumpeting three times, the white elephant died. The king at the time believed this to be an omen and that is why the magnificent temple was built here so long ago.

I walk on past rows upon rows of large polished brass bells towards the upper terrace where, after removing my flip flops and leaving them in a pile with many others, I find a multitude of smaller temples, ornate shrines, Buddha statues and golden umbrellas. In the centre of the terrace, I stand breathlessly in the bright glaring sunshine, bedazzled by a huge, gold, pagoda-style temple. It is so bright and shiny that I'm sure it can be seen from space. This is the impressive and magnificent centrepiece of *Wat Doi Suthep*.

After taking in the stunning views of the whole of Chiang Mai around me and strolling around the cloisters in the sunshine admiring everything ancient and colourful and shiny, I see a crowd flocking into one of the smaller chapels and I decide to follow them.

Inside, the chamber is lit by hundreds of candles and in the centre of the glow is a huge effigy of a lion. There is also a monk, who in Thai and then in fluent English, is telling the story of *Phra Singh* – the Lion Buddha – whose image is set with a really scary face.

He says this is to remind us 'that just like the lion it is our nature to live bravely'.

From here, feeling slightly braver, I notice a line-up of several other young monks entering another of the minor temples and I follow them too. They file inside and then sit cross-legged in rows on the mosaic tiled floor facing an ornately decorated altar filled with flowers and fruit.

Behind the altar is an enormous golden statue of Lord Buddha himself sitting serenely in the lotus position and with a look of tranquillity on his very beautiful face. Between all the gold, the saffron-wrapped monks, the gently burning incense sticks, and the candles, the entire room and everyone in it appears to be glowing.

With a cue from a leading monk, all the young monks begin to sing.

I feel every hair on my body stand on end. It is all so incredibly beautiful.

Wanting to listen to more of their singing and to their prayers, I sit quietly on the floor at the back of the chapel, along with several other visitors. I'm not religious or spiritual in any way. I'm an ex-protestant turned profound atheist, and I've never really had time to think about faith or my lack of it before – but I am captivated with the passion of the hypnotic chanting. I'm sure, from the serene expressions of those around me, that everyone feels just as I do because there is just *something* about these amazing temples, these fascinating multi-faceted deities, and these monks who live surrounded by priceless jewels and tonnes of gold without owning anything of their own except the saffron robe that covers them.

I close my eyes to concentrate on the incantation.

My soul stirs and my heart soars as I listen.

Then my busy mind quietens and I feel my heart slow to a tranquil beat.

Any bitterness inside of me seems to melt away. I realise I'm meditating.

It is a truly wonderful feeling.

When all the monks stand to leave, I open my eyes and stand to leave too. I'm just on my way out of the door, when I happen to notice another statue set into a shrine in the wall. It catches my eye because it's so joyfully colourful and because it has so many garland offerings around its neck and lit candles at its feet. It's a happy smiling image of a chubby dancing elephant deity with four arms, and human hands and feet, joyfully holding up what looks like a conch shell, a bowl of grapes, and a lotus blossom.

In contrast to the scary lion of earlier, this one isn't at all intimidating and, with his free hand, he's holding up a decorated palm as if to say to those who might pass him by: 'hey, stop and look at me and feel happy!'

So I buy a garland and a candle and I go back to the jolly elephant to offer him my gifts.

Kneeling on the floor in front of him, I close my eyes.

I'm not entirely sure how this works, so I try a silent prayer just like I might in a church.

Dear happy elephant, please help me to find happiness and purpose in my life.

When I open my eyes, I see a young monk has sat down next to me.

'What do you see when you look at Lord Ganesh?' he asks me in perfect English.

'I see true happiness. It's something I want for myself,' I confess to him in a whisper.

The young monk smiles at me serenely. 'Rest assured, if you are willing to open your heart, then Lord Ganesh will guide you. He will send a sign that will lead to your place of happiness.'

The young monk asks for my hand and so I give it to him.

And very carefully, without touching my skin, he ties

a small piece of twisted white string around my wrist. 'This is a *sai sin* bracelet of sacred thread. You must wear this until you find your place of happiness.' Then he begins his songful blessing: *Om mani padme hum. Om mani padme hum. Om mani padme hum. Om mani padme hum. Om mani padme hum. Om mani padme hum.*

Embarrassingly, I'm moved to tears.

When he sees I'm weeping, he leans forward to speak in my ear in a voice no louder than a whisper. 'There was once a lady who said to Lord Buddha, "I want happiness" and Lord Buddha told her that she must first remove "I" as that was her ego. Then, she must remove "want" because that was her greed. And then, she would be left with "happiness".'

I ponder the meaning of his advice all the way back down the three hundred steps.

But at the bottom of the steps, my mind is suddenly filled with confusion.

Surely, in leaving everything behind me, I have already let go of my greed and my ego?

And what will be the sign? Will it be unmistakable, or will it be cryptic?

He also said 'your place of happiness'.

Does that mean I'll find my happiness in an actual place or simply in a mindset?

I return my rented skirt. I then notice another Thai

lady sitting on the floor at the bottom of the steps with her jars of paste and pens and a small board with symbols on it. I see she's offering henna tattoos for just a few baht. I immediately notice that one of the symbols is exactly the same as the one I'd seen decorating Lord Ganesh's upheld palm.

It looks like an elaborate and swirly upside-down question mark.

'What does this mean?' I ask her, pointing to it.

'It means to bring you much happiness,' she replies.

'Then I'll take it,' I tell her, sitting down and holding out my right palm.

Back at the homestay, several mornings later, after I had avidly explored practically every inch of Chiang Mai and visited dozens of stunningly beautiful temples all over town and received so many blessings that I had a whole collection of white string bracelets on my arm, I'm sitting at my breakfast table in the garden, enjoying tropical fruits and eggs and strong coffee and pondering where in Thailand I should travel to next.

As the tables around me are being taken up, I see there are lots of new people at the homestay today. Up until now, most of the other guests have been young couples or family groups and I've felt awkward and self-conscious about being on my own. I've honestly never had to have a breakfast at a hotel on my own before this trip. I've never been sightseeing on my own before. I've never flown on a plane or travelled alone and I've found it all rather disconcerting. I've thought that other people might be looking at me and judging me in some way for being alone. Silly, I know. But today, I realise, I'm not the only person here travelling solo. Some are younger, but not exclusively. There are one or two who are middle-aged like me. I also get the feeling that no one here feels even the slightest bit awkward for being alone.

In fact, everyone has an attractive aura of confidence and purpose about themselves.

I feel reassured. I don't have to feel self-conscious or less worthy or invisible anymore.

Today, I feel it is okay to be alone. It is okay to be me.

Not the dull old me – homemaker and housewife – but the new enlightened backpacking me.

I've now started introducing myself to people I meet as Lori, not Lorraine.

Having a new name makes me feel different about myself.

As far as I am concerned, Lorraine is still back in the UK – married and betrayed.

Whereas Lori is a world explorer who is on an amazing adventure, meeting new people and having fun in the pursuit of happiness and purpose. Like the monks of Chiang Mai, she carries piety in her heart rather than her ego, and she travels lightly because she doesn't need material things to represent her wealth. Lori is mindful of her place in the universe.

She is brave and fearless like a lion.

Over breakfast, in the green coolness of the garden, I strike up a conversation with a woman sitting at the table next to mine. She's English and her name is Polly. I'm guessing, like me she's in her mid-forties. She tells me she is from London originally and that she is a teacher taking a yearlong sabbatical – time out to travel. I didn't know people did such a thing.

'I teach history at a private school in Cheshire, just outside Manchester. But I've been travelling for almost a year now. I'm starting to seriously wonder if I'll ever want to go back to my old job or my old life,' she says, laughing at the thought of it. 'I can't really imagine being stuck in one place again. Travelling is so addictive.'

'What will happen if you don't go back?' I ask.

'I expect the person covering for me will take my job and I'll have to find something else to do. I could always teach in Thailand. I'd just need a work visa. I must say I'm very tempted.'

I smile. 'It sounds to me like you've already made up your mind.'

'And what about you, Lori. Do you have a job waiting for you in the UK?'

I shrug. 'I was a housewife. But, like you, I now realise I have other options.'

'So how long do you plan to stay in Thailand?' she asks me.

'Well, I only have a thirty-day tourist visa and I've used up seven of those days already, but I'm thinking of heading south. I hear the islands on the Andaman Sea are stunning and, for some reason, I feel the need to be by the sea right now. Somewhere to relax in the sunshine.'

Polly rolls her eyes in pleasure. 'Oh, yes. Tiny tropical islands, palm trees, white sand beaches, warm clear waters. It's known as the Maldives of Thailand down there. From Krabi, you can island hop all the way down the Andaman Sea to Langkawi in Malaysia. I did it earlier this year. You really should go. Three weeks might be long enough, if you pace it right'

I stare at her in wide-eyed wonder and in envy of her confidence.

'And do you think it's best to fly back to Bangkok en route to Krabi?' I ask her.

Polly sips her coffee and shakes her head. 'I'd suggest from here you take the train to Bangkok and then the bus over to Krabi. Then you can use a combination of ferries and long-tail boats to take you all the way down the coast stopping off at as many islands as you wish.'

I take out my notebook and jot down her advice on a new page that I've titled, 'Top Travel Tips'.

'And so, when I eventually reach Malaysia, what would you recommend I see there?'

'You should definitely explore Langkawi and then head over to Kuala Lumpur. From KL you can head over to the Malaysian side of Borneo. I spent a month there and highly recommend it.' She flicks through photos on her phone and shows me one of her holding a gorgeous baby orangutan. 'This is Peanut. He's just one year old. He's just like a human baby. He lives at this orangutan orphanage in Borneo where I volunteered. He was rescued from the jungle and now he gets to play in the nursery with other older orphans and learn the skills that will eventually lead to him being rehabilitated and released back into the forest reserve to live wild once more.'

Little Peanut is so tiny and has such a cute face, with his round bright eyes and spiky red hair.

My heart swells just looking at him. 'That's so fantastic. Can anyone go there to help with the orangutans or do you have to have special qualifications?'

'You don't need qualifications, although relevant experience might help. I think you just need to care deeply about the animals and the rehabilitation programme. In return, you get meals and lodgings and to help an endangered species. It's so worthwhile.'

Polly happily scribbles down the name of this sanctuary for me in my notebook.

'It's called the Northern Borneo Orangutan Orphanage and it's run by the Goldman Global Foundation. If you do an internet search it'll give you all the details and contact information.'

'Thanks Polly. I'll look into it. I loved doing voluntary work back in the UK for various causes, including animal charities, so maybe they'd consider all of that relevant experience. And, just to recap, you say that taking a train is far the best way for me to get from here down to the coast?'

'Yes. It's a bit of a journey but it's the cheapest and certainly the most scenic way to get back to Bangkok from here. It'll take either all day or all night, but that's part of the fun, right?'

I feel so glad that I've met Polly. She's inspired me with confidence, given me some brilliant travel tips, and provided me with a lifeline as to how I might find direction and purpose in my new life. Later on, I check the train timetable and the bus route that she'd suggested to me.

I find she was right about the train taking all day or all night, as you could choose either the daytime train or the nighttime sleeper for the twelve-hour journey to Bangkok. Polly had said that travellers, especially backpackers, generally prefer the night train as it saves on the cost of a hostel and the fare for both journeys is much the same.

Conversely, I eventually decide on taking the daytime train, because that way I'll get to spend the whole day looking out of the window at the Thai countryside as I travel from north to south. I'm not at all fazed by the length of the journey. I'm already hooked on the romantic notion of taking an old train on what is said to be an iconic journey through Thailand.

It sounds to me like a great adventure.

Although, on further investigation, I think Polly has rather underplayed the second leg of the trip from Bangkok to Krabi by bus. I discover this journey will take another gruelling ten hours or possibly longer. So, I make an executive decision for myself and decide, that after taking the daytime train, I'll save being squashed into a small bus in the pitch dark with lots of sweaty hippies heading to full moon parties on the beach and spend a bit extra on staying overnight in Bangkok once more. That way, I have the more convenient option of a two-hour flight over to Krabi the following morning. It sounds like baht well spent to me.

Just as I'm about to leave the homestay for the train station, Noon and Polly kindly come out to wave me off. I hug them both and thank them for their kindness.

Noon bows gracefully and wishes me *kar deinthang mi khwam sukkh* (happy travels).

Polly wishes me good luck. 'Oh, Lori, I forgot to say just one more thing!' she yells, as I'm just about to depart in a tuk-tuk. I stick my head out of the cab in anticipation of another pearl of her wisdom. 'Yes, what is it?' I ask her eagerly.

'If you pay a few extra baht for the first-class carriage, you'll get air conditioning!'

Chapter 3

Return to Bangkok

At the train station at Chiang Mai, which was so authentically Asian that it looked like either something from a classic movie set or a bygone era of train travel, I stand for over half an hour in a long and sweaty line of people queuing for a train ticket. When it eventually gets to my turn, I'm told I should have pre-booked if I wanted to travel first-class, because today the carriage is full. So, I walk away past life-sized statues of elephants and garland-wrapped effigies, with my rucksack on my back and a second-class ticket in my hand.

Perhaps I should be grateful that I hadn't been reduced to riding third-class (on the roof perhaps?) but I must admit to feeling a little apprehensive at what might be in store for me over the next twelve hours or more on a packed train with no air conditioning.

On Platform 3, I see the train to Bangkok with its

bright jewel-coloured livery. She looks as gloriously original as I'd hoped she would and I'm thrilled to bits. This is like stepping back in time. I remember how, many years ago, when I was still new to the travel agency business, a client had asked me to organise an epic train journey for him on the Trans-Siberian route – the world famous six-thousand-plus-mile journey across Russia. During the detailed planning stages of his itinerary, I'd often dreamt of taking the epic journey too and after talking at great length to the client afterwards about his amazing experiences, I've been left with a romanticised view of long train journeys on classic trains.

I show my ticket to a uniformed guard and he kindly escorts me to my carriage.

It's several carriages along the platform and past the first class one with air conditioning.

As we trot past it, I try hard not to feel envious of those settling into big comfortable looking velour wrapped seats with headrests and elaborately curtained windows. I follow the guard along the platform to my second-class carriage and settle myself into a vinyl wrapped seat by a window that has no blind or curtain to filter out the heat or glare from the blazing sun.

As there are still plenty of empty seats around me and no seat number allocations, I get my pick and make sure to choose one benefitting from one of the very few electric fans fixed to the ceiling. Soon the carriage fills with other people – Thai students, migrant workers from bordering Myanmar, lots of backpacking Westerners, and several saffron-robed monks. I've prepared myself for the long journey by stocking up on snacks and drinks and it looks like everyone else has done the same, climbing on board with bulging carrier bags from the 7/11 store.

I see a young woman boarding the train. She's wearing a short crop top and exactly the same style of baggy red elephant pattern trousers as I'm wearing. She's petite, slim and pretty and has the most gloriously deep golden suntan and long shiny conker-brown hair worn in a high pony tail. She has artful looking tattoos on her upper arms and she carries a large tatty back-pack that has a yoga mat strapped to it. Both her bag and her tan suggest she's been travelling for quite some time. I guess she's in her late twenties or early thirties but there is something about her that makes me want to watch her as she places her belongings in the over-head storage compartment and slides into the seat next to me.

'Hi, I'm Summer,' she says in a soft American accent, holding out her hand.

'Nice to meet you, Summer. I'm Lori.' I smile and reach out my hand.

She immediately spots my henna tattoo. 'Oh, look, I have that one too.'

She shows me the same symbol – only hers is a real tattoo – on the inside of her wrist.

We laugh about wearing exactly the same elephant pattern trousers and I confess to having also bought the matching shorts. As our journey gets underway, the train rattles out of the station and into open countryside. I stare out of the window as we pass rice field after rice field. There is a scattering of simple homes and small farms, and surprisingly few villages, and very few animals in the fields – only a few long-horned cattle on occasion. I do see lots of people in the fields as we gather speed along the rails, both men and women, thin and small and bent, as they manually toil the land. They look as if they've been standing in those fields as part of the scenery all their lives. For many hot and sweaty hours, I stare out of that window, but disappointingly the backdrop never seems to change.

I start to think that once you'd seen one rice field, you've seen them all.

People around me are mostly sleeping. Summer has put her headphones in and closed her eyes. She's either listening to music or sleeping too. Occasionally, we stop at a small rural railway station, but they are few and far between. Nobody ever gets off and we only ever pick up one or two more passengers along our route.

When I decide it's time to visit the toilet, I wonder what to expect inside the small cubicle that so many others have visited before me. The awful smell of stale urine wafting through the carriage every time the door is opened has me waiting until I can't wait any longer.

Inside, I find a window with no glass and a fiercely hot breeze serving as ventilation.

There's a pan with a hole straight down onto the tracks.

I expect I came out looking a little awry.

Back in my seat, the heat in the carriage is making me feel drowsy. I know I could easily drift off to sleep, but while I have the benefit of a calm and passive mind and all these hours just to sit and think and reflect on life, I know that I should. I have a lot to think about.

I have some big decisions to make. I have plans to mull over. I have blessings to count.

My mum says it's a lesson in humility to count one's blessings.

Over the past week, I have grieved the loss of my husband and my marriage. I've wept with sadness. I've raged at my betrayal and humiliation. But I know this cannot go on. It must stop sometime, so it might as well stop now, before I lose myself in those tears of anger and shame.

I owe it to myself and I owe it to my sons to be strong and get through this with some dignity.

I reflect on my life back in the UK and the people there. My mum, my friends, my associates.

I happen to know lots of people – fortunate people – with health and wealth and property and love in their lives. And, mostly through my voluntary and charity work, I also know people who are suffering with very real problems – far worse than infidelity and divorce and loneliness. I'm talking about death, disease, pain and crippling debt. So, while I may still have my problems, I know I must always keep things in perspective.

I do still have blessings to count.

I have my wonderful sons and they are both healthy. I have my own good health too. What else? What am I looking forward to right now? Well, I'm looking forward to having some time at the beach to relax and to get a proper suntan. I'm looking forward to treating the next few weeks as a much-needed holiday. I should think of it as a convalescence – a time to heal and a time to move on with my life. I'm looking forward to travelling down the Andaman Sea from one beautiful tropical island to another and being lazy about it. I want to tick every single thing off my bucket list. I want to spend my time in a hammock, reading, snoozing, resting, and reminding myself that I'm travelling at long last and I'm experiencing the stuff of dreams.

I just hadn't expected to be making my dreams come true on my own.

Then, when I finally reach Malaysia, I'll decide what happens next.

I'd decide whether to head to Borneo to volunteer at the Orangutan orphanage or scuttle back to the UK to face Charles and sign the divorce papers. Such decisions. To think that just one week ago, I had been an ordinary woman living an ordinary life and making ordinary decisions. I would wake up in the morning and decide whether to have cereal or toast with my tea or coffee. At some point during my day, I would push a trolley around the supermarket, deciding whether to cook chicken or beef for dinner and whether to choose bio or non-bio washing powder. I'd had absolutely no idea then, that just one week later, everything would suddenly stop being mundane and I'd be choosing whether to take a plane or a train and where to go travelling next.

Then, with a sick feeling in the pit of my stomach, I realise that if I hadn't gone home unexpectedly early last week, all of this would never have happened, and I'd still be living a terrible lie. I'd still be thinking I was happily married and that everything in my life was fine.

Without that cruel twist of fate, I might still be none the wiser about Sally and Charles.

For a little while longer, anyway. Until he'd decided the time was right to leave me.

One week ago, I'd arranged to take my mum to the cinema. It was senior citizen day and they were showing one of her favourites – Casablanca. But we'd only just settled into our seats when Mum said she had a headache and wanted to go home – and that simple change of plan started a chain of actions that exposed to me my husband's affair and to my friend's betrayal. Somehow it felt like more than a week ago that I'd been a housewife.

And now I have neither a house nor a husband.

I have to ask myself which one I was married to – the home or the man?

Either way, I am now homeless, redundant, and my marriage vows are void.

But I have my life. I have my health. I have some money – and if I'm very careful it could last a while – and all those things add up to me being a free and independent woman.

I should be feeling excited not fearful. I'm right to count my blessings and to be positive.

The monotony of the hours rolls on and the hypnotic swaying of the train and the clacking of the rails is broken by the sound of the carriage door suddenly opening. A uniformed and rather grumpy-faced Thai lady is pushing a squeaky-wheeled trolley into our carriage. She doesn't make eye contact or speak to anyone but focusses on her task of distributing plastic trays. She slaps one down in front of every person and so I'm guessing lunch is included in the price of the ticket. I straighten up in my seat and pull down my tray holder expectantly. I realise I'm hungry. The sudden activity disturbs all my fellow passengers including Summer.

I investigate my meal by peeling the foil wrapper off what looks to be the main course. A warm waft of curry spices hits the air. I peer inside and see a portion of rice and a fish head complete with pouting lips and bulging eyes staring up at me from a slimy green sauce.

'Oh, I wouldn't eat that unless you want to spend the rest of the day in the toilet,' Summer says to me, pushing her own meal aside.

I reattach the foil lid and rifle through my 7/11 carrier bag instead.

'Here ... I have plenty' I say, offering Summer a sandwich, a packet of crisps and a bottle of water. For some reason, I've bought double of everything and far more than I need.

She thanks me and then rummages through her own carrier bag and produces a couple of cartons of cooked noodles, two hard-boiled eggs and a bag of fruit, which she offers me in return.

'Well, I guess we won't go hungry!' I laugh.

Like everyone else, we return our trays of train food untouched when the grumpy Thai lady returned to clear away. She practically snatches them away from us and slams them back into the trolley, glaring at us as if we're all ungrateful '*farangs*' (white tourists).

'Are you planning to stay in Bangkok or are you travelling on?' I ask Summer.

'I'm staying in Bangkok tonight then heading over to Krabi and Railay Beach first thing in the morning,' she tells me. 'I thought there'd be no point in dashing off to the airport tonight, when none of the boats to the beach will leave Krabi once the sun had gone down.'

'You have to take a boat to the beach?'

'Yes, Railay is surrounded by tall limestone cliffs, so you can only reach it by boat.'

'I'm sure I've heard of it,' I say, thinking aloud and digging out my guidebook.

'Well, it looks awesome. If we had wi-fi right now I'd show you some photos on my iPad. It looks stunningly beautiful. You simply can't go to Krabi and not see Railay Beach!'

'I'm flying to Krabi tomorrow morning too. Then heading on to Koh Lanta,' I tell her.

'Me too!' Summer says. 'I'm heading to Koh Lanta after my one night in Railay.'

'Oh wow, that's a coincidence,' I say, finding Railay Beach in my guidebook and ogling the photos.

Summer laughs. 'Not really. If you are doing the islands then most people will head to Koh Lanta first, which is fine. *But* if you are really savvy then you'd take a detour to Railay – it's not as busy as the other beaches, but it's supposed to be one of the best in Thailand.'

'It does look amazing.' I groan, seeing a photo of towering cliffs and a white sand beach and palm trees, and feeling like I'd missed a trick here and that I really should research more.

'Why don't you come along?' Summer offers. 'If you'd like, we can go together and then we can both take the ferry from Railay to Lanta together the next day?'

'Really?' I say, feeling thrilled at receiving such a kind invitation from a stranger.

'No, Railay!' She laughs at her joke, showing off her small perfect white teeth.

With her suntan and aura of casual freedom in mind, I ask where she has been and how long she has been travelling. Mainly so I can guess how long it might take me to acquire the same attractive qualities. Summer tells me she is a yoga teacher.

'Before I came to Thailand, I was in India for a while,' she says, sounding so effortlessly well-travelled that

India just rolls off her tongue. 'I went there to deepen my practice and to learn meditation with a guru in an Ashram. Then I came to Thailand because I was offered a job teaching yoga at a retreat on Koh Samui. I did that for a couple of months. Then I did a visa run and came straight back here so I could go to Koh Phangan for the full moon party.'

'Well, it must have been very sunny because you have a great tan,' I tell her enviously.

'Yeah, it's been really hot over the past few months. After Koh Phangan, I went over to Koh Tao for the scuba diving. I did my divemaster internship there and I'm planning on going back as soon as the monsoon season is over to do an instructor course.'

I open up my trusty and well-thumbed guidebook and looked up the islands mentioned.

'You mentioned scuba diving, Summer. That's something I'd really love to try, as well as yoga, of course. Is it hard to learn?'

'Not really, but it's important to find a good teacher. That applies to both yoga and diving.'

After several more hours of chatting and snacking we chug into Bangkok at sundown.

And, along with everyone else in our carriage, we're all leaning over each other to get a westerly window spot and to point our phones at the spectacular sight of a fiery red sunset filtering through the city smog before its time to disembark. Suddenly our long journey is over.

'Summer, I'm so very happy I met you and I'll look forward to seeing you tomorrow at the airport.'

'Sure. Me too. I'm so glad we met, Lori. I'll see you at the gate for Krabi tomorrow.'

We hug each other goodbye as if we're old friends and I head straight to the taxi rank.

I see Summer making her way down to the bus station to take a public bus to a hostel where she'd said she'd be spending the night. I'm looking forward to getting back to the Holiday Inn and taking a long leisurely soak in a bath. I'd been sitting on the train in the same clothes for so long that I can't wait to get freshened up.

But the traffic is slow through the congested city and the taxi ambles at a slow pace.

My fingers are absently playing with my *sai sin* bracelets as I look out at the bright lights of the city that looks a little less scary to me this time around. My thoughts again wander over the events of the past week. I consider how fate has played such a huge part in everything I've done. I reason that if I hadn't met Polly on my last morning in Chiang Mai, I wouldn't have thought to get the train to Bangkok because I'd have taken a plane instead.

And, if the first-class carriage hadn't been full on the

train today, then I wouldn't have sat next to Summer and I wouldn't be going to Railay Beach tomorrow.

Some people call it fate or they credit a guardian angel or a spirit with such guidance.

I'm pretty sure I'd found this special pairing in a temple somewhere in Chiang Mai.

I know how ridiculous that sounds. Just a week ago, I'd have dismissed it as complete rubbish, but I now strongly believe that this is all happening for a reason and I think I'm being guided and helped and that one day soon, I'll open my heart and be given a sign that will lead to finding my place of happiness.

That evening, in a standard single room this time rather than a decadent suite, and after a shower and dinner ordered from room service with a nice glass of wine, I sit on the bed flicking through my phone and looking at all the photos I've taken in Chiang Mai over the past week.

There are some simply stunning ones. The sky in every single shot is a clear backdrop of deep blue against a myriad of wonderful and ancient things made of gold and precious jewels and intricate mosaics and polished bells and monks in saffron robes. The light in every photo is so soft that it makes everything appear dream-like and glowing.

I post all my photos into an album on my Facebook page. I struggle to choose a favourite but then pick the one I'd taken of the old train in the station at Chiang Mai as my new Facebook cover picture, replacing the rather boring one of a tub of flowers from my garden back home.

Then I delete Charles and my ex-friend Sally from my friends and family contact list and update my current location to Bangkok, Thailand. I guess if my loved ones know where I am and what I'm doing they might worry less. They also might give me some space and time and leave me alone for a while.

Chapter 4

Railay

The next morning, I'm saved the expense of an expensive taxi by the free hotel shuttle bus to Suvarnabhumi airport. Once there, I find transiting through the domestic avenues rather easier than navigating the international ones. At the gate for the Krabi flight, I see Summer waiting.

Today Summer looks all bohemian and quite beautiful in a pair of light-cream flowing harem trousers and a white vest that shows off her deeply tanned skin. Her long dark hair is loose about her shoulders. On her arms, she wears lots of jangly bangles. In contrast, I'm wearing a baggy white cotton blouse and my old jeans that this morning I'd decided to turn into knee-length cut-off shorts. I've scraped back my humidity frazzled hair and tied it into a tight chignon, the way I'd always wore it at home. I had thought I'd looked chic as I left the cool ambiance of the hotel but now, having spent almost an hour travelling in a hot minibus with a dozen other people, I feel both overheated and underdressed at the same time.

I rush over to greet Summer and I'm full of apologies in case I'm late.

But she tells me our flight isn't even in yet and it might have been delayed. I offer to buy us both coffee and a muffin while we wait. A couple of hours later, our flight departs and we arrive in Krabi to sky-high temperatures and blue skies and body-soaking, pulse-pounding humidity.

'How far away is it to the boat?' I ask. My heavy denim shorts are now sticking to my thighs and chafing me uncomfortably, and sweat from my hair is trickling down my beetroot-red face.

'It's about half an hour on the bus.' Summer replies, coolly taking it all in her stride.

We walk past the taxi rank, ignore all the touting drivers, and we buy a bus ticket each for just a few baht from the transport office in the arrivals hall to take us from the airport to the pier. Soon afterwards, we are escorted to a minibus already packed full of passengers and we're ready to set off. It's hot and stuffy and crowded. Even with the air-con flowing it's quite suffocating on the bus. But everyone seems to be in a jolly mood and so there is lots of laughter and enthusiasm for seeing the famous Railay Beach.

In the bus with us are several young couples and a group of five young lads. The lads all seem to know each other well. Summer immediately gets chatting with them. They tell us how they all started out travelling solo around South East Asia but had met up in Vietnam and for the past few weeks had been travelling together. Three of them, Chad, Rick, and Brad, are loud chatty Americans with the same short, choppy haircuts, who all seem very keen on outdoing each other to impress Summer. Another lad is German and called Peter who, being European, speaks very good English. The fifth fellow in the group is a Brit who introduces himself as Nate, but the others immediately tell us they've nicknamed him Prince Harry, because of his short red hair and clipped British accent that makes him sound rather royal.

Poor Nate. To compensate for his poshness, I notice how he's finishing all his sentences with 'man' or words like 'gross/cool/awesome' to try to fit in with the laid-back Americans.

I guess they're all around the same age as my sons and suddenly I feel rather old.

What must they think of someone my age backpacking around Thailand?

The topic of conversation between the lads is entertainingly all about which of their bus journeys across Asia has so far been the longest and the smelliest (sixteen hours from Hue to Hanoi with someone who had vomited and missed the sick bag) and how many times they've all had food poisoning (at least twice each with bad seafood being the main culprit) and whether Chang or Leo or Singha is the best beer in Thailand (Leo, apparently, and then Chang and then Singha). Then there was the big debate on whether we were all going to find Railay Beach as beautiful as was promised or – like the not-too-far away island of Koh Phi Phi Ley (known as 'The Beach' because it has been used as a location for the movie of the same name starring Leonardo DiCaprio and was once voted the most beautiful beach in the world) – we would find it full of discarded plastics and totally ruined by mass tourism.

'It's a shame but I hear Koh Phi Phi Ley is now so overcrowded it's impossible to even take a selfie,' says Chad (or Rick or Brad) shaking his head in dismay.

'I hear thousands of tourists go there every day, all pouring out of long-tail boats like lemmings onto what once used to be a perfect beach,' says Rick (or Brad or Chad).

'Yeah, I heard that too, so I've already decided I'm gonna give it a miss,' says German Peter, trying to be heard over the loud Americans.

I listen in disappointment, as I too had bookmarked Phi Phi Ley in my copy of *Lonely Planet: Thailand* as a must see. But now, like the lads, I'm not so sure it would be worth the effort of taking a boat over there just to stand on a beach with thousands of other tourists.

'Not to worry, I'm sure there are other beautiful islands and beaches to see,' I say brightly.

When we arrive at the pier, we all pile out of the bus. I wait with our backpacks while Summer goes into the shop to buy us a couple of bottles of water. I'm far too hot. Sweat is pouring from every pore in my entire body, making me pant like a mad dog. I know my face must be a hot red swollen mess and my hair a fizzy muddle on the back of my head. I have my sunglasses on against the dazzling sun, but they keep sliding down my nose and I desperately wish I had a hat too, as the sun is beating down on me like a blowtorch. I scuttle sideways dragging our bags into the shade of the wooden canopy over the ticket office.

When Summer comes back, I see she's not only bought us a cold bottle of water each, she has strawberry ice lollies too. I haven't had an ice lolly since I was a kid and thoroughly enjoy sucking and licking it as fast as it was melting off the little wooden stick and running in scarlet dribbles down my chin and over my sticky fingers.

Soon, several long-tail boats turn up. A long-tail boat is named after the long prop shaft sticking into the water at the back of it that propels it forward. The boat itself is a traditional narrow wooden one with rows of bench seats – a bit like a large canoe – and to me it looks and feels wholly unstable. The front, where all our backpacks are being precariously stacked for the journey, has an extended bow and this is decorated with colourful garlands and wreaths of flowers that look really pretty but that I know are specifically there to provide good luck and to ask for protection from sinking from the spirits of the water. There is a roof of sorts, but it's just a metal frame tarpaulin, designed to offer passengers some protection from the sun or rain.

Our boat has sixteen passengers aboard and one Thai boatman, who operates the 'long-tail' with one bare foot while a cigarette dangles from his lower lip. The engine looks like it's something he'd salvaged from an old car and as he revs it up and steers us out into the open sea it pours out a reek of black smoke all the way from the pier and around the monumental headlands to Railay Beach.

I sit completely still on the wooden bench in the midsection next to Summer. The boat rocks and tilts as it smashes its way through the choppy waters. The large rolling waves that crash against the front of the boat are soaking all the bags and spraying those of us sitting at the front.

I'm petrified but trying desperately not to show it. I try to recall the last time I was on a boat.

It was in the Lake District, I think, when I was about twelve years old. In a little flurry of panic, I wonder if I can still swim? I try to remember the last time I went swimming. Properly swimming, I mean, because I can't count the time Sally convinced me to take up water aerobics and we never left the three-foot end of the local pool. I tell myself that swimming is like riding a bike. Once you've learned, it comes back, no matter how long ago you did it last.

Over the sound of the roaring diesel engine, I ask Summer if she's already got somewhere to stay at Railay. She shakes her head, flicking her long glossy hair from side to side like a show pony. 'No, but don't worry, it's early in the season. I'm pretty sure we'll find somewhere reasonably priced to stay for one night.'

I keep my eyes trained on what I can see of the horizon over the large moving expanse of deep water ahead of us. I worry about being seasick. To distract myself, I play a guessing game on where the lifejackets might be kept in case of a capsize. Then I hear Summer laugh.

She's enjoying another conversation with the gap year lads from the minibus.

They're all sparring over 'where is the best ... something ... in the world?'

I enjoy listening to their animated and enthusiastic conversation, probably because they are all so impressively well-travelled and confident. Their parents must be so proud of them, I think to myself, knowing how proud I am of each of my own two sons. This time, German Peter has asked for the consensus on 'where is the best full moon party in the world?'

'Without a doubt, Koh Phangan has the best full moon parties!' Summer tells them emphatically. I can see the lads all nodding their heads in agreement. Although I also notice they tend to agree with Summer whatever she says. And who can blame them?

'Yeah, you haven't lived until you've been to one of those crazy nights on Phangan!' yells one of the American lads, punching the air to make his point and to let everyone (most importantly, Summer) know that he's one of the cool cats who's actually been there and done it. Almost everyone in the boat nods in agreement with him. I guess I haven't lived?

'So where would you guys say is the best for scuba diving?' German Peter asks.

I listen keenly for the answer, grateful for another distraction. I'm starting to feel queasy.

Summer immediately pipes up again. 'That would be Geluk Island. I learned to dive on the reef there and it got me totally hooked on scuba. It's got the best diving in the whole world'

'Yeah, man, Geluk!' Nate yells. 'I went last year with the GGF and did my thesis in marine ecology and conservation. The reef is so alive, man. I swam with dolphins. It was awesome!'

The other's look at him enviously as they obviously can't make the same claim.

Prince Harry is suddenly winning big over the Americans.

'What's the GGF?' I ask him curiously.

'The Goldman Global Foundation. It's a conservation charity organisation.'

'That is SO cool, Nate!' exclaims Summer. 'I love dolphins.'

'Where is this island again?' I ask for clarification. 'And how is it spelt?'

'G-E-L-U-K,' Summer spells out for me. 'It's pronounced "gluck" and it's on the Meso-American reef in the Caribbean, the second largest barrier reef in the world after the Great Barrier Reef in Australia, only it's in much better condition and, like Nate says, the diving there is incredible.'

My eyes are wide with interest. Summer and Nate have painted such a vivid picture of this beautiful tropical island paradise. I immediately dream of going there one day to scuba dive.

I mentally add it to my bucket list.

I mean, why not, right? There's nothing to stop me because I'm a backpacker too!

Just then, our boat comes around the headland that

successfully cuts Railay Beach off from the rest of Krabi province, and we all gasp at the sight of the picture-perfect utopia in front of us. The photos in my guidebook did no justice at all to the incredible beauty of this place.

The soaring limestone cliffs look like giant fingers pointing into a cloudless blue sky.

Having entered the protection of the bay, I see the water all around us is now a flat calm shimmering emerald green sheet of pristine clarity. Just ahead of us is the much-anticipated white-sand half-moon curved beach with its backdrop of lush green forest and swaying palm trees. Our boat takes us right up to the shore line, beaching itself so that we can all clamber out, straight into the calf-deep, bathtub-warm water that is gently lapping the soft powder white sand. I look around me. Happily, so far, the place doesn't look too overcrowded or trashy.

The boatman throws us our backpacks. I grab mine and trudge with everyone else up the beach until we reach a sand path between the low-lying buildings sitting under the palm trees.

'Where shall we try first?' I ask Summer, thinking the hotels on the beach looked very nice.

'Oh, not here, Lori. Not for me anyway. These hotels are way above my budget.'

I shrug it off. 'Then they'll be over mine too. I imagine this place is pricy, right?'

Summer nods. 'Right. If you stay on West Beach you'll pay a fortune for the privilege of watching the sunset from your balcony when you could actually just watch it for free on the beach. But don't worry, I'm sure there are places far less expensive further in.'

'Okay. Let's go. I'll follow your lead,' I say to her, trying to hide my concern over ending up in a shared dorm with one bathroom and with all the lads from the bus and the boat.

As it is, on East Beach, just a five-minute walk away from the idyllic West Beach, while Summer checks out the shared hostel dorms, I find a pretty twin-bed wooden bungalow with private bathroom for rent. It's double the cost of the hostel – but when I point out if we shared it would be the same price, Summer agrees it would be far nicer than the dorm.

We decide to spend the rest of the day lazing on the beach. Summer wants to top up her tan and I'm hoping to develop one. Summer, looking the very definition of her name, is wearing a tiny white bikini on her tiny, toned and evenly suntanned body while I'm searching a local beach stall for a sun hat, a tube of factor thirty sunscreen, and a swimsuit.

The hat is no problem but the sunscreen is ridiculously expensive and the swimsuits (bikinis as they don't seem to do one-pieces) are all ridiculously small and nothing more than triangles of fabric and string.

73

Eventually, I find one with large enough triangles and we head for the sand and the sea.

The beauty of the enclave surrounding Railay beach is unreal.

It's so blissful to lie on the silky soft, white sand and feel the hot sun radiating over my body.

I keep closing my eyes and then opening them again just to make sure I'm not dreaming.

I see that Summer has gone off snorkelling with the lads. I watch them swim over to the rocks underneath the wrap-around cliffs. I can hear them whooping and shouting, 'oh wow look – you gotta see this!' I'm curious to wonder what they have seen in the water.

Soon Summer comes running back up the beach to insist that I go snorkelling too.

'Come on, Lori. It's amazing. There are so many fish. It's so beautiful – it's like a tropical fish tank, and it's so shallow and close to the rocks that you can stand up if you want.'

As comfortable as I am sunning myself on the beach, Summer won't take no for an answer and she is being so sweet to want to include me. It does look like fun. I reason with myself, that if I intend to learn to scuba dive then I really should try snorkelling first, so I agree to rent a snorkel and mask and join them.

Well, from the very first moment I put my face into the water, I find I'm utterly spellbound.

The sea is warm and clear. Below me, lying on the sandy seabed are starfish, and all around me there are tiny colourful fish. I've never seen anything like it.

It's like being in *Finding Nemo*. I float on the surface, with my face in the water and my arms and legs splayed out so I look like a starfish myself, watching all the fish darting about in the corals and rocks and sea grasses. It's so fascinating that I soon forgot to panic about breathing through a narrow tube or getting a little bit of water in my facemask.

I'd absolutely no idea that the underwater world could be this stunningly beautiful.

I've watched *Blue Planet*, of course, but even that hadn't done the real thing any justice.

From above, I watch the underwater creatures going about their fishy business, looking for food, having little fights, falling in love, chasing bubbles and each other, and all the while being unaware of the crazy world of people who inhabit the land above them with their lives and loves and wars and politics. I decide that I'd much prefer to be part of their watery world than my complicated earth-y one. I swim up and down that rock face for I don't know how long. I completely lose track of time. It's so peaceful, so very tranquil and calming.

Now I'm even more determined that while I'm on the islands I will learn to scuba dive.

I'm sure there will be scuba diving schools on the next island of Koh Lanta, which is the first and the largest island in the chain that I plan to visit and explore. Once I get my dive certificate, I'll be able to do even more scuba diving, and build up my experience and confidence in the water.

Eventually, despite the expensive factor thirty sunscreen, I'm sure I've got rather too much sun on my back, and so I decide to head back up the beach. Summer and the boys are all lying flat out on the sand and in the sun but I know that I must find some shade. It has to be the hottest part of the day right now. But I see that all the palm tree shade has already been taken.

I wander up and down the beach for a while, until I spot a just-vacated chair in the shade of a palm-thatched parasol and I run like a sprinter to plonk myself into it. It isn't long before a hostess comes over to ask me what I'd like to order. It seems the seat comes with a price. I order an iced tea and it's by far the most refreshing iced tea I've ever tasted and well worth the exorbitant cost.

Later on, that same afternoon, spruced up for the evening and while Summer is taking her shower, I'm feeling mellow and reflective so I take a walk along the shoreline. The beach is quiet and the tide is going out. There are just a few families still building sandcastles with their kids now the sun had lost its burning intensity. A few local people are walking their dogs. The lads have invited both Summer and I to join them for sundowners on the beach tonight. I can see the bar owners at the top of the beach are getting ready by expanding their pitch and putting out beanbags and rugs and low tables on the beach in front of their bars. I imagine that I've been invited out of kindness and because Summer and I are travelling together. They clearly all have the hots for Summer, and must be at least a little furious at me for finding the only available bungalow on the beach – when they'd all had high hopes of sharing a dorm with her! I smile at foxing their plans. I do remember what it was like to be their age. Young and high on hormones, trying to fit in, desperate to fall in love.

Even if it was a long time ago.

Although, generally, I think the youth of today are far more confident and self-assured than people of my generation were at the same age. That's a good thing. As a young woman, I hadn't known anyone who went on a gap year around the world. Or anyone who did their thesis in the Caribbean. I only knew one or two people who had managed to go to university.

Most people I knew left school and got a job and then got married and had kids. The end.

But now, being around lots of people who travel extensively makes it seem normal.

Today, while almost out of earshot, I'd overheard Brad (or Chad or Rick) asking Summer if she and I were mother and daughter. Summer had responded so sweetly. She'd told him we were just friends but that she wished she had a mother who was as cool as me, who might be old, but still brave enough to go travelling through Thailand on her own.

Old? I had laughed to myself. I might not be young but I'm certainly not bloody old!

I take a deep breath of sea breeze and toss back my freshly washed hair from my shoulders. Tonight, I'm letting it lie in damp waves down my back. Back home, I'd always considered my long hair too thick and too difficult to ever let it wild and loose, so I'd scrape it back off my face and twist it up on my head in a prim-looking topknot or I'd braid it out of the way to lie behind my back and out of sight. Once upon a time, my long hair had been my crowning glory, but now it's the only thing that makes me feel different in a town where every woman of a certain age has a shoulder length 'housewife' bob cut and they all look just the same. Although, every few weeks, I'd consider having it all chopped off.

Now I'm glad I didn't because when I'd come out of the bathroom tonight with my hair loose and damp from the shower, Summer had looked at me with some surprise and said to me so sweetly, 'Oh wow, Lori, I didn't realise you have such fabulous hair!'

'Really? You think so?' I'd said, feeling flushed with delight.

'Yeah. You look ten years younger with your hair down like that. It softens your face. You should wear it down all the time.' So, I've decided that from now on I will.

I stop walking at the midpoint curve of the beach, where the sun has created a golden line across the water, making it look something like a shimmering divine pathway. I hitch up the white cotton dress that I'd bought at the market stall in Chiang Mai and I wade in just past my knees. I look down into the clear warm water to see the white sand between my toes and the almost translucent fish swimming around my legs. I lift my face once more to the warm salty breeze and I look up at the towering cliffs all around me. Then I let my gaze wander over the traditional long-tail boats bobbing on the shoreline, decorated with their colourful ribbons and garlands and flowers and I take a moment to acknowledge how free I feel right at this moment. Today has been an unimaginably lovely day.

I pull at my wedding ring and with a twist it comes off my finger quite easily.

How strangely bare my hand looks without it.

I realise it's the first time I've ever removed it.

I raise my arm in the air and I throw the ring as far as I can into the sea.

I watch it twirl in the air, catching the golden light, until it disappears ... and is gone forever.

Chapter 5

Koh Lanta

The next morning, I wake up from a lovely dream to hear movement in our room. I realise it's still dark. In alarm, I put on the bedside light, to find Summer trying to get dressed.

'Oh, Lori. I'm so sorry. I was trying so hard not to wake you,' she whispers.

'It's okay. What time is it? Where are you going?'

'I'm going to the beach to practice my *surya namaskara.*'

'Practice your what?'

'My sun salutation. It's almost dawn. You wanna come?'

'No thanks. It's way too early for me.'

I pull the sheet back over my head grumbling something about it having been a late night.

'Oh, come on Lori, let's go and do yoga together while the sun is coming up on one of the most beautiful beaches in Thailand. I promise you'll be so happy you made the effort!'

And there was that word again – *happy* – and the actual promise of it.

My sleepy head reminds me that if I don't open my heart, I'll never receive the sign that will lead me to my place of happiness, and who knows if that place isn't in yoga?

Summer always has a serene look about her, not to mention really great posture, so it works for her.

To my surprise, we aren't the only ones on East Beach ready to do yoga just before the sun begins to rise. We start off standing in what Summer says is *Mountain Pose* in honour of the tall rocks around us. Then, in the moments before the actual sun comes peeping over the horizon, we hold our palms together at chest level and we focus on our inner sun.

We inhale noisily; this rushing breath is important and called *ujjayi* or 'ocean breath,' taking in great gulps of warm, humid morning air, sweeping our arms to the sky and stretching our bodies up while gazing at our thumbs. Then we fold our bodies down again before going into a lunge with our palms and soles pressing into the sand for the Downward Dog pose.

I struggle with the next couple of poses – a sort of planking that Summer calls *Chaturanga* and then we rise up into Upward Facing Dog followed by yet another downward one. I find it quite exhausting trying to keep the flow of movement, but I follow Summer and when we come back to the standing pose again with our palms together as if we're praying, I find myself silently thanking the sun for coming up this morning.

And I do indeed feel very happy.

After a hastily bought and quickly eaten store-bought breakfast of tinned iced tea, a carton of yogurt and a banana – all for the price of just a few baht – Summer and I head back out into the already blazing hot morning sun onto West Beach where, with our back-packs and lots of other people, including the lads, we must wait to be taken by long-tail boats out to the ferries.

The boys are taking a different ferry from Summer and I this morning, as they are going onto Phuket and we are making our way to Koh Lanta. We thank them for being a lot of fun and such great company. Last night, we'd all sat on the beach on beanbag cushions drinking beers, listening to pulsing music and watching around a dozen fire dancers twirling their brightly burning torches in a cleverly choreographed show. It was fabulous.

After the fire show, the dancers had set fire to a long, heavy and fuel-drenched skipping rope, and encouraged the audience to participate by offering a free bottle of beer to all those who managed ten skips.

Summer had instantly jumped up, thrown her phone to one of the lads for safekeeping and grabbed me by the hand to join in. The lads had clapped and jeered their encouragement at us but I really didn't want to go. I didn't think I'd be nimble enough on my feet to jump the flaming rope even once never mind ten times.

But for some reason, I found myself running across the sand with Summer towards it and in we went, jumping, jumping, jumping. As I leapt in the air, the rope and the flames whipped past my feet and my head and I worried that my hair or my dress might catch fire. The crowd were all counting 'one, two, three...' I was panting hard and breathing in the awful kerosene fumes from the twirling burning rope.

But I couldn't stop or I'd get burned.

When we got to 'nine' I simply couldn't jump anymore. My legs felt so heavy trying to clear the burning rope. Each time I landed, my feet were becoming ever more deeply entrenched in the sand. I felt like I was digging my own grave. Then, hearing 'ten' and seeing the rope slow, I saw my chance to escape. I tried to exit sideways as gracefully as I could, but unfortunately, I misjudged things and got the rope caught around my legs.

The lads came to my rescue, picking me up and dusting me down and telling me what a great sport I was. But I see this morning that I have two angry red welts across both my ankles.

After our fond farewells on the beach, Summer and I wade into the sea and hand over our backpacks and flip flops to our boatman before climbing aboard via a short slippery metal ladder that has been hooked insecurely onto the side. Then we sit on the rough plank seats and bob about waiting until the boat is full of people and their luggage.

I watch those clambering on board. Only one or two are un-savvy types who have brought suitcases on their travels rather than backpacks. I watch them drag these painfully heavy suitcases across the sand on their useless wheels over to the boatman, who rolls his eyes and struggles at the effort of manhandling these fancy slippery hard-shell cases on board. I'm also excruciatingly aware that under any other circumstances, I'd absolutely be one of those un-savvy travellers, too.

I know that once Summer and I arrive on Koh Lanta we will be parting company, as she is going into a rainforest yoga retreat in the centre of the island and I'm hoping to find somewhere to stay near to a beach. My plan for the next few days here is to sunbathe, read, swim in the sea, get lots of Thai massages and eat lots of delicious Thai food. According to my guidebook, Koh Lanta is the largest island on the Andaman Sea. It is known primarily for its long coastline and beautiful beaches and for being a little behind the times with regard to tourism – a bit like me, I suppose, a slow developer in the world of backpacking. It's also said to have the last of the original and authentic Thai fishing villages and is home to a semi-nomadic people – the sea-gypsies known locally as *Chao Ley*.

For some reason, the very idea of a sea gypsy evokes in me a fantastical and romantic image of magical mermaids and handsome mermen. When I tell Summer this, she laughs, and suggests that while I'm on Koh Lanta I should find myself a real-life *Chao Ley*.

As we approach the island, we can see many of the surrounding uninhabited islets and rocks just off its coastline. Tall limestone rock formations protrude from the sea and there are clusters of small islands that have been formed from ancient collapsed volcanos.

I spot Koh Haa (this is a group of five small islands known for soft corals and marine life) and Koh Muk with its emerald cave, Koh Phi Phi (that's the one of *The Beach* fame again) and Koh Rok with its reef of amazing rainbow corals. These islands are also famous dive sites.

I remind myself that I'm absolutely going to give scuba diving a try while I am here.

Before we part company and get caught up in the ensuing chaos on the landing pier on Koh Lanta, Summer and I make sure to swap phone numbers and to connect with each other on social media. I've enjoyed being in her lovely company and want to keep in touch.

'I'm excited to know where your next adventure will take you, Lori,' she says with an affectionate hug. 'I really hope we get the chance to meet up again somewhere someday.'

I wave my hand in the air and blow her a kiss as she disappears into the steaming throng of touts and taxi drivers and welcoming committees who are all crowded on the pier here. Then I take a tuk-tuk for my ten-minute commute into town, where I sit in a roadside café with free wi-fi and an iced tea, checking out the accommodation possibilities nearby using my guidebook and my phone. I'm in an area called Long Beach, which boasts a main street lined with lots of rustic, open-fronted shops and massage parlours and stalls and bars and restaurants, all running alongside a five-kilometre stretch of golden sand beach. I haven't really had a chance to book anywhere in advance but the general consensus from all those I'd met travelling, was that this early in the season, there is plenty of choice for places to stay and reasonably low prices.

Indeed, I soon find a place listed nearby on an internet booking site.

It offers cute looking individual rattan-and-wood-framed palm-thatched huts set back from the beach. I finish my tea and decide to set out and investigate. Then, as I'm ready to settle my bill and get on my way, I hear my phone ping and see that Summer has already tagged me in a couple of photos she's just uploaded to Facebook.

One of them is of both of us sitting together on the beach last night.

We are so happy and we are smiling, holding up our sundowners and saying 'cheers' to the camera. It made me smile. It's such a good photo and it's clear from the rosy glow on our faces that we'd just spent the whole day on the beach and in hot sunshine.

The second photo is a close-up of me on the skipping rope. I stare at it in amazement.

In the photo, I'm poised in mid-jump with my legs tucked up beneath my white dress and my arms are held out wide. My dress looks like gossamer wings against a backdrop of pitch black night sky. In the trailing blurry yellow flames of the skipping rope my body is twisted in mid-air and my face is obscured by my riotous mass of flying golden curls.

I hardly recognise myself. I look like a mythical fire-sprite.

Within moments, friends and family back home are clicking 'like' on these photos.

Then to my alarm, I also get an immediate comment from Paula Chadwick, who works as Charles' secretary. *Amazing photos, Lorraine. Looks like you are having fun in Thailand!*

I feel my stomach churn over. I wonder if she's showing this photo to Charles right at this moment. My finger hovers over Paula's profile to delete her but then something stops me.

I realise it's my old ego.

What if she does show this picture to Charles or indeed to Sally?

It might not be a bad thing for my self-esteem because it is an amazing photo.

My finger falters over the delete button and then I remember the Chiang Mai monk's words.

There was once a lady who said to Lord Buddha, 'I want happiness' and Lord Buddha told her that she must first remove 'I' as that was her ego...

And so, with a sigh, I accept the lesson graciously and press delete.

I rent the hut near to the beach. It sits under the cool shade of a line of pine and palm trees with open views to the sea. There's just one room space inside and it's small but spotlessly clean, with a polished wood floor and a double size bed covered in a white sheet and a mosquito net. There's also a small fridge, a few items of furniture and a bathroom. No air conditioning, but I do have a sea breeze and a ceiling fan to keep me cool.

I settle in and hang up the few clothes that are still clean in the wardrobe, rinse through the ones that aren't, and hang them out to dry on my little raised balcony under the roof thatch. It is a perfect little home, just steps from the sand, and it's all mine for the next few days. From my balcony, I look out across the vast expanse of beach, where the only other person in sight is a man throwing a stick for a little black dog.

The man sees me and he waves and I wave back. I realise then that I've stopped feeling invisible at last. I feel like a whole person again. I lie down on the bed, which feels so soft that it's like floating on a cloud, and I allow a warm and rather decadent feeling of satisfaction to wash over me. I really feel like I've come through a storm and stepped into sunshine again.

I'm also feeling hungry. It's late afternoon, so I go out barefoot to explore the beach and soon come across a charming place called Driftwood Bar. It looks like a hippy hideout, perched on a rock in a haphazard sort of way and, like its name suggests, it looks to be built entirely out of driftwood.

I climb the wooden steps and look about me to see a little black dog sleeping in the shade. Thinking the place is closed because there are no other customers, I hesitate at the bar for a moment, but then notice a young man working in the little kitchen tucked behind it.

'Hello. Are you open?' I ask him.

He pops his head round the door and flashes me an attractive smile.

'Sure. Take a seat. I'll be right over!'

I sit on a beanbag that has been arranged on top of what looks like a small prayer mat under the shade of a bamboo canopy. Once I get down there, the cushion is perfect for lounging back on and there is a little bamboo table designed to be sat at cross-legged and yogi-style for dining. The bar area is decorated with homemade chains of colourful paper lanterns and windchimes made of seashells and carved pieces of coconut shell that tinkle in the warm wafts of breeze. It is so peaceful and pretty and laidback here. I decide I love it.

I sit back and relax and wait to be served. A few moments later, both the man and the little black dog come over to me. I realise now that I saw them earlier on the beach from my hut.

'An' what can I getcha?' the bartender asks me cheerily, as he steps out from the shade into bright sunshine to hand me a menu. In that moment, I actually hear my jaw click as it dropped open. This guy looks like he should be starring in a TV advert for a chocolate and coconut bar. He's all toned abs and darkly tanned skin, chiselled jawline, and oh my goodness ... the most beautiful and bluest eyes I've ever seen. They're like sparkling deep blue swimming pools.

He smiles at me, showing the whitest and straightest of teeth.

I notice his eyes have a few fine smile lines spreading out from the corners, giving him even more appeal, and giving me the impression that he might not actually be as young as I'd first thought. Have I been duped by his incredibly good looks into thinking he's in his late twenties when he might really be in his late thirties?

Or is that just wishful thinking on my part?

'Erm, I'd like a cold beer please?' I squeak.

'Sure. D'ya need a minute to look at the menu?'

I want to say no – I need a few more minutes to look at him.

From his accent, I'm guessing he's an American, perhaps from the southern states. He has a tall, athletic looking body and he's wearing surf shorts and a tie-dye T-shirt. Along with his boyish casual good looks, he has rock star-length, shaggy, dark brown hair that could have once, many moons ago, been a short city-boy cut. His feet are bare and he has the sort of deep brown tan that says he's spent not weeks, but months, if not years, ripening under the hot tropical sun.

My breathing has quickened and my heart feels like it's doing a crazy drumroll in my chest.

And in my (surprisingly fertile) imagination – he looks exactly as I'd imagined a *Chao Ley*.

My mouth has gone dry. My pulse is palpitating. What the hell is happening here?

I glance briefly over the menu. 'Erm, do you do Pad Thai?'

'We do the best goddamn Pad Thai you've ever tasted,' he tells me, quite seriously.

He points over to a driftwood sign nailed to a palm tree.

It reads: *We make the best goddamn Pad Thai you've ever tasted!*

I start to laugh. 'Well, I'm quite a fan of Pad Thai, so shall I be the judge of that?'

He whoops at the challenge. 'You're on. Y'want shrimp with your Pad Thai?'

'Well, if that's what makes it the goddamn best?' I say, giggling and blushing and grinning like an idiot. 'I'm Lori, by the way.' I offer him my hand.

'Good to meet ya, Lori. I'm Jack.'

He takes my hand and gives it a firm shake. His is so warm that I don't want to let it go.

But he quickly pulls it away to bring me my beer and then he disappears into the kitchen.

His dog stays to keep me company, panting at me from under the shade of a palm tree. He looks like a mixed breed. Maybe one of his parents was a black Labrador and the other a wire-haired terrier of some sort. He has a sweet face and soft brown eyes. My mind wanders across the miles to think on Molly, my little dog back home, and a searing stab of pain goes straight through my heart as

I imagine her sitting patiently at the door waiting for me to come home. I suddenly feel horribly guilty, as if I'd carelessly abandoned an innocent child.

I wonder if dogs, who have such a huge capacity for love, are capable of forgiveness.

When a few other people, mostly couples, come walking by and stop off to take in the laidback ambiance of Jack's beanbags, he reappears behind the bar to serve everyone. Then once his customers are all happily lounging on cushions, chatting, drinking, and enjoying the views of the beach and the sea and all the tiny nearby islands and interesting rock formation, he disappears again, only to reappear moments later, with my steaming plate of Pad Thai and shrimp. It looks, smells, and tastes amazing. I savour my meal and sip my beer and admire the view – and I don't mean the seemingly endless length of beach.

What on earth is going on with me today?

I haven't even noticed another man in decades never mind lusted after one.

Does sunshine help the body to produce hormones like it helps it to produce vitamin D?

That's the only explanation.

When I get up to pay my bill, Jack comes over for my verdict on the food.

'Well?' he says, folding his arms in a way that emphasises his bulging biceps.

'Yes. I have to say, that was the best goddamn Pad Thai I ever tasted,' I tell him honestly.

He laughs loudly. 'I knew it. I just goddamn knew it!'

Ridiculously, my heart is thumping like that of a teenage fan at a boyband concert.

'Your dog and I are now good friends,' I tell him. 'He's very cute. What's his name?'

'He's Hey Joe. Same as the Jimi Hendrix song. An' like me, he appreciates a pretty woman.'

My face feels like a furnace as I hand over the money for my tab.

I'm melting. Am I suddenly menopausal? Is this my first hot flush?

I decide to ask Jack where I can find an accommodating dive school.

'Erm, Jack. I'm guessing you know this area quite well, so where would you recommend I go to learn to scuba dive? Bearing in mind, I'm a complete beginner and a bit nervous.'

'Sure. I'd recommend the Dive Shack. An' lots of people start out nervous. It's only natural, right?' Then he gives me another smile and I feel like I'm drowning in his deep blue eyes. 'It's just down the beach there.' And he points a long finger in its general direction. 'If you tell them I sent you, you'll get a discount on your gear.'

'Okay. Thanks!' I say, trying to recover enough so as not to fall down the steps to the beach.

'Hey, Lori...' he yells after me. The way he says my name almost makes my knees buckle.

I turn to him and smile. 'Yes, Jack?'

'Happy hour is between six and seven.'

I wave. 'Thanks Jack. I guess I'll see you later.'

And he waves back. 'Cool. See ya'!'

I continue walking along the beach in the direction Jack had indicated, feeling a little lightheaded, and still asking myself what the hell just happened to me? I find the Dive Shack nearby. It has several flags outside flapping in the sea breeze and lots of dive posters on display showing happy smiling young people in wetsuits. The doors are wide open and inside I can hear a radio station playing Western pop music and I see tidy racks of dive equipment hanging up, wetsuits and facemasks, snorkels and fins and a wall of metal air tanks. I hover by the door.

Soon a sporty-looking woman with short, wet, slicked-back hair appears. She's wearing a wetsuit and a welcoming smile. 'Hi, can I help you?'

'Yes. I was just chatting to Jack, over at Driftwood Bar. He recommended I came here to learn how to scuba dive.'

'Cool. I'm Carly, one of the instructors. Jack sent you to exactly the right place!'

'I'm Lori,' I say, shaking hands with enthusiastic Carly. 'Although I have to confess I'm a bit nervous about doing it – diving, I mean – deep in the sea on an air tank.'

'Can you swim?' Carly asks, crinkling her brow and looking totally sympathetic.

I nod, wondered if yesterday's snorkelling in four feet of water counts as swimming.

'Then there's no problem,' says Carly. 'How about taking a Discover Scuba Diving course?'

Carly tells me it's a one-day course and training starts in the pool in small groups.

'Or we can offer you individual tuition if you prefer. All our instructors are highly trained and very experienced and we are used to clients being a bit nervous at first. Once you've mastered a few basic skills in the pool, you'll come out with us on the boat to do a supervised shallow dive and to see some amazing corals and colourful fish. It'll be just like *Finding Nemo*. How does that sound to you, Lori?'

She makes it sound wonderful and so easy. As I'd fully expected to be thrown out of a boat into the deep sea straightaway, training in a pool before a shallow dive sounds safe enough.

'It sounds great. Okay, when can I do it?'

'Tomorrow, if you like. We can do the paperwork now. Here are our course prices. If you find that you love Discover Scuba then you can go straight onto doing Open Water Diver – which will give you a dive qualification recognised all over the world.'

I fill in the form and Carly gives me another of her megawatt smiles and a high-five.

'Okay, Lori. I'll see you back here at 8 a.m. tomorrow morning.'

I've never been high-fived before in my whole life.

I got back to my hut to relax and sit on my porch reading *The Beach*, which I'd picked up in a second-hand book store next to the 7/11 on the main street here. But I can't get past the first line of the story because I can't stop thinking about Jack and how amazingly good-looking he is. I wonder, what the heck is going on with me? Just over a week ago, I'd been a dried-up old housewife with not a glimmer of a sex drive whatsoever, and now I'm practically a goddamn cougar.

Feeling embarrassed and even a little bit freaked out by my sudden and unexpected interest in A Man, I decide I can't trust myself to go back to the Driftwood Bar for happy hour in the hope of ogling Jack again. I mean, what if, after a couple of cocktails, I make a complete and utter fool of myself?

I decide to go out for a relaxing massage instead. I have a knot of tension between my shoulders that needs to be worked on and I've already walked past at least ten massage parlours on the street between the 7/11 store and my hut. Back in the UK, it's an expensive treat to have a massage. I usually got them as a birthday or anniversary or Christmas gift – as everyone knew I'd appreciate a spa treatment voucher – but here in Thailand I know I can afford to have a massage every single day if I want to. I head for a spa I spotted earlier because it had a glass door and a proper window – a feature not many of the others possess – which leads me to assume it also has air-conditioning. It's so incredibly hot and steamy out here on the street that I'm already drenched in sweat and I can't imagine myself feeling relaxed if I'm not feeling cool.

Standing outside the Pretty Lady Spa, touting for customers, is a tiny young Thai girl.

'Pretty lady! Massage!' She trills at me like a little songbird. She has such a sweet smile and a clean spa outfit and a frangipani flower in her hair, so my first impressions are good.

I smile and nod, and she bows and invites me inside.

I leave my flip flops at the door and follow her into the inner sanctum in the anticipation of an hour of pampering and bliss. Inside, it is clean with soft music and fragrant candles.

I'm asked to sit in a comfortable chair and I have my feet gently washed and patted lightly dry by this gentle girl. I'm now fully expecting to be guided by her into a private room for a gentle massage, when another, much older woman, appears from behind a beaded curtain.

This other woman is short and wide and has the formidable look of a sumo wrestler about her. She holds out a muscly arm and with a grunt she points a wide finger to indicate that I should follow her behind the curtain. Dutifully, I do as I'm told and I find myself in a room with a row of mattresses on the floor. Each is covered with a clean white sheet and has a privacy curtain but they are all so close together and the curtains are so thin that it is possible to see the shadows and hear the sounds of other people – both men and women – being massaged behind them. I'm not sure I like the look of this, but I have a feeling it's far too late to turn and run.

My muscled masseuse waits with crossed arms and a determined expression while I strip off my shirt and shorts and slide quickly under the sheet in just my scarlet lace thong.

Moments later, she has both her elbows pressed into the small of my back, pinning me into the mattress. I manage to let out a high-pitched squeal – so high that perhaps only a handful of dogs roaming outside might have heard it – before being smothered and crushed by her full weight. Then, with no air left in my lungs, I can't make another sound.

After the smothering and the crushing comes the

slapping and the stretching and the pummelling. I'm being beaten up and I know I'll be horribly bruised afterwards, but if I try to move or raise a limb in protest she yells, 'Relax! Lady! Relax!'

When I hear my back crack, I groan, and she says, 'Very good. Now you loosen up!'

Then she climbs all over me, standing on my back, stamping on my spine with her short flat feet and with her short wide arms she bends my poor limbs into all sorts of strange positions.

And, in my excruciating embarrassment, I stupidly just let it all happen.

After exactly an hour of this torture, feeling bruised and humiliated, I practically crawl out of the shop having handed over not only the requested fee of four hundred baht but also a tip of one hundred baht. So much for feeling calm and relaxed.

I limp back to my hut to take a shower and to climb exhausted into bed.

Chapter 6

Koh Lanta (ii)

At 8.30 a.m. the following morning, I turn up at The Dive Shack nervously wearing a bikini under my shorts and T-shirt. I'm not quite sure what to wear for scuba diving training. I needn't have worried though because as soon as I arrive, I'm met by a very enthusiastic Carly and given a shorty wetsuit to wear, which I immediately take into the changing room and squeeze myself into.

Catching sight of myself in the mirror, I actually think I look rather fetching.

The tight neoprene fabric forces up my boobs, squeezes my tummy flat, and lifts my bum.

I sashay into the equipment room, feeling like a Bond girl in my wetsuit and expecting to find Carly, but instead I walk slap bang into – Jack?

'Hey Lori! Carly's just told me I'm your instructor for Discover Scuba Diving today.'

'You...? You're a dive instructor ... here?' I splutter.

Jack is wearing only half his wetsuit, as only a true merman can – with the bottom part of it balanced precariously on his narrow hips while the rest of it hangs low and open leaving him half-naked and bare-chested while standing right in front of me. I stare at his muscle-toned chest, his full set of rippling abdominals, flat stomach, and the soft line of dark hair that trails from his navel to lower down on his otherwise smooth and darkly-tanned skin.

I think I might have heard myself groan.

He laughs, flashing his perfect white teeth at me. 'Yeah, I work here when I'm not needed at my bar. It's a perfect life!'

Again, I find myself gazing into those blue eyes of his and not knowing what to say next.

'It's pool training this morning,' he says, rubbing his hands together as if he's warming them up for me. 'We'll run through a few scuba skills, so you feel comfortable in the water breathing through a regulator. Then, after lunch, we'll go out in the boat. We'll go divin' in a shallow cove where you'll see lots of colourful fish. It'll be fantastic. Any questions, Lori?'

It does sound fantastic. He sounds both knowledge-able and encouraging.

I have no doubts about Jack's competency as a dive instructor but how on earth am I going to cope with being with him alone all day long – in such close proximity – when I have such an excruciating crush on him? It feels like I'm drowning before I'm anywhere near water.

The swimming pool for dive training is in part of a large hotel complex behind the dive shop. At the bottom of that pool, wearing all the gear – which includes a very heavy air tank – I kneel in front of Jack and watch as he demonstrates to me how to purge water from my face mask by tipping it back with a forefinger and blowing air into it through my nose.

He makes it look so easy but as soon as I try to do it, I get water in my eyes and make straight for the surface in a panic. Jack comes up after me, gently explaining why I must not do that again.

'Lori, we gotta come up nice and slow and in control. Because we're breathin' compressed air from a tank, comin' up too quick, even in a shallow pool, can be dangerous.'

'You mean, I could burst my lungs?' I say to him in horror and new understanding.

'Sure. It's possible. That's why, if we learn a few skills in the confined space of the pool, we can be safe out there in the open sea. Remember, today's just an introduction. I'm only gonna show you the basics so we can go out divin' this afternoon and have some fun together.'

His words 'have some fun together' take away any

fears and reservations I have. Once I'd practiced tipping back my mask and popping my breathing regulator in and out my mouth a few times, I find I can do it easily, and it's not so hard after all.

We swim up and down the pool together, Jack by my side, with his hand supporting the weight of my air tank, while guiding me through the water. His breathing and his bubbles are as loud in my ears as my own. I can't wait to get to the sea and for the fun together to begin.

'Well done. You got it!' he says to me at the surface, taking out his regulator. 'Fantastic!'

I watch him run his hand through his shiny dark wet hair and slick it back from his forehead.

I see glistening drops of water clinging to his eyelashes until he blinks them away in the bright sunshine. I realise I have a crushing desire to kiss away those tiny droplets of water trapped in the cupid's curve of his perfect upper lip...

But of course, instead, I just wave my arms in the air and grin at him like an idiot.

'All thanks to you Jack. You are a great teacher!'

'No problem. And you, Lori, are a fast learner!'

At lunchtime, Jack disappears for an hour. I think he might have gone back to the Driftwood Bar. I'm relieved because being with Jack is making me breathless, even with a tank full of air, because I can't stop myself from fancying the neoprene pants off him. It's exhausting.

While we were underwater, he maintained constant eye contact and gave me hand signals for 'watch me' for whenever I was supposed to be paying careful attention to him. But I didn't need telling.

I can't take my eyes off him. I'm captivated.

I buy a sandwich and a bottle of water and sit at a picnic bench outside in the shade of palm trees with all the divers who've just come in from the morning dive boat. They're a welcoming and chatty bunch who are full of enthusiastic dive talk. It feels cool to be amongst them. It's fun to be one of them. A real diver. A mermaid amongst other mermaids and mermen.

'Did you see that sea snake on the rocks at Koh Haa dive site?' one of them asks another.

'Yeah, a banded sea krait – highly venomous!' comes the reply.

I almost choke on my sandwich. Then, they start making fun of one of the divers called Eric, who had apparently been attacked by a Trigger fish that morning. They've captured the whole thing on a GoPro underwater camera and they're playing back the video over and over again and are laughing so hard that they're all creased up. They play the video with the volume up high so that everyone can hear Eric's underwater squeals.

'Haha – you squeal like a little girl!' Poor Eric.

Luckily, Eric thinks it's hilarious too. I don't. I didn't think there was such a thing as snakes in the sea and the thought of a fish attack terrifies me just as much as a shark attack. 'Where did it bite you?' I ask Eric, once he has stopped giggling.

'Nowhere. It didn't get me. It just chased me away from where it was nesting. I got a scare because it was such a big fish. I didn't know triggers could get that big!'

He holds his hands apart like the proverbial fisherman to show me how big it was.

I gawp at him in horror. Five minutes later, I'm supposed to be in the equipment room with everyone else getting my gear together for the afternoon dive but instead I'm still outside like a jabbering wreck, wringing my hands until Jack comes back.

'Erm, I don't think I'll go diving after all. I feel a bit queasy,' I tell him.

'What'd you have for lunch?' Jack asks me with concern.

'A tall tale of attacking trigger fish and poisonous sea snakes...' comes a voice from behind me. It was Carly. She then continues to tell Jack all the details of what she had seen and overheard from her office at lunchtime. 'I saw poor Lori's face going paler and paler while she was listening to those goons. Pay no attention,

Lori. Any snakes you'll see out there are beautiful and totally non-aggressive. They have far too small a mouth to bite anything more than a pinkie finger and would even turn it down if you offered it to them. As for the trigger fish – well, they all knew she was there, they'd been pre-warned in their dive briefing. It's the breeding season and Eric got too close to her. He got chased off, not attacked, because he's an idiot and for no other reason.'

Jack is standing with his hands on his narrow hips looking at me with an expression of concern. I feel bad for him. He's probably thinking that he's just wasted his whole morning trying to teach me to dive and I'm now too afraid to go into the sea.

'Okay. I'll do it,' I relent. 'But promise you'll keep me away from snakes or trigger fish?'

Jack gives me a big smile. 'I promise. Come on. Let's go divin'!'

As we head out to sea on the dive boat, I stand on the open sun deck to work on my tan and to watch Koh Lanta's pretty coastline getting further away and the scattering of islands on the horizon getting closer. The dive boat is large and impressive. It's a traditionally built wooden boat with two decks and with a mostly Thai crew. On board, working for the instructors are the teams of dive masters, whose job it is to look after the customers and the equipment and the air tanks that are secured on racks, until everyone is ready to gear up.

As I'm the only one doing a try-diving course rather than a certification course, I decide to keep well out of the way of the hustle and bustle going on downstairs until we are at the dive site, and all the divers who are training are in the water with their instructors.

I strip down to my bikini and start applying lots of sunscreen because the afternoon sun is beating down intensely, and I can feel my shoulders starting to burn already. I didn't expect Jack to come up to the top deck as he'd been busy downstairs chatting with the other instructors since we'd left, but suddenly he appears, with a bottle of water and a book on fish identification, both for me. He's still in his wetsuit, which has been pulled down off his torso.

I can hardly take my eyes off him.

'Hey, Lori, ya need some help?' he asks, indicating to the tube of sunscreen.

I gulp and take the bottle of water from him. 'Thanks. Yes, that would be great.'

I'm suddenly excruciatingly aware of how much flesh I have on show. Other than a few triangles of fabric and lengths of string, I'm basically standing naked in front of him.

I know my skin is glistening with perspiration and I feel awkward and exposed.

My face is glowing with embarrassment.

He gives me a wink and a boyish grin. 'No problemo! It's one of the perks of my job.'

I hand him the sunscreen and turn my back on him. I lift my hair off my shoulders and reason with myself not to be so stupid. He must be so used to seeing women in bikinis every single day. This is normal to him. Like a gynaecologist sees lots of lady parts every day and thinks it's normal too. I hold my breath as my body anticipates his touch.

I realise if I had a spray sunscreen, he wouldn't have to touch me at all but this is a cream in a tube and so he'll have to rub it in really well. All the nerve endings in my entire body are now tingling in expectation. I feel him gently picking up a few loose strands of my hair from the sensitive nape of my neck and from my shoulders and move them aside. I shiver, eager for his touch but also reticent, because I know from the churning feeling in my stomach and the throbbing heat in my pulsating groin, that I'm highly aroused.

I haven't felt like this since I was in my twenties.

His long fingers work in circles on my shoulders. I bite my lip to stop myself moaning.

He dabs the cream down my back, along my spine, and then he starts to massage it in.

I want to cry out in pleasure.

But instead I wince in pain. 'Ouch!'

He jumps back in alarm. 'Oh sorry, Lori. Did I press too hard?'

I explain about the monstrous Thai massage I'd suffered the night before and while he sympathises he also finds it incredibly funny. 'Yeah, most people have tales to tell about a Thai massage. I've had one or two like that myself. So, that would explain why you didn't come to the bar last night. I was waitin' for you. I was gonna mix you my special sundowner.'

I laugh to hide my aching disappointment at not being there.

'And, I imagine, it would have been the best goddamn sundowner I've ever tasted.'

He continues to rub the cream into my shoulders, so gently and so carefully now, that his fingers feel like a trail of kisses across my shoulders and down my back. I have to stop myself from gasping when they sweep along under the border of my bikini bottoms.

I grip tightly onto the handrail on the side of the boat and I'm actually dizzy with desire.

Isn't he the least bit aware of what he's doing to me?

'There, all done. You have protection.'

Excuse me? Was that a question?

Oh, for heaven's sake – what am I thinking? Have I lost my freaking mind?

He puts the top back on the tube for me and sits

down on the bench seat, opening up his book on fish identification. I hurry to compose myself and then I turn to face him. It's in that fraction of a second – when his face is level with my chest – that he looks up from the book.

For what seems to be an indiscernible amount of time, his eyes gaze appreciatively at my breasts which, being on the sizable side, were bulging out of my triangular bikini top.

I gasp. And, when he realises he's been caught, he quickly turns away.

I see that he's still smiling but that he also looks a little flustered.

Feeling flustered too, I sit down next to him and try to pay attention to the book on his lap but realise that what I'm actually staring at is his bulging neoprene covered groin.

Jack taps a finger on a picture of a brightly coloured fish. 'On this page, are the kinds of fish we might see today, if we're lucky. Sweetlips…'

I look up from the book, at him. Our lips are so close, and I realise that if I lean forward just a little, I could steal a kiss from him. I can't help but imagine what that might feel like. When he speaks, I can feel his warm breath on my face. He smells minty. I nervously lick my own lips before I avert my gaze from his mouth, up and into the deep blue sizzling depths of his dilated eyes to see an unfamiliar – yet quite unmistakable – look in them.

It's a look I haven't seen in a man for a very long time but my memory still serves me well. I'm left in no doubt that the frisson between us is real and also mutually acknowledged.

'I like the way you look at me, Lori. It makes me feel real good,' he says in a low voice.

My heart leaps and panic fizzles through me. I don't know what to say. What have I done?

He quickly puts his hand onto my bare leg and he squeezes my thigh gently.

Then he removes his hand just as quickly in order to point at another fish in the book. Did I imagine what happened just then? Was it my imagination playing a trick?

'Erm, did you just call me sweetlips?' I ask him, using humour to defuse the tension.

Jack laughs. 'I promise it's the name of the fish. Look, here's an Oriental sweetlips and a clownfish and a batfish and a grouper. They are all very common in this area.'

Having just been groped myself I say, 'A groper fish? Ooh, well, I'll have to watch out!'

He creases up laughing. 'No. It's called a grouper, Lori, and the sweetlips thing – oh my that's so funny. You're so funny!'

Our laughter slices through the heavy sexual tension in the salty air and we both breathe a sigh of relief. We go downstairs and Jack helps me gear up.

The diving experience is great. We go down to a shallow cove that has a stunningly beautiful coral garden. He stays by my side every moment, guiding me, keeping one hand on my air tank and pointing out interesting colourful fish in the waving corals and the scuttling crabs in the sand and even an ugly looking eel poking its head out from the rocks. The dive is supposed to last around forty minutes but the time passes so quickly. I'm so in the moment and I love every single minute of being underwater. I love every single minute of being with Jack.

'Do you think you'll wanna do a dive qualification now?' he asks me afterwards.

'Yes. Absolutely,' I tell him. 'I want to get my Open Water certification.'

'Great. Cos I know Carly has an Open Water group starting tomorrow, if you feel ready?'

I'm suddenly and heart wrenchingly disappointed. 'But Carly told me that I could go with a group or I could have private one-to-one tuition. I'd really like to continue with you as my private instructor, Jack. Will you teach me?'

He looks at me and, for moment at least, I see something else in his eyes.

Hesitation?

'Sure. It'll be my pleasure. Will I see you tonight at the bar – for happy hour?'

I reach Driftwood Bar just as the sun is setting. I'm still high on happiness from the wonderful day that I've just spent with Jack and I'm excited over having had my first diving experience. I'm still tingling from his fingers on my skin. I'm still basking in the glow of the unmistakable way he looked at me on the boat and the way he squeezed my thigh, sending zaps of carnal lust and errant longing straight to every erogenous zone in my body. He's woken me from my long sexual coma and sent me into a lightheaded tizzy spin of reckless thoughts.

I suddenly feel like a teenager again. I feel like a very naughty and sexy minx.

Oh my … I'm so out of control!

The night is warm and balmy, there's a thin sharp slice of moon tonight and an inky sky full of stars. I'm wearing a loose cotton dress and I've taken some time over my hair, washing out the salty seawater and teasing a slick of coconut oil through the length of it with my fingers, so that it dries in long tousled waves down my back. My only accessories are my sacred string bracelets and a beaded anklet that jangles as I walk, my only make-up a slick of strawberry lip balm. I dearly wish

I had a fragrance to wear. I wonder why I hadn't thought to treat myself to a bottle of Chanel or something nice in duty-free on the way out here?

It's this simple nonchalant thought about perfume that stirs something inside me.

That something is a rather bitchy reprimand. A sharp reminder that I hadn't bought any perfume at the airport because I'd been in a completely distraught state over finding out about my husband's affair with my best friend. That my shopping at that time had been about frantically grabbing whatever might be suitable because I was running away from my adulterous husband – not flitting off on holiday on my own in a cloud of fragrance, in the hope of having a quickie with another man!

I'm totally shocked at how my own consciousness could slap me down so viciously.

What's this all about? What am I doing?

Do I have a need for revenge? Is that what this is?

Am I looking for a quick fling to make things right? A romp for retribution?

A quick affair to get payback at Charles?

An eye for an eye. A tooth for a tooth. Sex for sex?

As I approach the bar from the beach, I can see there are lots more mats and beanbags laid out on the sand. All are occupied by couples, laughing, chatting, clinking glasses, sipping beer or cocktails and sitting under colourful paper lanterns and twinkly lights that are strung up high or wrapped around the trunks of the surrounding palm trees.

There is live reggae music floating on the air. A Bob Marley lookalike with long dreadlocks is strumming a guitar and crooning *One Love, One Heart* into a microphone.

I make my way up the steps to the bar where Hey Joe is sitting. When the little dog sees me, he beats his tail on the deck in welcome. I slip onto an empty bar stool. To my surprise, there is someone else serving behind the bar tonight. It's a woman.

She's immediately friendly and asks me what I'd like to drink. I detect from her accent that she too is an American like Jack. She's attractive. Blonde. In her late thirties?

I'm not sure why I'm suddenly into guessing other people's ages.

I'm just about to tell her that I'll have a beer, when Jack appears from the kitchen.

'Hi Lori!' he says immediately. His blue eyes and his smile light up when he sees me.

And for some reason, instead of just saying hello like a normal person, I wave my fingertips at him and giggle, which looks ridiculous and girly and comes out sounding like a strange purr.

'This is Jules. Jules this is Lori,' Jack continues, happily introducing us.

'Nice to meet you, Jules,' I say.

I can see by the amused look on Jules's face that she's already clocked my crush on Jack.

'Nice to meet you too, Lori. We've got two for one in our happy hour just now.'

Jack points to a driftwood sign on the bar: *Cocktail of the Day: The best goddamn vodka martini you've ever tasted!*

Jules rolls her heavily mascaraed eyes. 'Oh, an' they truly are the goddamn best!'

'Okay. I'll try your goddamn martinis!' I laugh, trying desperately to pull myself together.

Jules mixes my first cocktail while, to my disappointment, Jack disappears back into his kitchen. I watch Jules reach for the vodka bottle from the shelf at the back of the bar where all the spirits are in a tidy row and then I notice, propped up on this shelf, there is a certificate of thanks for money raised for an animal charity on the island.

It reads: *Thanks to Jules Perry and Jack Perry and the patrons of Driftwood Bar.*

And I realise that Jack and Jules have the same name.

This information hits me like a brick and takes my breath away. I feel sick.

I realise I've been flirting with him all day, giving him all kinds of signals that I was interested in him, thinking it was just a bit of innocent fun.

And he had responded by coming onto me – *when he was married!*

I suddenly feel like you do after a great night out of fun and dancing and drinking when the crazy alcohol-fuelled rush of excitement is over, and the nausea has set in and you think you might throw up. Jack the merman-sea-gypsy was taken. *What a goddamn tragedy.*

I finish my drinks quickly. I'm drowning my sorrow in the best goddamn vodka martinis I've ever tasted. I really want to flee without drinking them but knock them back, knowing I have nothing other than a bottle of water back in my beach hut and I need the alcohol hit to deal with what's just been revealed to me. The bar is suddenly incredibly busy and everyone is ordering food and drinks, keeping Jules busy mixing cocktails and Jack in the kitchen.

I leave my tab on the bar and walk back down the beach feeling completely stupid.

What on earth had I been thinking?

Gazing into his eyes like a silly teenager. Flirting with him like a bitch on heat.

Why didn't I even think to question if he was married?

Is this some kind of reverse karma in play?

And what kind of woman does that make me?

No. I would *never* ever want to steal another woman's husband!

Poor Jules. With a husband like Jack – so good-looking and flirtatious with other women – she's probably seen it all a thousand times before. To think, when he'd laid his hands on me, he'd said it was the perk of his job. Bloody men!

Two-timing no-good heartbreaking bastards!

Jack and his two for one on the goddamn side.

I return to my beach hut feeling foolish and jaded and angry all over again.

The following morning, I wake completely soaked with sweat and wrapped up in my bedsheet. I've had the most horrible and scary nightmare about being deep down in the sea. So deep I could look up and just about see the rippling surface and hazy sunlight far above me. In the dream, I was diving with Jack, but he was pulling me down into the unfathomable black depths below, trying to drown me. I was trying to scream but no sound would come out of my mouth – only air bubbles. In desperation, I tried to claw at him with my fingers to loosen his grip, but he had lots of hands and lots of arms, each with tentacles like those of a giant octopus. My clawing was in vain and I floundered in the water, spinning and sinking deeper and deeper, with nothing left in my air tank.

Gasping and choking for breath as I wake, it takes me a while to calm myself down and shake off my fears.

I make myself a cup of strong coffee and gulp it down before taking a shower and heading down to the Dive Shack on shaky legs. I arrive a little earlier than planned but I need to speak to Carly. I want to tell her that I've changed my mind about having one-to-one tuition with Jack. That I now want to be part of her group for the camaraderie and support.

Carly is absolutely fine about it. She introduces me to the others starting the Open Water course and sets us all up in the classroom to watch dive training videos and do quizzes called knowledge reviews. Most of the study at this stage is about dive safety and water depths and what effects water pressure and breathing compressed air has on the body.

I feel daunted by all the study and struggle with the science behind it all. I know the standards are incredibly high in preparation for a tough online exam. Some of the others have their own laptops but as I don't, I'm given one to use.

There's a lot more to learn than I ever imagined and there's an unspoken pressure to progress at the same level and timeframe as the others, who are so much younger and who seem so much smarter than me. Only after passing the theory exam can we go onto pool training and only after that can we put everything we've learned into practice in the open sea.

Carly says that most Open Water trainees complete

the course in three to four days. I realise that I need to stay on Koh Lanta for a day longer than I'd originally planned. But that's okay. Being a qualified scuba diver is a big tick off my bucket list.

After a whole day in front of a computer screen, I drag myself back to my hut carrying a pile of manuals and homework. To reach my hut, I have to walk past Driftwood Bar.

To my surprise, I see Jules waving to me as soon as she spots me coming up the beach.

She looks a little agitated. I cringe but there's no avoiding her.

'Hey, Lori! What happened today? Jack said he was expecting to start a dive course with you this morning, but you'd gone and joined Carly's group instead?'

I look at her incredulously. Okay, I'd flirted with her husband and he'd flirted with me but that was as far as it had gone. What I do in my own time is really none of her goddamn business.

'It's no big deal. I just decided I'd be better off learning with a group, that's all.'

'So you weren't unhappy with Jack?' she demands to know.

I can hardly comprehend the question. 'Unhappy with him? What do you mean?'

'It's just, well, my brother was worried you might think he behaved unprofessionally towards you. Jack prides himself on being an absolute professional. He's a really good dive instructor and—'

'What did you just say?'

'That Jack was worried he might have been inappropriate towards you yesterday. I know he really likes you, Lori, but he told me he thinks he may have overstepped some boundaries.'

'I meant about what you said about him being your brother?' I clarify.

'Yes. That's right. He's my big brother – but you knew that, right?'

'No. I thought you were his wife?'

Jules's hand flies to her mouth. 'Oh my gosh. What on earth gave you that idea?'

'Look, Jules. Tell Jack I'll pop down for a drink later and we can talk about this, okay?'

Jules nods. 'I'll tell him. He'll be back soon. He's had to take Hey Joe to the vets, or he'd have been here himself. He's been waiting all day to talk to you, Lori.'

'Oh no, what happened to Hey Joe?'

'He slashed his paw on some coral washed up on the beach. That stuff is razor sharp.'

'Okay. I'll come over later. But I have to study first.'

My mind is whirring. Jack and Jules are brother and sister?

I take a shower and change into clean shorts and a vest and sit on my bed. I have so much work to do but

I also know that I must take an hour out to see Jack. I have to explain why I changed my mind. He's obviously upset at me joining Carly's group without telling him. Although, I still think it was a good decision. The course is tough and Jack is a distraction.

Everyone in Carly's group is so supportive and we encourage each other. I know that when it gets to the Open Water training, it will be even more important to have that kind of camaraderie, and my lusting after Jack would not be conducive to me passing this course.

Feeling exhausted, I close my eyes for a moment.

What feels like seconds later, I'm woken by a tapping sound.

My eyes spring open to find it's pitch black in my room.

I flick on the bedside light to see my dive manuals scattered all over the bed sheet.

My first thought is that I've managed to miss happy hour and talking with Jack.

Then there is that tapping sound again. It's someone at the door.

'Who's there?' I yell, feeling a little confused and disorientated.

'Lori. It's Jack.'

I open the door to a cacophony of tree frogs and crickets and geckos, and to the sight of Jack standing on my porch looking anxious. 'How's Hey Joe?'

'He's okay. A few stitches but he's revelling in all the attention it's got him.'

'Look ... I want to apolo—' we both say in unison.

'Come in,' I say, keen to shut out the noise and humidity and marauding mosquitoes.

Jack follows me inside and closes the door. I'm left standing in the middle of the room under the ceiling fan with my arms crossed defensively. This feels really awkward and a little surreal.

'I wanna apologise, Lori. I'm sure I've offended you. I came onto you yesterday and I shouldn't have because it was unprofessional. I mean, it's also kinda against the rules, too. So, when you changed your mind about me training you, I felt really bad. I felt terrible, actually.'

'Jack, I changed my mind because I thought that you and Jules were husband and wife. I was a terrible flirt with you yesterday. Although, it's not really like me to do that kind of thing and when I thought you had betrayed her by flirting back with me, I was horrified.'

He rolls his beautiful eyes in confusion. 'Oh Lori ... she's my sister. We own the bar together and I guess I sorta just assumed you knew. I'm sorry. I never thought to explain.'

'Anyway, I'm glad I joined Carly's class. They are a such a supportive group. I feel like I fit in and if I work really hard and focus then I know I can get my qualification. I can't focus around you, Jack. I think we both realise that now.'

He takes a step towards me, smiling softly and reaching out to take my hand.

My breath quickens as he makes contact and pulls me towards him.

'It's a good decision. You'll do well, Lori. You're a natural in the water.'

He leans in to kiss me and a moment later his warm soft and beautiful lips are on mine.

I can feel my legs weakening and my whole body melts against his as both his arms come around me. His body is pressed against mine and his tongue slides inside my parted lips to flick against my tongue. My insides tremble. My erratic heart beat pounds in my chest and in my ears. I lean into him to increase the delicious pressure of our togetherness and I breathlessly kiss him back. Then, as his hands move up my body, moulding to my breasts, and his thumbs find my stiffened nipples through my vest, I gasp and arch my back.

I throw my head back and moan with pleasure as we twirl together in a locked embrace across the room and towards the bed. The dive manuals hit the floor as we hit the mattress together. He kisses me even harder, bruising my mouth, nipping at my lower lip, grinding his hips into mine.

Oh, he tastes so good – I'm getting a minty mix of mouthwash and vodka martini.

He smells of sandalwood and citrus cologne.

And, oh my goodness, his body is so hard and hot and wonderfully heavy on mine.

I wrap my arms around him and pull myself towards him wantonly, lifting my hips against his, desperately wanting the fire ignited deep within me sated by him. He drives the fabulously hard and impressive bulge in his shorts against me at the same time as his tongue delves into my throat to show me how deeply he wants to take me.

My mind is swimming and I'm lost and dizzy and senseless with lust.

It's only when his fingers turned their attention to the waist band of my shorts that I suddenly come out of my passion-fuelled state and start to question my sanity. In that same moment, I clamp my hands over his to stop him going any further.

'No. Stop. I'm sorry Jack. This is as far as it goes. This is madness!'

'Yeah, complete madness,' he agrees, not really listening, as his fingers fight mine for possession of my panties.

'Jack, I really like you. I do. But in three days I'm leaving here, and I'm probably never coming back, which means that I'll never see you again.'

'I understand, Lori...' he says, his breath rasping and hot on my neck. 'That's exactly why we should value this short but precious time together.'

'No. I don't think you do understand, Jack. I'm sorry but I've changed my mind. I can't do casual sex. I really don't know how to be so free and easy.'

He whispers into my ear. 'Relax, babe, and let me show you...'

And to me, that line sounds so crass and so sleazy, that my unbridled passion for him fizzles out like a wet squib. Jack might be the most good-looking and sexiest goddamn man alive, but I don't want to relax and I don't want to be shown how to be casual and easy by anyone.

I'd rather be lonely than have meaningless sex.

Don't get me wrong. After all this time, I'm more than happy to have my libido back and to feel young and sexy and wanted again, but I'm certainly not just giving it all away to the first man who wants to love me and leave me.

So, I ask Jack to leave without making a scene, and he does.

After that night, I never see Jack again. For the next three days, I walk along the road rather than the beach to get to the Dive Shack, so I can avoid walking past Driftwood Bar. I go on to pass my theory exam with flying colours. Then, I spend two long and difficult days in the pool practising all my dive skills repeatedly and another day in the sea, proving I had all the skills to be a competent and responsible Open Water diver.

Until finally and deservedly, I complete and pass my course and achieve my certificate.

When I leave Koh Lanta, on the early morning long-tail boat for the next paradise island on my list and along this coastline, I'm not only a qualified diver, but also a wiser woman.

I might still be in search of true happiness and purpose in my life, but I now know that no matter how pretty the package, those things are not going to be found in a man like Jack Perry.

Chapter 7

Koh Ngai

Getting up so early over the past few mornings, staying up so late at night studying and working through the intense days of training to get my Open Water certificate, has really taken its toll on me. I'm physically and emotionally exhausted from my time on Koh Lanta.

Consequentially, I intend to spend the next two days on a tiny and very beautiful little island called Koh Ngai, relaxing in a hammock with a book or lying stretched out on the beach deepening my tan before moving on to the other islands for the excellent scuba diving there.

I'm pleased to report that my suntan is really coming along at last. I remember being so envious of Summer's golden tan and, although I'm nowhere near as deeply tanned as she is yet, I'm making great progress. I know it's not good for you to be tanned. Exposure to the sun dries out and ages your skin, but I can't help but feel better when I'm sun kissed. The locals must think the Westerners lying stretched out on the beaches or by the pool in the full sun are completely crazy. I suppose we are because the sun is so intense here. It's hard to gauge over-exposure and I do see people with badly-burned faces or with great red welts and white patches where yesterday's swimsuit had covered the skin that today's does not.

Pale skin can burn in just minutes here, even with copious quantities of high factor sunscreen. I was in despair over my arms and legs turning into a horrible mottled mess. I even had a heat rash that, together with my mosquito bites, made it look like I had chicken-pox for a while. However, with the help of nightly slathering of coconut oil (a tip from Summer to soothe sunburnt and fly bitten-skin) and with the protection of a high factor sunscreen and a cover-up and a hat over the past week, my body is now the satisfying colour of a light gravy rather than a boiled lobster.

Koh Ngai, my next destination, is not too far from Koh Lanta, so today I'm travelling by long-tail boat. I buy my ticket from a hut on the beach and wade into the water with my rucksack, with several other travellers who are heading the same way. For once, I'm actually looking forward to this boat ride. Going out on a dive boat and doing my dive training in the sea has given me a much greater confidence. In so many ways, being on Koh Lanta has been a positive and confidence-boosting experience for me and I'm grateful for lessons learned.

It's another perfect day. The sky is blue and cloudless. The wind is light and the temperature is scorching. We head out to sea and the scenery all around is breath-taking. We pass close to and in between some of the most spectacular limestone rock formations along this part of the seaboard. Some of them are massive rounded mounds in the sea, that have been worn completely smooth by the monsoon winds and rains, so they look like giant cupcakes topped with rich green icing. Others are incredibly imposing and rise up like tall chimney stacks. Many might have started out this way but over countless years have been worn away at the base by the strong tides and now look like top heavy ice cream cones with verdant sprinkles. My favourites are the ones that look like tribal heads complete with happy smiling faces and protruding noses and ears, with dreadlocks of hanging vines. Or perhaps the ones that look like animals or birds – I kid you not. You only need to look at Koh Kai (also known as Chicken Island) to know why it was so named.

Our boat driver, who is a skinny old barefoot man with the crinkled skin of an old brown snake, is standing at the helm with a cigarette dangling from his lips. He's steering the long-tail prop with one bent leg while balancing on his standing leg. He yells to us and points a bony finger to a tiny and derelict long-deserted stick hut that is balanced precariously on a rock on one of these barren and uninhabited outcrops that we are passing by.

'Look. It's your hotel!' he shouts, gleefully cracking himself up over his joke.

After less than an hour, we reach the beach on Koh Ngai and everyone grabs their backpacks and scrambles overboard into the shallow warm and clear turquoise water, eager to get their toes in the sand and to secure some accommodation on the island.

The photos in my guidebook do no justice to Koh Ngai. The place is idyllic.

I see the interior is a steep dense jungle all the way down to the beaches. I'm told there's sketchy wi-fi here, but no villages, no towns, no convenience stores, no ATMs, no roads or motorised vehicles. It's a quiet island and there aren't any wild parties.

A real 'no news no shoes' kind of place. It sounds perfect.

I've actually managed to plan ahead this time and I've booked a room at a small resort on the beach. Many travellers, I know, are not too fussed and will happily just show up and take a shared mixed dorm (and shared bathroom) or even be prepared to sleep on the beach with the crabs and sandflies. I'm not quite that kind of traveller yet and wonder if I ever will be.

My chosen resort is lovely. It's one of several set back from the beach behind a line of pine-like casuarina trees and swaying palm trees. I'm met off the boat by a young boy with a wheelbarrow who is waving a sheet of paper with my name scribbled on it. He takes my rucksack from me and puts it in his barrow and I follow him up the beach and through a garden planted with flowering musky-fragranced frangipani. There is a circular tikki-style palm-thatched bar and a reception area and a small swimming pool and all the accommodations are typical of many in this part of Thailand – simple, raised, teakwood bungalows with rattan wall panels and palm-thatched roofs.

This time, I have paid a bit extra (okay, a lot extra) for air conditioning (I know Summer would consider me a total spendthrift) but I hope it deters the bugs and mozzies and other biting flies that have bothered me in Koh Lanta. Inside my bungalow is a double-sized bed draped with a mosquito net providing double bug protection. My bathroom is gorgeous and has a hot water bamboo showerhead, a sink carved out of a sanded tree stump, and the very best thing of all – my little outside balcony has a hammock.

I end up spending the whole afternoon in that hammock, reading and snoozing and feeling deliciously decadent. I'm reluctant to move even when I see the sun going down, but I'm suddenly hungry, so I wander inside to take a shower and dress in something light and floaty.

In the dusky evening light, I stroll barefoot through the trees and flowers and along a sandy path, accompanied by a cacophony of croaking frogs and chirping crickets to the beach where, on a narrow stretch of sand in front of the resort, I see tables for two have been set with white cloths and tealights and little arrangements of flowers. It looks terribly romantic.

This is when I suddenly get a little concerned. Alarm bells start ringing in my head.

I hadn't considered before coming here that this dreamy resort might be the preferred haunt of newly-wedded honeymooners and cosy couples. But as there's hardly anyone around, it's hard to tell, so I take a bar stool at the tikki bar where a smiling barman asks me what I'd like to drink and I ask for a glass of white wine.

I sip my drink and browse the menu.

I decide to go for a spicy rice dish as I'm hungry. I order the *massaman* seafood curry.

'Table for one, madam?' I'm asked, which I think makes me sound lost and lonely.

I'm shown to a table on the beach. The other seat and set of cutlery are both quickly removed.

I try not to mind being on my own. I try to relax and take in the ambiance.

I listen to the gentle sound of the waves that are so close they're almost lapping at my toes.

As others arrive to take up other tables, I see I'm right. It's all loved-up couples here tonight.

Now I feel a bit awkward. I wish I'd brought a book with me although, of course, it's far too dark to read with just one tiny flickering tealight on the table. My meal comes quickly and is delicious but once I've finished eating, with the only sounds being the waves kissing the shore and loved-up couples kissing each other, I want to head back to my hut and lock my door.

I try unsuccessfully to get a signal on my phone to pick up any messages.

I sigh deeply. To think that I'd stupidly thought that no wi-fi would be A Good Thing.

With nothing else for it, I go back to my room, close my curtains and climb into bed.

I'm not tired but I am bored.

I pick up my book but with only two chapters left to read, I soon finish it.

I try to cheer myself up by thinking about what I'll do tomorrow. I decide I'll have a delicious breakfast. I'll sunbathe all morning. Then I'll have a light lunch. I remind myself to check to see if there is a book swap shelf in reception, so that I'll have another novel to read while I'm lazing in my hammock again in the afternoon. Then, I'll have a drink and dinner ... again. I'm bored just thinking about it.

The problem with being bored is you also have time to think. It is a vicious circle.

Now that I've stopped being busy, I'm suddenly feeling strangely bereft and lonely.

I'm not angry anymore. I'm not bitter either. I'm just feeling, well ... horribly empty.

I have been so busy preoccupying myself and planning and travelling and sightseeing and praying and socialising and flirting and learning how to scuba dive, that I've done a pretty good job of making sure I don't have any spare time in which to overthink everything and become depressed again. So now I'm thinking about my marriage and I'm feeling like a failure.

My marriage is over.

I say it out loud, just to make it even more real.

I'm one of *those* women whose marriages has failed.

I'm going to be a divorcee. A stigma. A sad statistic.

I start to cry. Marriage is such a big and all-encompassing thing, I tell myself. It's a husband and a house and a car and, in my case, two children. It takes up such a big space and the longer you are married the more space it takes. I'm now starting to see it as a big black soul hole. It might start out like a bright shiny star that dazzles you with its promise of light but then it sucks you in with its gravitational pull, taking over everything and every single part of you until one day, it simply can't sustain itself anymore and it starts to implode.

And that's when it spits you out and leaves a black hole in your life and your heart.

My marriage has pulled me down. It's crushed me. It's squeezed the life out of me.

It's far stronger and much weightier than any Thai sumo-wrestler masseuse.

I sob for everything I feel has been taken away from me. Not only my marriage and the loss of my home and my dog and all my personal possessions, but the loss of my friends and my boys and my mum. They all seem so very far away now. I'm in the middle of nowhere, surrounded by nothing but emptiness. My pillow is now sopping wet and my face is a red, swollen mess.

I must have cried myself to sleep because when I wake it's morning.

I get out of bed and stand outside in my vest and shorts. I walk down onto the beach, almost down to the waterline, where I sit cross-legged and close my eyes. I tip back my face and let the warm orange glow of the early morning sun's rays coming over the horizon be the bright light I see through my closed and swollen eyelids.

I breathe deeply. I stand up and I raise my arms into

the air above my head and press my palms together. Then, I open my eyes and I open my heart and I realise I am saluting this beautiful new day. Today, I'm determined to keep busy.

I'm still in shock over how upset I was last night and although I'm over it now and can see it for what it was – simply another stage in my grieving process – I certainly don't want a repeat performance. So, I've decided that today, instead of sitting around, I'm going to do something adventurous instead. I've seen a half-day trip advertised in the reception area, to a nearby island called Koh Muk. It's part of the National Marine Park and the island is famous for its Emerald Cave. Instead of spending my morning sunbathing on the beach or reading in a hammock, I'm going on a trip. The Emerald Cave is a sea cave, which means access to it is via the sea. I'm told you can swim through the narrow eighty-metre long tunnel of the cave into the inner chamber that is formed from a huge sink hole. Once you have passed through the tunnel, the cave opens out into a hidden lagoon with lush tropical plants and its very own beach. It sounds amazing.

I read in my guidebook that it is called the Emerald Cave because the light from the sun reflecting on the water in the lagoon shines on the surrounding walls, giving them a deep green colour. It also used to be a favourite spot for pirates to hide their treasure because the tunnel into the lagoon is underwater during high tide and only accessible at low tide.

I do love the idea of a hidden cave and a secret lagoon and pirate treasure!

I ask Mr Lee, our resort manager, if it's possible to hire a long-tail boat for the morning and head out there myself after breakfast (thinking that I'd rather not be squished up on a boat full of kissing couples), but he tells me that it can be quite dangerous to go there alone.

He explains that if you get left inside when the tide's turning, you'll be stuck in there until the next day when the cave becomes accessible again. Heeding his warning, I sign up for the organised trip that's leaving this morning at nine-thirty to meet with the low tide.

After breakfast, wearing a sarong over my bikini, I grab a bottle of water and realise that as I'll be swimming through a cave, I'll have to leave my phone behind. There'll be no photos for Facebook today, unfortunately. The ride to the cave is calm and smooth and so the trip is uneventful and pleasant. There are seven of us on this excursion – myself, our guide, two young Chinese couples who chat exclusively to each other in Mandarin and our Thai boatman who only speaks Thai. I'm grateful to chat to our English-speaking guide and our topic of conversation is our mutual amusement over our Thai boatman's T-shirt which reads: *Good guy goes to Heaven. Bad guy goes to Pattaya.* A slogan claiming that Pattaya, a beach resort on Thailand's east coast, has a well-deserved reputation for debauchery.

When we arrive at the cave, we're almost the first. There's just one other boat at the entrance and around a dozen people already in the water, all ready to disappear into a small crack in the rock face. We are given orange life vests to wear and head protection in the form of Styrofoam bicycle helmets. Once we're in the water, we're instructed to follow our guide – who has a flashlight – through the tunnel in a single and orderly line.

It feels so good to finally slip over the side of our boat into the cool water after sitting under the heat of the scorching sun, despite it still only being early morning. The water outside the cave is calm and crystal clear and when I look down, I can see lots of fish swimming around. We swim into the cave entrance following our guide. Beams from his flashlight make the dark cave look magical and the echoes of our voices sound quite eerie.

It takes us around ten minutes to swim along the tunnel. I find it really enjoyable but I suppose, if you were in the slightest bit worried about closed dark spaces, it might be rather scary. Soon we reach the place where the cave opens up into a big sunlit lagoon.

I immediately leave our group to swim out into the middle of the lagoon and lay on my back in the cool emerald coloured water, looking up through a hole in the top of the headland at the walls of emerald rock with hanging vines and tropical foliage.

It's beautiful and quite fascinating in a romantic and swashbuckling adventure sort of way. With this lagoon being accessible at low tide, it is indeed a perfect place to hide pirate treasure. As more and more people come through the cave into the lagoon, I head ashore to the little half-moon shaped beach to dry off and warm up. I lie back on the sand and close my eyes and try to ignore everyone else and their shrieks and yells and splashes. I have a little fantasy about being here long enough that everyone leaves and the tide turns and I have this absolute paradise all to myself. But my imagination can't hold onto the fantasy for very long because more and more people in bicycle helmets and orange lifejackets are flooding through from the tunnel into the lagoon and the whole place is reverberating with their gasps and cries and yells and shouts.

Very soon, I expect there will be no space left in the lagoon or on the beach and everyone will be swimming on top of each other in an effort to either stay or to go.

I remember what the lads had said about The Beach on Koh Phi Phi.

'*Thousands of tourists pouring out of long-tail boats like lemmings onto what used to be a pristine beach...*' I think about what a shame it is that all these amazing places are now so ruinously popular with tourists that the pristine perfection has been spoilt.

Soon, I've had enough. I decide I'm heading back through the tunnel.

Going back out, I realise I'm swimming against the current. It's also problematic to swim in the opposite direction to the infinite line of incoming people swimming in such a narrow space. I'm glad of my head protection, as I'm rudely pushed aside a couple of times, knocking my head on the sharp rocks that are jutting out from the side of the cave.

Feeling annoyed, I keep to the side saying, 'excuse me please' to no avail.

I really want to get out of there. But just as I reach the mid-point of the tunnel, where I can see no natural light at either end, although there are plenty of flashlights being waved about in all directions, someone suddenly starts screaming.

The screams are ear-splitting in such a confined space and they ricochet off the walls.

There's also a lot of splashing and then even more shouting. It's chaotic and awful.

I feel deafened by it all. I try to turn around to see what might be going on.

I want to see if I can do anything to help whoever it is in a total panic.

But once again, I'm slammed into the wall of the tunnel by someone rudely trying to push past me and in my attempts to right myself, I manage to hit my knee and catch my foot on what feels like a very hard sharp rock. Cursing at the pain and the discourtesy of some people, I can only hope that the screaming and claustrophobic person has managed to get themselves dragged either in or out of the tunnel, because there are so many people in it now and so much chaos and yelling and thrashing about that it's impossible for me to swim back in and offer any help. So, in pain with my knee and with the cut in my foot stinging in the salt water, I make my way back outside. Once I make it, I find myself swimming amongst what had to be twenty or more long-tail boats all at anchor outside the cave and they all look the same.

I haven't a clue which one is mine.

I swim around for about half an hour or more, searching for my boat and the one and only recognisable feature amongst them all – our boatman wearing the *Good guy goes to Heaven. Bad guy goes to Pattaya* T-shirt.

Eventually, I find him. Thank goodness. If I hadn't, I'm sure I'd have been swimming around outside the Emerald cave until I bled to death from the deep gash in my foot. When our boatman sees that I'm injured, he looks very concerned and takes me straight back to Koh Ngai.

Back on the island, I thank him and wade from the boat to limp my way back up the beach with my bashed knee and my bloody foot. I know there's no pharmacy or medical facility on the island, but I hope the resort manager, Mr Lee, can offer me some ice for my knee and an alcohol wash and bandage for my foot.

'That is a nasty gash. No get wet,' Mr Lee advises me when he sees my cut foot. 'Seawater full of germs. So keep foot always dry so not get infected.'

I return to my room and grit my teeth while I apply an ice pack on my bruised knee.

I give the graze on the top of my foot and the cut on the side a good clean.

The top of my foot, with the loss of several layers of skin, looks like a slab of raw liver.

All in all, I suppose it could have been worse, but it annoys me to think that I now wouldn't be able to go swimming or snorkelling or diving again until it heals up. *Damn it.*

I limp back over to reception with my foot bandaged and with my finished copy of *The Beach*. I need something else to read to while away my afternoon in my hammock.

Disappointingly, the only books left on the swop shelf are in every language other than English. I limp over to the bar for a drink instead. I order a glass of white wine and, after a couple of reviving sips, I'm feeling perhaps a little less sorry for myself.

A young woman wearing a sarong approaches from the beach and orders a couple of beers. She has short dark hair and a friendly round face. She says 'hello' and smiles at me and, realising she speaks English, I say 'hello' back and we strike up a conversation. She spots my bandage.

'Did you cut your foot on the coral here?'

'No. I did it this morning in the Emerald Cave,' I tell her.

'You'd better watch it doesn't get infected,' she advises.

'I know. No swimming. No snorkelling. No diving. It's depressing,' I lament.

She winches in sympathy for me. 'I'm Jodie, by the way.'

'Nice to meet you, Jodie, I'm Lori. You don't happen to have a book you might want to swap, do you? I've just finished this one.' I wiggle my book at her hopefully.

Jodie smiles. 'My girlfriend just finished a Wilbur Smith she picked up on Koh Lanta. It must be good because she's hardly had her nose out of it these past couple of days. I'll ask her for you.' She takes her two beers back to the beach but soon comes back to the bar accompanied by another girl, who she introduces as Laura, and who is carrying a big hardback book. Her eyes light up once she spots my battered paperback.

'Cool! I've always wanted to read *The Beach*,' she enthuses.

'Great. I'll swap you,' I say.

'Jodie tells me you've cut your foot. You'll need to keep it away from the sand. If you get sand in it, you'll get an infection.'

'Yes. I know. No sand and no water. That rules out everything to do around here.'

The girls sit at the bar and we chat for a while. They're really nice and friendly.

With the book swap done and their beers finished, they make a move back to the beach where they've been sunbathing. Feeling brave and dreading another evening in my own company, I ask them if they'll be coming back over to the bar later, and if I might join them for a drink.

I realise I'm missing Summer and the lads and all the people on my dive course and I'm even starting to think about Jack and to have regrets – which I know can't be a good thing.

I feel like I need cheering up with some interesting company and conversation.

Happily, we arrange to meet up again here again at the bar for sundowners at six-thirty.

Feeling a lot less grumpy, I spend the rest of the afternoon reading and relaxing in my hammock, which takes the pressure off my swollen knee and helps to stop the blood seeping any further through my bandaged foot. All considered, it's a pleasant way to while away a few hours. Then with the sun low in the sky, I put the book down, realising I need to think about my onward plans for the following day as I'd only planned to stay here for two nights after extending my time on Koh Lanta.

The next island further along this chain is a similar island to Koh Ngai and is called Koh Kradan. I had planned to spend a whole week there because it has the most beautiful sandbars. Not the kind of bars for buying drinks, but the white sand kind of sandbars exposed only when the tide goes out, that you can swim out to and sit on and feel like you are on your own private tropical island like a castaway.

The next tiny 'no news, no shoes' destination in this idyllic chain after Koh Kradan, with beaches that are always ranked up there in the top beaches of the world, is called Koh Bulon – and Koh Bulon is supposed to be even more idyllic and perfect.

But what use are perfect beaches, quiet retreats, and undeveloped, off-the-grid islands with sandbars and fabulous tropical reefs full of amazing marine life, if I can't walk on the sand or swim or snorkel or go diving until my foot heals? I know I'm going to be horribly bored.

I want to spend time in a hammock but I think I might go crazy if I can't do anything else, and the thought depresses me. It seems my plans are completely ruined.

My only option seems to be skipping Koh Kradan and Koh Bulon completely.

This will mean heading straight on to Koh Lipe, the last island in the chain that also serves as the border between Thailand and Malaysia. If I'm lucky, because it's en route, I might get to see the other two islands that I'm giving a miss from the boat as we go past them.

At least from Koh Lipe I can get to Langkawi, where I'll have far more options, and I can gather my thoughts and reorganise my plans.

I shower standing on one leg with my bandaged foot covered with a plastic bag.

Then, once I'm dressed, I hop over to reception again. Mr Lee tells me that there is a speedboat transfer sched-uled to pick people up here in the morning and take passengers south.

I put my name down as a passenger and head over to the tikki bar to order a drink while I'm waiting for Laura and Jodie. They arrive after a few minutes later looking sunny and smiley and glowing after their day on the beach. 'How's the foot?' they both ask me at once.

'Getting me down, actually,' I tell them and I'm unable

to hide the extent of my misery over my time here now being totally ruined. We order more drinks and they both listen sympathetically. 'I was hoping to put my new dive qualification to good use,' I moan. 'Now I'm at a complete loss what to do. I guess I have no choice but to leave here tomorrow and head to Malaysia until my foot heals and I can decide what to do next.'

I shrug and sulk, until I realise I'm lowering the mood of the mellow evening.

'Anyway, tell me about your travel plans?' I ask them, before they can decide to dump me.

'We are heading onto Koh Phi Tao tomorrow. There's a turtle conservation project on the island. It's funded by the Goldman Global Foundation and we're volunteering for the last two busy weeks of the nesting season. We did it last year too and it was fantastic.'

Jodie sounds really excited and I can't blame her. It sounds wonderful.

'It'll be especially good, as we're joining the same small group we worked with last year,' Laura adds with equal enthusiasm. 'There are a couple of smart Australian boys, George and David, and there's our project leader, Ethan Jones. It's going to be so much fun as well as totally worthwhile because we'll be saving endangered turtles.'

'That sounds amazing. You know, I met someone recently who'd been volunteering in Borneo at an orangutan sanctuary and that sounded really worthwhile too. I was even thinking of doing the same thing myself. I'm sure it's funded by the same foundation.'

'It probably is. Mr Goldman is a billionaire philanthropist,' Jodie explains to me. 'He has conservation projects all over the world and I hear he has a special interest in orangutans. I've never actually met him but he's my hero. Someone who makes a real difference in the world.'

Laura laughs. 'Ethan Jones is my hero. He works for the Goldman foundation and he's so cool. He's always off having wild adventures all over the world, so I call him Indiana Jones!'

Jodie rolls her eyes. 'Ah, so that's why we're going back. You're lusting after Ethan!'

'No. I don't fancy him. I want him to adopt me and be my dad!' Laura protests.

'So, tell me, what do you do on the island exactly – to help save the turtles?'

'We mostly monitor their nests and protect the eggs from poachers,' Laura tells me.

'You mean to say that people actually steal turtle eggs?' I ask.

'Yeah, they're a delicacy in Asia,' Jodie explains. 'Green turtle numbers have declined more than twenty per cent over the past few years because of poaching or beach erosion. We also guard against natural predators too and, like Laura said, we monitor the nests until they've hatched. I love the moment the baby turtles emerge. They're so cute and full of energy and determination as they dig their way out with their tiny little flippers flapping away.'

'That's the most dangerous time for them, you see...' Laura elaborates. 'Getting safely from their nest into the sea. We make sure they have a clear run across the beach and we cheer on each little brave turtle.'

'It's heartwarming. I get so emotional about it,' Jodie says, with a sigh.

'And the poachers? How do you stop them? I mean, is it dangerous?' I ask.

'No. It's more like a standoff. We are simply a presence on the beach to discourage them.'

'It all sounds so fantastic. I've not heard of this island. Is it between here and the border?'

'Yes, it's sort of between Bulon and Lipe but it's well off the tourist trail. The name means "the island of the old turtle" and there's nothing much on it except lots of monkeys and turtles and the research station. It's not listed on tourist maps and so no one else really goes there.'

'So how did you first hear about it?' I ask, becoming even more fascinated by the idea of this hidden island of green turtles, with its very own Indiana Jones.

'Through volunteering with the Goldman Global

Foundation. We've been involved since our university days. Mr Goldman usually recruits student volunteers from Biology and Ecology courses, although not exclusively – he wants people of all ages and practical skills to volunteer too. Year on year, we all keep in touch with each other and we share news of any new opportunities or ongoing conservation projects where we can volunteer.'

'I love the idea of it all. It makes perfect sense to me,' I say. 'Why simply backpack around the world when it is possible to volunteer for important projects to help people or animals and the environment and really make a difference?'

'If you really are interested, Lori, you can come with us. We were supposed to be bringing a friend along with us to Koh Phi Tao but she couldn't make it at the last minute. It sounds to me like a perfect way for you to spend the next couple of weeks?'

There is a moment of silence before I feel my eyes practically pop out of their sockets. Before I realise what's being offered to me.

Then I remember my damned foot injury.

'I'd really love to come, but what use could I be to the turtles if I can't stand on the sand or in the sea?' My voice is so full of woe that I sound like I might start weeping.

'That won't stop you from helping out. There's always

lots of camp jobs – cooking and stuff that we generally all share and there's admin too because all the turtles need to be identified and catalogued,' Laura insists.

'Then, after a few days, when your foot is better again, you could stick a bag on it and help us patrol the beach and monitor the nests. You should think about it,' Jodie tells me.

I'm already sold. I decide I'm going with Jodie and Laura to Koh Phi Tao.

I'm excited, but they warn me that facilities at the camp are quite basic and the island is quite remote, with only weak access at best to a mobile phone signal or to the internet.

So on my way back to my room, I pop into reception, which seems to be the only place I can get a decent wi-fi signal on my phone on this island, to message my sons and to tell them I'm going offline.

I'm going to a remote island with some friends to help save turtles. Don't worry if you don't hear anything from me for the next two weeks. I'll message once I get to Malaysia. Love, Mum xx

Chapter 8

Koh Phi Tao

I have a horrible dream. In it, I'm desperately trying to escape from a tiny island in the middle of nowhere. I'm living with a tribe of backpacking couples but I've ran away and now I'm trying to hack my way through an impenetrable steamy jungle inhabited by giant monkeys. When I finally reach an idyllic-looking beach, I discover that the only way off the island is through a long dark sea cave full of snakes and sharks and razor-sharp rocks.

I wake at sunrise in a terrible sweat. I give myself a good shake, tell myself that dreams are just random and, after heading for the shower, I grab a cup of coffee and my backpack.

An impressive looking speedboat with three outboard engines has arrived to pick us up.

There are already a few passengers onboard who are also heading south. Laura, Jodie and I climb onboard and strap ourselves into our seats and soon the wind is whipping back our hair as we travel down the Andaman Sea in style, skimming the waves at great speed under fabulous blue skies and on a flat calm sea.

We stop off at Koh Kradan and also Koh Bulon along the way, to let out some of our fellow passengers. I immediately realise on seeing these beautiful islands, that if I hadn't been going onto Koh Phi Tao with Laura and Jodie, I'd have been weeping with regret because they look so picture perfect.

We continue on our way with three other people who are travelling down to Koh Lipe and the Malaysian border. Around an hour later, we spot the shape of a tiny island ahead of us. The boat's engines slow and everyone on the boat unclips their seatbelts and stands up as the island appears to us from a veil of vaporous mist. It has a tall volcano-shaped mountain at its core and a dense green interior jungle tumbling all the way down from the misty peak to its rocky coastline. The island is ringed by a calm, dark blue lagoon and is protected by an azure green coral reef. Suddenly, the mist clears from the volcano, and we see a rainbow appear.

It looks so perfect and unreal, like a Garden of Eden.

As we get closer, all eyes are now on the bay with its shimmering, blindingly white sand beach fringed with gently swaying palm trees. The other passengers immediately demand to know where we are. It's as if they can't believe their eyes.

'Oh boy, where is this place?'

'Jeez ... what's it called?'

'This is not on my map!'

Jodie grabs her backpack and answers them. 'This, my friends, is paradise.'

The high tide allows our boat to pass safely over the coral reef and into the lagoon. We wade ashore. The water here is warm, clear and shallow, and the sand is soft underfoot. As the boat speeds away, we are met on the beach by a small welcome committee of four people. Three men and one woman. I hang back while Laura and Jodie enthusiastically greet the men and introduce themselves to the woman. There's a lot of hugging and kissing and backslapping before it's my turn to be introduced.

'Hey, everyone, this is Lori,' Laura announces. 'She's kindly agreed to come along to help us out and to replace Kim, who had to bow out at the last minute.'

'Hi Lori and welcome!' the welcome party chorus.

'Nice to meet you, Lori. I'm Marielle,' says the woman in a heavy French accent. She shakes my hand and kisses me on both cheeks. I'm really pleased to see another woman here who is around my age. She is very slim, unlike me, gorgeously suntanned, and wearing tiny white cotton shorts and a loose-fitting top through which I can see a blue patterned triangle bikini. She has straight, fine, mid-brown, shoulder-length hair. She's not what you would call a classically beautiful woman – she has full lips and a strong nose and deep-set eyes – but she is so completely natural-looking that she is quite striking to look at.

'This is David and this is George,' Marielle tells me, introducing two guys, who stepped forward to shake my hand. I see they are both around the same age as each other – mid-twenties, I'm guessing – blond, tall and lean, both wearing board shorts and the same style of sunglasses. They give me a cheery Australian greeting. 'G'day, Lori'.

I didn't realise Australians really said that – I thought it was a myth.

'Hi, I'm Ethan,' says the last, very good-looking, man.

And I realise I'm now looking at Ethan Jones. The real-life Indiana Jones, hero and sugar-daddy-figure, who Jodie and Laura have told me about. 'Hi Ethan. It's great to meet you.'

I shake his hand and he bends forward to kiss me on both cheeks just as Marielle did.

Ethan is tall and slim but wide across the shoulders. He's wearing khaki shorts and a loose-fitting, bright yellow-and-green pineapple print shirt, so I guess he has a sense of humour.

His eyes are narrowed against the sharp morning

sunlight as he looks at me. His hair is dark, short, and flecked with a little silver grey at the sides, which together with his morning shadow of facial stubble, makes him look classically distinguished rather than middle-aged.

I realise his good looks and his kisses have me blushing.

'I'm the project manager here,' he tells me, taking my rucksack and insisting on carrying it up the beach for me. 'Thanks for helping us out, Lori. We really appreciate it.'

'I'm happy to be here,' I tell him, realising he also has a very nice soft Scottish accent.

He asks about my foot. 'What happened there – shark attack?'

I laugh. 'Nothing as exciting, but it really hurts and look, I managed to get it wet again.'

'We'll get you a dry bandage. You don't want to get it infected.'

We walk up the beach to the tree line where there is a sign that reads *No White Lights!*

It's then I see the camp. It's much nicer than I imagined it to be.

From the way Laura and Jodie had described it as 'extremely basic', I had envisaged nothing more than little tents on the sand and no electricity. But there are in fact several large wooden open-plan buildings on wooden stilts with palm-thatched roofs and I can hear the hum of a generator. One such building has tidy racks of scuba gear hanging up in it and air tanks lined up in orderly rows. Another looks like a kitchen and dining area with dining tables and chairs.

On the beach, between the trees, there are several hammocks strung up in the shade.

It all looks wonderful. I thank Ethan, recover my rucksack from him and follow Marielle and Jodie and Laura along a narrow sandy jungle path between the buildings towards our lodgings. It's almost unbearably humid. It must be nearly noon. The sand underfoot is burning my feet through the rubber of my flipflops and sticking to my sodden dirty bandage.

As we make our way along the path, enormous monitor lizards, sunning themselves and looking like prehistoric creatures, scatter back into the edges of the jungle fauna. High in the trees, I spot a black-haired monkey with a long tail and white patches around its eyes. It's the size of a small child and it's watching us. It's just like being in Jurassic Park.

To my surprise, our lodgings are in four small wooden palm-thatched bungalows, all set back in a staggered row under a dark and dense canopy of tall trees. 'Wow. I thought we'd be roughing it but these bungalows are gorgeous,' I enthuse.

Jodie laughs. 'Hold on, you haven't seen what's inside them yet. Don't expect a soft bed!'

'This place used to be an eco-resort and that's why we have nice buildings,' Laura explains.

'You will be sharing with me, if that's okay, Lori?' Marielle says to me, indicating to her bungalow. 'Of course, that's fine by me,' I reply, smiling at her warmly.

Inside the bungalow it's surprisingly dark and dingy and earthy smelling. I note there is only one small window with a mesh screen and no glass. There's no air-con – not that I expected it – but I can't see a fan either. Jodie is right about there being no soft beds as there are no beds at all – only a couple of hammocks with mosquito nets hanging over them.

They look like large white cocoons hanging from the ceiling.

'That one is yours, Lori.' Marielle says, pointing to a hammock. 'They are surprisingly comfortable once you get used to them. *Le salle de bain* is just through there. It's outside but it's private.'

I put my rucksack down and go to check out the bathroom through the door that Marielle had pointed out at the back of the room. There's a Western-style toilet and a vanity sink and a pretty pebble-clad shower area courtesy of a bamboo pipe. I also spot a clamshell soap dish that has a startled looking green gecko sitting in it. The area is clean and enclosed but it has no roof, so it's completely open to the canopy of the surrounding jungle and presumably to the stars at night – as well as bugs and mosquitoes of course, but I would have to get used to that.

I come back into the room smiling. 'I love it!'

Marielle looks relived. '*Tres bon*, but please don't ever leave the doors open as that will invite in all sorts of trouble. I've had monkeys sneaking in and stealing my stuff before now.'

I nod, thinking of far worse consequences – like snakes for instance.

'What happened to your foot?' she asks me, looking concerned.

'Oh, I cut it in the sea. It's going to take a couple of days to heal and then it will be fine.'

'Then you should go and get it cleaned and rebandaged. It will be time for lunch soon.'

I grab the first aid supplies I'd brought with me, and follow Marielle back to the common area. 'If you need more bandages, our first aid kit is always kept here,' she says, pointing to a large box on a table. 'Help yourself to whatever you need. The last thing we want is for your foot to get infected here. That would be very – how you say – problematic?'

I sit down on a bench and start to remove the sea-soaked bandage, thinking that the constant warnings about not getting this damned foot infected were starting to feel like a curse.

I wince in pain as I peel the gauze off the sticky and

bloody wound. To my disappointment, the cut is still an open flap of skin and the graze looks just as angry as when I'd first done it, although that's hardly surprising, when in the last twenty-four hours I've had to climb off two boats and wade twice through the sea. I give it a good clean, wash it thoroughly with clean bottled water and then dab on an antiseptic cream before protecting it again with a clean dressing and a plastic bag.

All done. I wash my hands and join everyone for lunch.

We sit around the table like one big happy family, chatting and laughing, while we eat our meal. Marielle is the cook and she has prepared steamed coconut rice and fish curry.

It's delicious. I compliment her on her cooking.

'*Merci*. We usually take turns in the kitchen. Can you cook, Lori?' she asks me.

I nod with enthusiasm. I'm in my comfort zone with that particular question.

'Yes, until recently, I was a housewife with a family. So I know my way round a kitchen.'

Everyone looks absolutely delighted that I have proven culinary skills.

Ethan also looks surprised 'A housewife? What prompted such a lifestyle change?'

I immediately regret mentioning my family. This is

the first time in the past couple of weeks that anyone has picked up on something I've said in passing about my family and asked me about it directly. I feel myself blushing. 'Well, my two sons, Josh and Lucas, are both grown up now and my husband and I have recently separated.'

I say this in such a matter-of-fact tone that I even surprise myself with my composure.

'Well, we are very glad you are here with us, Lori,' Marielle says, just before she mentions my injured foot again. 'While your foot is healing, would you consider being our chef?'

I try to hide my disappointment. I haven't come here to cook. I've come here to help save the turtles. Feeding the people who save the turtles isn't really the same thing at all.

'I'll be happy to cook our meals, as long as I can also do my shifts on the beach,' I insist.

'Of course!' Ethan agrees, while spearing his piece of fish with a chopstick. 'Although we should warn you, we only have a limited range of supplies and we can't always get fish. It's hard to be creative with a couple of vegetables, but if you can do something a bit different with rice, we would all appreciate that very much indeed. Wouldn't we gang?'

Everyone shouts their mutual appreciation of something a bit different.

'I'll do my best,' I tell him. 'And I'll wrap up my foot so that I can still do beach patrols.'

When the meal is over, strong ice-cold coffee is served, and we all continue to sit around the table for what Ethan calls the afternoon briefing. This is apparently when the shift rota is discussed and jobs are allocated and any problems anyone has are addressed.

From what I can tell, Ethan runs a tight ship here.

'Okay. We're now into the last two weeks of the turtle nesting season on the island. So, this briefing today is mostly for the benefit of our lovely ladies Laura, Jodi and Lori. We currently have thirty nests in the hatchery and twenty-two of them are due to hatch at any time. There're thirty-two more on the beach. So, we all need to be extra vigilant in keeping a lookout for any signs of emerging hatchlings. Also, David and George have today moved two nests from the far end of the beach where they were laid last night and transferred them into the hatchery.' Ethan looks at me to explain. 'This is because we often have poachers coming ashore at night in that area of the beach.'

'Ah, they come to poach the eggs,' I say to him, nodding in my understanding of the situation. Then, realising what I've just said, I suddenly catch a terrible fit of the giggles.

I feel terrible about it but I can't stop myself.

It seems so terribly rude to laugh at something like

that. I'm sure it's totally down to nerves. But now I can't seem to stop giggling. My eyes are streaming and my face is red and I look like I'm crying. I truly want the sand beneath me to open up and swallow me whole.

'Haha – Lori just cracked an egg joke, everyone!' George gaffs, snorting with amusement.

'I've got one for you, Lori.' David laughs. 'What day do eggs hate the most?'

I can't speak so I shake my head.

'I know, that'll be fry-day,' Laura groans.

'Hey, I got a new one. What do you call an egg on safari?' asks Jodie.

'An eggs-plorer, perhaps?' Ethan offers.

'You guys crack me up...' George groans, and everyone is laughing again.

Ethan smiles at me with a school-boyish gleam of appreciation in his eyes. And that's when I notice his eyes are the colour of seagrass, dark green, with twinkling light brown speckles.

'Strangely, we never get bored of egg jokes here,' he says to me. 'But yes, we do have a problem with poachers from the mainland. So, I've drawn up a new shift rota. David and George are on the early shift tonight from sundown to midnight. Then it will be Laura and Jodie on the midnight to dawn patrol. Marielle and I did the second shift last night, so we are the lucky ones who get a night off and we will take over from Laura and

Jodie in the morning. Lori, if you'd like to join any of the teams then you are most welcome.'

'Why don't you come out with David and I tonight, Lori?' George offers.

'Thanks, that'll be great,' I say, grateful for the invitation. 'I have so many questions about the turtles. I hope you won't mind me taking notes, so that I don't forget anything.'

'If you like, I can give you the grand tour right now?' Ethan says to me. He is sitting back in his chair now, his long legs stretched out, somehow making these small hard and rickety bamboo chairs look comfortable. 'Then you can ask as many questions as you need.'

My tour begins at the turtle hatchery, which is situated near to the common area building. The hatchery is a large rectangular area of flat sand that's raised up from the beach with its sides supported by long lengths of bamboo. It has a low fence around it made of netting to protect it from predators and inside are cone-shaped metal and net frames that identify the site of each individual turtle nest buried in the sand. I count the nests. Twenty-two of them have red markers on them. These are the ones Ethan says are due to hatch any time.

'The hatchery is where we transfer the eggs that we think might not hatch successfully in their original site on the beach,' Ethan tells me. 'It could be because a nest is too close to the end of the beach where the poachers are likely to come ashore. Or, because it's too close to the tideline and in danger of being washed away. Or, maybe we think that the nest is likely to be disturbed by natural predators. We have a lot of monkeys and lemurs and lizards here that will dig up any nest they find. But, we will only move a nest if we think it'll stand a better chance of survival in our hatchery. If we think it's going to be okay where it is then we just mark the site very discreetly, so we are not alerting the poachers to its location, and we monitor it.'

'And how long does it take for the eggs to hatch?' I ask him, with my pen poised over a fresh page in my notebook.

'Incubation is around sixty days.'

'And how many eggs are laid at one time by the mother turtle?'

'Usually around a hundred or so and she'll come back and lay up to five times in one season. The same female uses the exact same beach where she was born decades ago to lay her eggs. So we often recognise her.'

'But how do you know her again? Does she have a marker or a tracker device attached?'

Ethan smiles. I can tell he is amused by my many questions.

I'm thinking about my dear old dad, who'd kept

racing pigeons in a shed at the bottom of the garden. They'd each had a ring on their leg to identify and track them over great distances.

'Nah, we take her photograph and make a note of anything that marks her out as an individual. You see, every turtle has unique markings on their head and some might also have a scar or a chunk out of their flipper or shell which helps us identify them on our database. If she's new to us, we'll give her a name.'

'A name? How lovely!' I exclaim. 'I can't wait to see a nesting turtle for myself.'

We wander over to the office building that Ethan calls Turtle HQ. Inside is a desk, a computer, and a wall-sized white board with lots of squares and names and numbers on it.

He points to the whiteboard. 'This chart and these squares represent the nests we are monitoring right now. For example, this one...' Inside the square it says: *Choosy: (2) 10/11. 22/23*. 'This means that a turtle named Choosy, laid her second nest of the season on the tenth of this month, and it's located on the beach between markers twenty-two and twenty-three.'

'That's a great system. I love all their names!'

There's Bubbles and Seashell and Shelly and Speedy ... just to name a few.

'It's been an amazing year so far,' Ethan tells me proudly. 'We've had a record number of turtles coming ashore and hatchlings born this year. It makes being here on the island for a couple of months every year really worthwhile.'

'Yes, it's such a big commitment. How many years have you been coming here?'

'Too many to count. This was my very first turtle project, so it's very special to me.'

'Well. It's my first and so it will always be special to me too,' I tell him sincerely.

And he gives me a lovely warm smile that gives me butterflies in my tummy.

'Ooh – and there's a computer in here,' I say. 'Does that mean we have internet?'

He laughs and drags his fingers through his short spiky hair. 'I wish. We do occasionally pick up an internet or cell phone service because we are quite close to the mainland, hence the problem with the poachers. But I wouldn't hold your breath.'

'Sounds a bit risky. I mean, what if something happened here, like an emergency?'

'Oh, don't worry, it might feel like we are castaways but we do have radio coms.'

'Oh, I'm not worried,' I tell him truthfully. Everything about Ethan Jones is so reassuring.

Next on my tour is the scuba hut. 'Here we have all the equipment needed to go diving including a compressor to fill the air tanks. Sometimes, when we aren't monitoring the turtles, we'll do some reef diving. In fact, there's another team arriving on the day we leave here, who will take over from us and then focus on house reef conservation for the next couple of months.'

I proudly tell him I have my Open Water Diver certificate. He seems impressed.

'If you like, when your foot's better, you can do your advanced diver course here. I'll teach you. It'll only take a day or two and then you'll be able to dive deeper to thirty metres.'

'Really? You mean you're a dive instructor too?'

'Aye. When I'm not managing projects like this one, I'm usually off somewhere in the world teaching diving so that our project ecologists can become marine biologists too.'

'Actually, I'd only done a handful of dives when I managed to cut my foot.' I tell him this in case he's under any illusion that I'm some kind of expert with hundreds of logged dives.

But I'm now convinced that Laura and Jodie were right. Ethan *is* a modern-day Indiana Jones.

Ethan hands me a pair of rubber boots. 'These will help keep your foot clean and dry.'

I put them on. They're a little too big, but if I can also find a pair of socks, they'll do the job nicely. We walk along the beach, me in my welly boots and Ethan in his bare feet.

He points out the areas between the palm trees where we'll need to keep a keen eye for any hatchlings exiting the nests. 'There's a full moon tonight. It will act as a beacon to bring the last of this season's nesting turtles ashore,' he tells me. 'Two months ago, we had a super moon, and that's why we have so many nests due to hatch right now. I expect we'll be very busy over the next few days.'

'And that's why I'm here to help!' I enthuse.

'There are twenty-six palm trees between here and the end of the beach,' he tells me. 'The trees are our markers. So, for example, when we saw Choosy's nest marked as 22/23 on our whiteboard, it means it can be found between the twenty-second and the twenty-third palm tree. That's our system. Simple but strategic.'

'You didn't explain why she's called Choosy?'

'That's because she's always a little choosy over where she'll make her nest. We don't know exactly how old she is, but from her size and condition we can take a guess she's getting on for around fifty years old now, much like myself.' He gives me another boyish grin and I feel my heart flip over.

I could listen to Ethan talk about turtles and his conservation projects for hours. He speaks so passionately about it and yet he is so practical and clear about what needs to be done to help.

174

Then there is his Scottish accent, which is incredibly attractive and even, dare I say it, sexy.

I'm really enjoying being in his company. We wander along slowly and my eyes are continually scanning the sand for baby turtles. I hardly dare blink. Then I see something.

A little something crawling on the sand.

'I think I see one. Is that a baby turtle?' I point a finger to the spot.

We kneel down to take a closer look. Ethan uses one long finger to gently excavate the sand.

I'm so excited, I'm holding my breath. But then I see it is, in fact, a little crab.

That evening, after dinner, which is a plain but satisfying dish of rice and beans followed by a rice and mango pudding cooked by Marielle, I take one of the hammocks strung up between the trees at the front of the camp to relax for a while. I'm thinking that if I'm going to be up late tonight, it might be a good idea to take a nap in this hour before dusk.

But it's hard to close my eyes and focus on the lulling sound of the distant waves crashing over the coral at the other side of the lagoon, when I'm being stared at so intensely by a creature in the tree directly above me. I've never seen anything like her before. I say 'her' because this creature, which looks like a cross between a large fruit bat and a fox, has a little wide-eyed fur baby clinging to her belly. When George and David appear ready to patrol the beach, I ask them about the creature, because they are scientists and will probably know about the animals here.

'Ah, it's a lemur. *Cynocephalus Variegatus* also known as the Sunda flying lemur, except it is not actually a lemur and nor does it fly. It's an arboreal gliding mammal found all over South East Asia,' George informs me knowledgeably.

'Well, it's very cute,' I say, rolling out of the hammock to pull on my socks and rubber boots, while trying not to show how much pain I'm in from my throbbing foot. But once we are patrolling the beach, with the evening sunset firing up the whole sky, my pain is forgotten.

All I want now, is to see a turtle coming up the beach to lay her eggs in the sand or to see a nest erupting with a hundred little baby turtles all wanting to run free to the sea, and I'll feel very fortunate and very privileged indeed.

George hands me a torch. 'We have a no white light policy here, so you'll see the torch shines a red light. All the lights we use at night in the camp after dark are red lights too. This is because turtles can't see red light.'

'It's not just natural erosion or poaching that has endangered the turtles. Many of their original nesting beaches are now so developed that white light pollution from hotels and bars and other buildings confuses them and then the poor turtles have nowhere to nest,' David explains. 'If a turtle can't nest on the beach where she was born, then she'll have no choice but to evacuate her eggs at sea and they'll all die.'

I feel so bad for the poor mother turtle, imagining her confusion and stress.

Learning about these turtles and their struggle for survival, and how the only time they will ever leave the sea is to come ashore to lay their eggs, has really brought it home to me how important this work is and I feel so honoured to have been given a chance to be part of it.

'I think that one of the most amazing things is how they know to come back to the same beach where they were born,' I say, recalling Ethan also telling me this interesting fact earlier.

'Yeah. It's instinctive. But no one really knows exactly how they remember.'

The last shimmering glow of the sun has now disappeared over the line of the horizon and the white light of a brilliant full moon has taken centre stage, illuminating everything around us and casting shadows across the beach, into the line of trees that marks the start of the jungle, where strange noises emanate and where birds roost and huge bats flutter.

George and David tell me that what we are looking out for are distinctive tracks made by a turtle coming ashore. I'm told they look like tyre tracks in the sand, coming from the tide line and straight up the beach.

It's not long until we see an enormous silhouetted shape moving slowly from the surf and up the beach. My heart is doing somersaults in my chest when I realised I'm seeing a huge old green turtle. 'Oh, my goodness ... she is absolutely gorgeous!' I breathe ecstatically.

As the turtle heads up towards the tree line in earnest, we follow her at a safe distance and we speak only in whispers. I make sure to keep a step back from David and George, so I can watch what they do to help her in this situation. Then we sit and simply observe her for a while, as she is busy mooching around in the area where the beach meets the jungle and where the fine white soft sand is mixed with soil and vegetation. Like Choosy, she seems to be quite particular as to where she will lay her eggs and she combs the area for the very best place.

Then, when she finally settles herself down to begin digging her pit, the sandy soil and the scent of damp forest begins to fly in all directions from her thrashing thwacking front flippers.

'Okay, she's gonna be a while. Let's check the rest of the beach,' George whispers.

We creep away. My heart is racing with excitement. I feel so lucky to be witnessing what looks to me like a miracle happening. A turtle, who is perhaps even older than I am, has come ashore on this moon-drenched beach to the very place that she herself was born to give life to her own babies. I'm so moved by it all that I'm almost in tears.

Further along, towards the end of the beach, near to the big, round, weather-hewn rocks, I switch on my torch to illuminate the place with red light and I see another set of furrows in the sand coming from the water line. 'Look! More turtle tracks!'

We follow the deep tracks to where another green turtle is heaving herself towards the top of the beach and again we watch and wait until she has settled herself down to nest.

'You know, Lori, we're gonna have to move this one,' George whispers to me. 'It's way too close to where the poachers come in.' He turns his red flashlight to where the dark water ebbs and flows against the rocks that might disguise a thieving poacher's boat.

And then, I remember, aside from all the excitement, that we are primarily here to defend these turtles. We are their first, their last, and their only line of defence against their predators.

Going back to the first turtle, we find her deeply entrenched in her pit and starting to lay her eggs. George explains to me how, once they start to lay, they can't stop and they seem to enter a trancelike state. He tells me that if we are really quiet and respectful around her, then she probably won't even notice that we are here, while we go about our work identifying her.

David passes me a notebook and a camera and tells me it will be my job to record and identify this turtle and her nest. I make a note of which palm trees she had chosen to lay her eggs between, and then I creep about taking some close-up photos of her, making sure to get clear images of all her markings, both on her head and on her enormous shell, which I also measure. It's 1.2 metres across. Enormous!

Then, leaving David to monitor proceedings, I follow George up the beach back to the second nesting turtle, where I repeat the identification process. This time though, as George needs to mark the exact location of this nest so he can return to move it later, he attaches a long green piece of string to the trunk of the nearest tree and feeds the length of string into the pit with the eggs. 'This string,' he explains in a whisper while the turtle is in her trance, 'will help us find the nest later. Because, when she's done, she'll do such a great job of camouflaging that it will be very difficult to know where it is.'

Several hours and many more nesting turtles later, George and David and I are sat on the beach watching a mother turtle leaving her perfectly camouflaged nest site to drag her heavy and exhausted bulk back into the sea. I feel incredibly emotional.

My eyes are filled with tears as I watch the turtle making her way slowly past me.

She's so close to me but she is totally focussed on returning to the sea and trusting that in sixty days – or in two full moons' time – her babies will be born and able to follow her down this beach that they in turn might one day, in decades to come, return to, to start the whole process over again. Then David says something to make me stop and think about this passage of time.

'I've decided, I'm going to do my very best to come back here in thirty years, in the hope that the turtles I see coming ashore will be the ones I helped to the sea as hatchlings.'

'Oh, that's such a lovely idea, David,' I say to him, wishing I could do the same thing.

George agrees. 'Yeah, that would be so cool. Let's do it!'

The two lads shake hands to seal their pact.

George laughs. 'To think, we'll be really old by then. We'll both be fifty-two!'

And both seem completely oblivious to my own dilemma.

If I could possibly return here in three decades' time, I'd be seventy-seven!

Chapter 9

Koh Phi Tao (ii)

Early the next morning, after a night without very much sleep thanks to the world's loudest bullfrog living in our bathroom, I roll exhausted out of my hammock. But, the moment I put my foot on the floor, I'm racked with intense pain. It's so immediate and so painful that it feels like someone's just driven a hot metal stake right through my foot.

I hop over to a bench seat by the window, and sit down and peel off the dressing to find my foot is now horribly infected. This is the one thing I've been warned about – so many times – and the one thing I've been trying to avoid. I now need something more than an antiseptic cream to treat this injury now or I could be risking blood poisoning.

As it's still quite early, and Marielle, who it seems can actually sleep through the bullfrog noise, is still stirring in her hammock, I hop down to the communal area to go through the first aid box for something I can use. It's here that I see Ethan having his breakfast alone.

Today he's wearing another pair of baggy shorts and a bright loose-fitting shirt with a yellow banana pattern on it. He gives me a wave and a smile and gets up from his seat in concern when he sees I can't put my foot down. I explain my problem and ask if there are any antibiotics available. I feel terrible using so many of their medical supplies and promise to somehow replace them.

'No problem. We have plenty. We'll run out of beer before we run out of antibiotics,' he tells me, reassuringly.

I sit down with a box of sterile dressings and alcohol washes and grit my teeth.

Ethan pulls up a chair to sit opposite me. 'You need any help? I'm a trained paramedic.'

Is there anything this man isn't qualified to do?

'Sure, thanks very much.'

He takes my foot and rests it on his lap. 'On a scale of one to ten how bad is the pain?'

'Nine...' I say, without any hesitation.

'Oh, that's bad...' he says, snapping on a pair of latex gloves and starting to gently work a swab against the layer of creamy pus that's now covering my open graze.

'Ouch! And I've been so careful about cleaning it and trying to keep it dry,' I wail.

'Sorry, Lori. But this is a very nasty infection. It must be eviscerated properly or we'll never get it to heal. That's the problem with all this tropical heat and humidity, it's so easy for any cut to get infected and if you're not careful, it can lead to sepsis.'

I try to be brave but every dab feels like my foot is being hit with a hammer and every wipe is like being slashed with a shard of glass. I've never experienced anything like it.

It seems to take Ethan forever to completely clean my wound and to apply an antibiotic powder. He gives me a course of antibiotics pills too and some painkillers.

Soaked in sweat and shaking with stress from all the pain, I thank him for his care but then I doubt I can stand up. Seeing my paling face, he helps me to my feet. I lean into him for support. He feels so strong and steady, like a rock, against my weakness.

'There. All done. Dr Ethan prescribes a hammock for you today, young lady.'

'But I can't. I must help. That's why I'm here after all. The very least I can do this morning is sit on those rocks at the end of the beach and put any poachers off coming ashore.'

Ethan shakes his head, laughing. 'My dear mermaid, with that pretty face and that lovely long blonde hair of yours, you are far more likely to lure them in!'

I blush furiously, seeing that the others are now

having breakfast not too far away from us and suspecting they will have overheard our conversation and Ethan's flattering compliment.

'Besides, it's my turn to cook both lunch and dinner today,' I retaliate.

Ethan shakes his head again. 'Sorry Lori, but you've got to keep your foot elevated. I don't think you realise quite how serious it is to get an infection out here. It can be life-threatening. I'm not joking. If I don't see any improvement in your foot over the next two days, you will have to be taken off the island to the nearest hospital for treatment. Two days. Now go and put your foot up. I'll bring you breakfast in your hammock. It'll be the island version of breakfast in bed.'

I do as I'm told. I hop over to a hammock feeling a little intimidated by his warning.

I also feel totally useless and something of a burden. So much for helping to save turtles.

Ethan soon brings me over some fruit and cereal and coffee on a tray.

I smile at him sheepishly. 'Thank you. You are being very kind.'

'Yeah, I know and it's fine. Don't worry. Dr Ethan is going to make you all better.'

While everyone's busy, I lie in my hammock and try to read, but I'm constantly distracted by all the goings on at the camp and on the beach and in the hatchery.

From my hammock, I have a good view over all the procedures. Ethan has spent most of his morning patrolling the beach with Marielle, after which he fixed part of the roof on Turtle HQ. Now he's busy servicing diving equipment on a bench outside the dive hut. He's sitting in the shade, wearing just his baggy surfing shorts. His lively looking banana-pattern shirt has been discarded, leaving him bare-chested. He's concentrating hard on the task in hand.

He is impressively toned. I'm sure he must work out to have a body like that at his age.

I can see George and David are transferring the second nesting turtle's eggs from last night into the hatchery. I watch, fascinated by how patiently, methodically and carefully they handle the soft, white, papery, ping-pong sized eggs, making sure they put them into the new nest at precisely the same depth (about an arm's length) and in exactly the same order that the mother had originally laid them. Then, once they are done, having loosely replaced all the sand and placed the cone over the top over the site, they disappear inside Turtle HQ to record the details of the new nest.

When they come out again sometime later they come straight over to me.

'Hey, Lori. Of all the nesting turtles that came ashore last night, we have positively identified all but one of them from the database. That means, the first one we all saw was a first-timer and Ethan says you get to name her.'

'Me? Really? What an honour!'

I look gratefully at Ethan and he glances up from his work to smile at me.

I'm so thrilled, I'm jabbering with excitement in my hammock, trying to come up with a suitable name for her. 'Erm ... let me think?'

'If it helps to narrow it down for you, we already have most girls' names beginning with T and all those associated with the teenage mutant ninja turtles,' George tells me.

'Well, I did notice, on the top of her head she has a curved mark that looks like a smile. And, as meeting her has given me so much happiness, I'd like to name her Happy!'

'Happy it is!' George announces, heading back into Turtle HQ to record my decision.

The next hour or two is quiet. Lunchtime comes and goes but I'm not feeling hungry.

The afternoon is baking hot with hardly a breeze coming across the beach. There's not a cloud in the bluest of skies and the sun is intense. Even the jungle seems to have been silenced by the cruel pulsating afternoon heat and I'm alternating between reading and napping while everyone keeps asking me in passing if I'm okay and offering me water.

With most of the chores now done and in respite between the shifts, Laura and Jodie have gone snorkelling in the lagoon with George and David. Marielle, having cooked lunch for us again, is now doing something in the dive equipment room. Ethan is sitting in the shade on the wooden steps of Turtle HQ alternatively strumming his guitar and jotting in a notebook.

He's concentrating hard and he looks like he might be composing a song.

I enjoy hearing him sing. His voice is soft and smooth and he sounds a bit like Jack Johnson.

Back in my shady hammock, I'm sweaty and sticky and sweltering and feeling seriously miffed that I can't go and cool down in the sea. I curse under my breath. I reason that if I hadn't cut my foot, I could be out snorkelling or diving right now and enjoying myself. Ethan had even said that I could have done my advance diver certification here.

It's easy to feel sorry for myself right now.

But then I remember where I am – on a sun-drenched tropical island in a hammock – and I think about life and the weather back home in the UK, where it is no doubt freezing cold and dark and much more miserable than here. I remind myself of my blessings, and how if I hadn't cut my foot that I probably wouldn't be here at all because I'd have just carried on with my plans to go to the other islands instead of coming here with Laura and Jodie.

I would have missed out on all of this and seeing with my own eyes the miracle of nesting turtles coming ashore in the moonlight to lay their eggs. An experience I will undoubtably treasure for the rest of my life. I really should trust in fate and remember that things always happen for a reason.

Suddenly Ethan appears like a handsome mirage in the steamy air and hands me a cold beer.

'Here, I brought you something for the pain,' he tells me and gives me a sexy wink.

I'm confident he's not at all aware it was a sexy wink. It's just my interpretation.

I thank him for the beer and feel myself blush while safe in the knowledge that my face is already so red and sweaty that he can't possibly tell that he has embarrassed me again.

I watch him walk away and I can't help but admire what I see.

My eyes are fixed for a moment on his muscular mahogany-tanned body, the broad width of his shoulders, the way his back tapers down to the attractive round firmness of his bum in those surf shorts. Not only is he a turtle-saving hero, a dive instructor, a Mr Fix-It, a marine biologist and a trained paramedic, he's also a talented songwriter and musician and a fun, friendly, helpful, incredibly good-looking man. Plus, he's shown such care and concern over attending to my infected foot that, even during the agony of the 'evisceration' (as he called the cleaning of my stinking pus-filled appendage), I couldn't help but close my eyes and enjoy his warm hand firmly gripping my lower leg.

Ever since my crush on pretty-boy Jack on Koh Lanta, I've had a heightened awareness of my reawakened libido, which I must confess is still troubling me. I'm not sure whether it's a good thing or a bad thing to have an active imagination and a rampant sex drive at my age.

And I can't help but wonder where the heck it's been hiding all this time?

Perhaps Charles is to blame? He was always just a quick fumble and a few thrusts under the bedcovers kind of guy. I think, to be honest, that's why I was so shocked at seeing him with Sally. Not that any wife wouldn't have been traumatised at catching her husband in bed with her best friend, but what had really stunned and angered me was not what they were doing but how they were doing it. They were both going at it like they were at a bloody rodeo. Maybe it's me, perhaps I'm to blame? I haven't been interested in sex for years.

But surely, in those early years of our relationship and marriage, there must have been something about

Charles to make me fancy him and want to be with him physically?

But now that something, whatever it was, completely escapes me.

Now, I can only wonder how I never realised a lot sooner that I was married to someone with so little in the way of charm, intelligence, personality, or attractive physical attributes?

I can't help but to compare him (rather badly) to Ethan. Ethan is interesting and intelligent and he looks in really good shape. His lifestyle as a scientist and a diver and a world traveller obviously keeps him in peak physical condition. Whereas Charles spends most of his working day at his desk or driving around in his car and his evenings asleep in front of the TV. Charles looks every single one and more of his years, with his long and lanky untoned body and his cracked teeth and thinning hair. So, all I see in him is a cheating and soon to be ex-husband, who now seems very boring and ordinary.

I'm starting to believe that I've had a lucky escape from him.

I while away another woozy hour in the hammock thinking about Ethan.

The beer and the painkillers are definitely working. I close my eyes pretending to nap. I say pretending, because I'm now in a full-blown romantic fantasy. In my imaginary world, Ethan comes to my room with my dinner on a tray, after he has insisted on my bed rest. Unlike in real life, where I'm cohabiting with Marielle and my room is dark and sparse, in this particular daydream, I'm in a large, light-filled room and I'm lying on a big soft king-size bed, surrounded by pillows and cushions and fine white sheets and a billowing voluminous silk mosquito net. As Ethan enters my imaginary boudoir with a quiet knock, the early evening sun is streaming in from the large open window making the room look steamy, and I'm wearing a La Perla negligée. He sets down the tray and asks me sympathetically how I'm doing. I wave a hand dismissively, saying something about how I'm trying to be brave, and he tells me with a sexy wink, 'I brought you something for the pain...' and then he opens a bottle of wine and...

I suddenly hear Marielle yelling my name.

'Hey Lori! *Venez ici* ... we have baby turtles in the hatchery!'

My eyes snap wide open and I literally fall out of the hammock in my scramble to be there.

I hop over to the hatchery to see dozens of tiny almost-black, fully-formed baby turtles, emerging from the sand and flapping their four little flippers like they're wind-up toys.

Marielle is sitting in the sand right next to the nest, the cone removed, and she is picking up each of these flapping adorable creatures and putting them into a large clean bucket. She's ignoring my squeals of delight and coos of joy because she is counting in the newly-born babes.

Very soon, everyone is standing around in excitement and we have over a hundred flapping and flailing little turtles in the bucket. I can't quite believe how much energy they have in them.

With a final examination of the nest (again, a whole length of arm inserted into the hole) a couple of stragglers are lifted gently to the surface and it occurs to me that these little chaps or chapesses might not have made it without Marielle's intervention as they'd been so very deep down in the sand. I'm allowed to hold one of them in the palm of my hand and I find myself giving this newly born turtle a silent blessing for a long and happy life.

A short time later, a runway to the sea has been carefully prepared at the top of the beach where the original nest site had once been. The sand has been levelled and a small sand bank has been formed on either side of the track to keep them all going in the right direction.

I have permission from Ethan to attend the hatchling release, as long as I promise faithfully to return straight to my hammock afterwards.

'And they're off!' Ethan yells, as one hundred and

twenty-six turtle hatchlings are released from the bucket at the top of the beach.

'It's a bit like crab racing but far more thrilling and much more important,' Jodie tells me.

I'm reminded of my son's graduation days. That feeling of being ever so proud, but at the same time frighteningly aware, that from this moment on your precious ones are living their lives independently of you and there's nothing you can do about it.

Ethan comes to stand by my side and explain the proceedings. 'It's very important that they get down the beach to the sea entirely under their own steam. That way, they will imprint this run into their instinct to survive, and eventually find their way back here to lay their eggs in decades to come.'

I can't help myself. It's all so beautiful and mystical, the way all this works, that I burst into tears and wobble unsteadily on my one good foot. Ethan puts a strong arm around me and pulls me close to him. He feels so solid and warm and manly.

I slide my arm through the crook of his arm for support and hug his waist while I sniffle.

I happen to notice Marielle watching us. I see that she doesn't look happy.

And for a moment, I feel incredibly uncomfortable under her sour scrutiny.

Ethan's laughing but there are tears shining in his

eyes and he lifts my chin with his index finger to see tears running down my face. 'Don't get me started. I'm a softie for a good cry myself.'

I like seeing a big manly man like him showing his emotions. It tugs at my heartstrings.

'I'm sorry. This is such a special day,' I tell him. 'I'll never forget it.'

'It's okay. We know how you feel. It's what we do here. Look around you...'

And when I look around, I see that Laura and Jodie are wiping away tears too and George and David are kneeling at the water's edge, crying their encouragement to all those brave tiny swimmers who're trying really hard to get out to sea but whose little flapping flippers don't seem to be getting them anywhere, and to those tiny souls who're being thrown back and upended onto the sand by the incoming waves.

'These hatchlings would normally be vulnerable to being picked off by birds and lemurs and lizards and even monkeys, but today these little guys are getting the red-carpet treatment,' Ethan tells me.

'Come on, run, run. You can do it *mon petite!*' I hear Marielle urging.

And she too is wiping away her tears.

It's the second day of my beachside hammock confinement. I'm still in a heck of a lot of pain and I'm really worried that if the infection isn't under control by tomorrow that I'll have to leave the island to go to a hospital goodness knows where. So, I'm still doing as I'm told and keeping my foot elevated. Jodie and Laura and George and David have been really kind, coming over to check on me, bringing iced coffee or water and asking me if I need anything.

I keep asking what is happening with the nests and how many nesting turtles have come up the beach while I've been so inconveniently indisposed. Out of everyone, I feel Marielle is the least sympathetic to my plight. I've seen her rolling her eyes at the sight of me with my foot on Ethan's lap over the past couple of days, while he has insisted on checking and cleaning and dressing my foot for me. I don't know if it's because she's seriously irritated with my chronic uselessness or if she's had her smouldering eyes on Ethan all along.

I have a theory that she sees me as some kind of threat which, of course, is absolutely ridiculous – although I have been monopolising a lot of Ethan's attention lately and he did hug me very tightly on the beach during the hatchling release.

It irks me how busy everyone is here except me. Last night, I'm told, there were literally dozens of nesting turtles on the beach and today, George and David have been busy rehousing two nests – and around two hundred and fifty eggs – into the hatchery.

This morning, Jodie and Laura reported a suspicious small boat at the other side of the rocks in the lagoon and they staged a sit-in on the beach for several hours before the suspected poacher (who was trying to pose as a lone fisherman) eventually gave up and went away again.

I can't help but feel like I'm really missing out and I'm so very bored of sitting around.

I keep checking to see if I might have a signal on my cellphone, but I never do, even when one of the others is jumping about holding their phone in the air yelling 'signal!'

I also keep forgetting to charge my phone when the generator is running.

Lunch today is just plain rice, cooked by Marielle. She's obviously bored cooking for everyone. This also makes me feel bad. I'd love to get into the kitchen and start creating.

I've been drinking so much iced coffee and water this morning to try and stop myself feeling hungry – another downside to boredom – that it is a real bother to have to get out of the hammock to go to the bathroom every hour or so. With effort I hop over to the bungalow, having to go past the kitchen window, which is much higher than I am tall, when I hear Mariella's shrill voice mentioning my name. I stop to listen.

'I think it was a very bad idea for Lori to come here

with you. I don't understand. Why would you even think to bring her to this island when she has such an injury?'

The voice responding belongs to Jodie. 'But, Marielle, we weren't to know her foot would get worse!'

'I wouldn't mind if she could cook our meals, but she is quite useless!' Marielle's voice rattles through the window at me like the sound of a venomous snake.

I feel my face flood with heat and embarrassment. My eyes fill with tears, because I know she is right. I am quite useless. Worse, I'm a burden. I really should leave here as soon as possible. When I get back to the beach and before I can climb back into my hammock, I see Ethan is waiting for me, brandishing the first aid kit again.

'Right, come on, for better or worse. Let's see how it looks this afternoon.'

I sit down in front of him on the bench so he can remove the dressing.

I'm thinking this is probably as good a time as any to tell him that I'm planning to leave here anyway, whether or not he decides I need to go to hospital. I do know that tomorrow is the day we have a boat delivery of water and fresh food supplies. So, I'll be able to buy a lift to the next island. But he speaks before I can get my words out. His voice is still full of concern.

'How are you feeling, Lori? Do you still have a temperature?'

'Erm, I don't really know,' I answer him honestly. 'It's hard to tell in this heat.'

Then the dressing is off and we both look down at the offending foot.

'Very good. Excellent! It's nice and clean and it's started to heal,' he tells me triumphantly.

'Really? The infection has gone?'

'Aye. No doubt all thanks to those post-surgery strength antibiotics you've been taking.'

'I think it's down to you that I haven't ended up with blood poisoning,' I tell him gratefully. I'm tearing up again. I seem to be doing an awful lot of crying lately. I'm like a ball of pent up tense emotions and anxiety. 'I mean, there's a really good chance you've saved my life and I don't know how I'll ever be able to thank you,' I blubber.

I'm really going to miss Ethan. I'm going to miss getting to know him better.

He takes both my hands in his and pulls me towards him. 'You are very welcome.'

Then Marielle's head pops up from the shrubbery and her shrill voice cuts through the moment I am about to tell him that I'm planning to leave tomorrow. 'Hey Lori, I just heard Ethan say your foot is *beaucoup* better today. Does that also mean you are able to cook dinner for us all later?'

'Sure. Yes, I'm much better today,' I yell back to her.

'*Tres bon!*' she replies, managing to look peeved and relived both at the same time.

It's almost 3.30 p.m. and as I've now been cleared for kitchen duty, it's time to prep some food for dinner. I take a rummage through the larder and I'm quite impressed by the tins and jars and packets of dried herbs and spices and other condiments in there. We have some fresh vegetables left too. We have no fish today – everyone has been far too busy to catch any – so I decide I'm going to put together a papaya salad, a spicy bean and vegetable dish that I can serve up with rice and a caramel sticky banana and mango dessert.

While I'm prepping, I have a good view all around me from the open plan kitchen.

I see Laura and Jodie patrolling the beach. David and George are in the hammocks, reading.

Ethan and Marielle are standing in front of the hatchery and their body language catches my eye and also makes me catch my breath. I see he is standing in front of her with his back to me but from his stance, with his legs apart and his feet planted firmly in the sand, one hand on his hip and the other raking desperately through his hair in exasperation, there is no mistaking that these two are having some kind of an issue.

I can see he is listening attentively to her while she is telling him something in a way that only a French woman can – with an elegance that challenges the twisted rage on her angry face.

I'm stunned. What the heck is happening here?!

He seems to be challenging her, trying to explain something, but she is shaking her head as if she's refusing to listen. I watch in horror as Marielle's long thin brown arms flail about in fury. She's yelling at him now. I can hear her voice but not what she is saying, and anyway I think she is speaking French. Then suddenly her hand makes violent contact with the side of his face. I hear the slap. George and David hear it too and I see them look over to the hatchery.

Ethan shakes his head in recoil and then he storms angrily away from her up the beach.

I realise I am shaking. I put my prepping knife down before I accidently cut myself.

Is this my fault? Was I wrong to think he was unattached?

I'm confused and upset and suddenly I feel desperately alone again.

I feel so foolish about taking such a liking to Ethan. For the first couple of days, until my foot got infected, Marielle was really nice to me and then, in the days that have followed, she's progressively become more distant and surly towards me.

Now I know it wasn't just because she thinks I'm totally useless.

Her venomous attitude and her outrageous display of violence on the beach towards Ethan today suggest that there is something much deeper going on here. I believe that she must think that either I've been flirting with Ethan or that he's been flirting with me.

Why else would she attack him like that?

Oh my ... how awful. I've become the other woman even if only in my imagination.

But was I flirting with him? Really? Just in being friendly and enjoying his company?

My daydreams and fantasies are, after all, just my own private thoughts.

But have I failed to veil my attraction to Ethan?

Has the connection we've made and the sparks that have flown between us been visible to everyone? If so, then I'm really going to have to keep my libido much more firmly under control. I finish prepping the meal and immerse myself in cooking it.

After a while, I see Ethan and Marielle coming out of Turtle HQ where they've been arguing for the past couple of hours (annoyingly in French, so I can't understand what they are actually saying) and then they both disappear into his bungalow. I can't help but wonder (enviously, to my shame) if they are making up their differences in private. I felt regrettably foolish.

Despite my cooking up a meal to impress, Ethan and Marielle don't appear for dinner.

I save what's left of the meal for them in case they reappear and want it later.

After our dinner, the rest of us sat around the big wooden table on the beach, allowing our stomachs to rest before the first evening beach patrol. We occupy ourselves by playing a game of poker. Everyone has their eyes down while considering their cards and nobody says anything at all about what happened at the camp between Marielle and Ethan but the atmosphere is tangible. I'm staring down at my cards and my mind is a whirl of anguish and guilt. I still can't believe that after being here for almost a week, I didn't realise that he and Marielle have something going on between them.

But then, if they're in a relationship, why is she sharing a room with me?

It doesn't make any sense. My stomach is tied up in knots.

Has Marielle seen the lust on my blissed-out face over these past few days, while Ethan's been bandaging my foot. Has everyone else seen it too?

Omygosh ... maybe they, too, blame me and think this is all my fault?

Then we hear raised voices coming from Ethan's bungalow.

I can't stand it anymore, so I blurt out the words playing in my head.

'I didn't realise they were a couple. I really had no idea. Do you think this is my fault?'

Jodie looks up casually from her cards. 'No way. This has nothing to do with you, Lori.'

'But, Jodie...' I reason. 'I overheard Marielle saying to you in the kitchen earlier today that she didn't like me being here and that she thought I was useless with my infected foot.'

David slaps down two of his cards on the table, making me jump out of my skin.

'No, Lori. Jodie's right.' He sighs. 'This is just a replay of what happened last week.'

'And the week before that...' George confides. 'That's married life, I guess?'

'Marielle moved out of his bungalow soon after we got here,' David divulges.

I'm so shocked that my cards seem to scatter everywhere under their own ruse.

'They're *married*?' I gasp.

Chapter 10

Koh Phi Tao (iii)

This morning, for the first time in days, I'm relieved to have no pain in my foot. I also wake to find that Marielle is up and out of our hut before me despite coming back late last night. I heard her creeping back to our bungalow and into her hammock in the early hours. I had feigned sleep to avoid a confrontation with her and hardly slept a wink, mulling over every second of every day since I arrived here, searching for clues that might have told me that Ethan and Marielle were married. I couldn't come up with a single one.

I'm now thinking there must be something seriously wrong with my relationship radar.

I mean, I hadn't a clue that my own husband and my best friend were in a long-term affair.

And, when I'd developed a crush on Jack, I'd wrongly assumed he was married.

Now I'd done it in reverse by wrongly assuming Ethan wasn't.

Oh, Lord. What a terrible mess. I really should know better and I really should apologise to Marielle this morning. I'll tell her that I'm leaving today.

When I walk into breakfast, I see my chance. Marielle is sitting having breakfast alone.

I assume that everyone else, including Ethan, is down on the beach already.

'Marielle, I just want to say that I'm so sorry about what has happened. I hope that you and Ethan can find a way to move on from this and that you can be happy together.'

She takes off her dark sunglasses and looks at me. Her eyes are tired and bloodshot.

'And I didn't know you two were married,' I stammer, getting to the point.

I plonk myself down in the chair opposite her without asking first because my legs feel weak and wobbly. She shrugs her skinny brown shoulders at me and wears a glib expression.

'*Merci* ... but it is impossible. We have tried too many times. This time, I know we are not right to keep trying. *Nous sommes touts hors d'amour* – we are all out of love for each other.'

I stare at her, blindsided, mouth open, wondering what to say next.

'We fell in and out of love on this island!' She stabs a long fingernail into the table between us and I leap back in fright. 'You see, here is not real life. That means the love is not real either. It's not possible for love found here to last beyond these shores. *D'accord?*'

I nod my head like one of those little nodding desk toys.

'But it is sweet of you to say this to me, Lori. Because I know I have not been so sympathetic to you. Ethan has told me he was very worried about you and your foot. It was very bad, no?'

'No. I mean yes. Well, I'm all better now. Thanks to him,' I say to her meekly.

She pats my hand to be reassuring but it feels more like a violent slap.

'*Bon*, I'm glad. Anyway, I must get packed. The supply boat will be here soon. *Adieu.*'

I stand up. 'You are leaving?'

'*Oui*. I have no wish to stay. Now they can all appreciate your cooking, Lori.'

I open my mouth to say that I'm leaving too, but then close it again while reconsidering.

The only reason I'd decided to leave today was because I thought I'd offended Marielle and because she'd said I was totally useless. But clearly, if she's leaving, then I might have a second chance and another whole week here in which to make myself thoroughly useful.

Now that my foot's healing, I can be mobile again and help save some turtles.

I offer her two kisses on the sides of her face. 'Bon voyage, Marielle.'

When the boat comes in, we all help to unload the weekly supply of ten five-gallon drinking water containers, three boxes of vegetables and dried goods and a crate of beers. Then we all stand on the beach and wave to Marielle as she leaves us. All except for Ethan. He stands among us but keeps his hands in his pockets and a frown on his face. Then, when the boat and Marielle are finally out of sight and we've all turned to start back up the beach, I hear him sigh heavily. As the others are already way ahead of us, I hang back to ask him if he's okay. He nods and shrugs and kicks the sand with his bare feet.

'Aye, I'm okay, thanks. You know, I really don't understand why she even came back here again. We've been separated for three years and hardly seen each other. Then, for some reason she decides to come out to the island again to see if we are "still meant to be together". Those were her words. It was all her idea. Not mine. I tried to do the right thing and give it a shot. But it was a big mistake.'

'I'm sorry to hear that. At least you tried.' This is the only thing I can think to say in response.

He raises his hands in the air as if surrendering or

praising something. 'Now she wants a divorce. Well, I say fuck you, Marielle. I'm glad it's finally fucking over!'

I breathe a sigh of relief on his behalf. 'Well, if you are not too upset, then that's good.'

'Yes. It is good. Everything is fine. Don't look so worried, Lori.'

I laugh. 'Well, it's just that I haven't ever heard you swear like that before.'

'Did I offend you? If I did, then I apologise. I really should mind my manners.'

'No. I like to swear too sometimes. If I do then the F-word is the one I like to use best.'

Ethan roars with laughter. 'Yeah, there's something satisfying about it, isn't there?'

I giggle and he gives me the biggest smile I've ever seen on him.

We walk up the beach together. I'm trying to digest what he's just told me.

'How long have you been married?' I ask him, hoping I'm not prying too much.

'Four years. What's that old saying? Marry in haste, regret at leisure. And you?'

'Twenty-five years and two grown up kids.'

He stops walking and looks at me in awe. 'Oh, that's a long time. I always wanted kids but I'm glad we didn't have any. We would have made terrible parents.'

'I feel we did a good job with ours. I'm very proud of them both.'

'So no regrets then?'

'No, I don't have any regrets. Like you, I'm just ready to move on.'

'You said you and your husband were recently separated?'

'Yes. He wants a divorce too.'

'And do you? Do you want a divorce?'

I nod. 'Yes. I do. It's the only way forward.'

He takes my hand and gives it a squeeze. It feels like he's taken hold of my heart and squeezed it too. 'Aye, let's look to the future. Thank you for listening and for being here, Lori. I'm sorry you're going through the same thing, but it really helps to know someone understands, eh?'

'I think *Never Look Back* should be our mutual mantra,' I say to him.

'And *Don't Look Back in Anger* should be our song,' he laughs.

Then he points to my foot in a bandage dressing and a clingfilm wrap.

'And how is your foot feeling today, Lori?'

I smile back at him. 'It's much better thank you, Ethan. I'm reporting for duty.'

I spend most of the day in the kitchen preparing both lunch and dinner and I enjoy myself. The new supplies make it easy for me to put together a vat of Tom Yum soup, a green mango salad, a delicious vegetable and dhal red curry, and a coconut tapioca pudding for dessert.

Everyone is ecstatic. It's amazing how good food can lift everyone's mood.

After dinner (it was the guys' turn to wash dishes) Ethan invites me to patrol the beach with him. I still have to wrap up my foot to protect it from water or sand, but now I'm using a plastic bag rather than a rubber boot, to make sure nothing agitates my fragile newly-healed skin.

'Before we go to the beach there is something I want you to hear, Lori.'

'Okay. I'm listening?'

'Not here. In the jungle.'

'Will there be snakes?' I ask him, sounding a little reluctant.

'No snakes. Anyway, they are more afraid of you, than you are of them.'

'That's not true,' I categorically insist.

But I follow him and his narrow red beam of light into the jungle.

Thankfully, we don't walk in too far before Ethan stops and turns out the light from the torch, plunging us into complete darkness. With the tree canopy over-head, there isn't even any moonlight. I feel him take my hand in his and I squeeze hold of it tightly as we stand side by side in the tropical fauna. 'Listen...' he says in a whisper.

So I do. I take a deep breath of dense damp and steamy jungle air and then try to slow my breathing and concentrate on the cacophony of sounds all around me. At first it all sounds like an overwhelming commotion of shrieks and clicks and rattles in the forest but then slowly I begin to pick out the individual sounds that make up the multi-dimensional mass.

I hear the rustlings of lemurs and the howl of monkeys in the trees. I recognise the sound of crickets and the rhythmic chirping of tree frogs and bull frogs croaking in baritone in the undergrowth while the warbles and squeaks of romancing lizards on the ground sound too close for comfort. Then there's something else too – a repetitive and quite distinctive sound that echoes all around us. I can hardly believe what my ears are hearing.

'Fuck you. Fuck you. Fuuuuck youuuu!'

I start laughing. 'What the...? What *is* that?'

'That is the tokay gecko,' Ethan tells me proudly.

'That is a gecko ... and it's actually swearing?' I clarify.

'Aye. Otherwise known as the fuck-you-lizard. It's common all over South East Asia. I just wanted you to know I'm not the only one on the island who has a penchant for swearing.'

I listen in amusement to lots more calls of 'fuck you' coming at us from all directions.

'It's ... well ... incredible and quite unbelievable!'

'It's the mating call,' Ethan says, hardly supressing his chortles.

We laugh until our sides ached and alternately repeat the cry all the way back to the camp. The lads and lassies (Ethan, being Scottish, likes to call the girls 'lassies') seem more amused that I hadn't ever heard the night time call of the tokay gecko before now.

'I can hardly sleep for the ones shouting *fuck you* all night in our bathroom,' Laura tells me.

'Well, that's because I have the Barry White of bull-frogs in mine,' I groan. 'He's louder than anything else on this island. If anyone wants to come in and catch him for me I'd be very grateful. I've hardly managed a wink of sleep since I got here.'

Ethan and I are on night shift patrol together tonight. I realise, as we leave camp for the beach with our red-light torches, we are being watched by the others. It seems that we have become interesting by default now that Marielle has left. We head towards the rocky inlet that poachers have been using to hide their boats and all the while we are looking for turtle tyre tracks coming up from the surf line. Not seeing any turtles, we sit on the rocks for a while because Ethan has spotted a small boat off shore. He thinks it could be poachers pretending to be fishing.

So, we keep our torches switched on, so they will know we are there and watching them.

'The plan is always to be non-confrontational. If the person knows we are watching, they might feel intimidated enough to go away and then our job is done,' Ethan tells me.

After a while, the boat does go away and so we start our walk back down the beach.

With great excitement, I immediately spot some tracks and we follow a huge old turtle to the top of the beach, where she rummages around with great effort under her massive weight before eventually settling down to dig her nest pit. We sit back quietly to watch her.

'This nest will need moving, won't it?' I say, noting the proximity to the poacher's inlet.

'That's right, Lori. First thing tomorrow morning, it will be our job to transfer all her eggs into the hatchery for safe keeping.'

I have to stop myself from squealing with excitement because at last I'm going to be doing what I actually came here to do – help save some turtles.

We monitor the nesting mother until she finishes digging her pit and enters her trance like state while laying her eggs. Then I approach carefully to take her photo and make a note of her unique markings. She is a fully mature heavy turtle. One and a half metres across her shell. She's showing her age too, as her shell is rough and looks a little worse for wear in places. Ethan says he recognises her from a triangle shaped chunk missing from the outer edge of her shell. 'This is Pizza,' he says. 'She's been here twice this season already. I've a feeling this might be her last nest for a few years or possibly for good, because she's getting really old now.'

I feel so honoured to be here for what might be Pizza's last efforts to make babies.

I also feel a great responsibility of care for her eggs when we transfer them tomorrow.

At midnight I go back to my hut, in which I'm now alone, and climb into my hammock. I enjoy being cocooned in the dark because it somehow feels symbolic of my life right now. I'm in the process of great change, like a caterpillar, waiting to become a butterfly.

I don't get much sleep though, thanks to Barry the bullfrog White in the bathroom.

But hanging from the ceiling wrapped up in white netting is certainly conducive to thinking.

And it's Marielle's words that are at the forefront of my mind right now.

They are on repeat in my head like some kind of ethereal warning.

We fell in and out of love on this island...

The way she spoke, so passionately, hit a nerve with me.

I understand what she was trying to convey and therefore I feel I understand her.

To some extent I even sympathise, because I've been that angry too, and not so long ago.

Even though she'd violently struck out at Ethan, which was quite unforgivable, I completely understand why she did it – why she lashed out, why she wanted to hurt him.

She had lost him. It was already over. She'd lost her marriage.

Her words and her pain take me straight back to a time not so long ago, in my own life, when I'd had a split second to choose between the knife or my passport.

It had been bone-jarringly painful to walk away and leave everything behind me.

And, woman to woman, I know that's what Marielle had to do today too.

Here is not real life. So the love is not real either.

I agree that this place is as far from reality as you can possibly imagine.

It's not possible for love found here to last beyond these shores.

And these are the words that hit me the hardest.

What's that old saying about holiday romances? That they'll never last?

Because they are only ever perfect while you are in the perfect place?

The next day, I'm up at first light, keen to help move Pizza's eggs into the hatchery.

Ethan, always the first to rise, is having breakfast. 'Good morning, Lori.'

'Good morning Ethan. I see it's another beautiful day and you are wearing another very beautiful and colourful shirt – are those birds of paradise you have on there?'

'Aye, another perfect day in paradise.'

But his voice is flat and he's not looking up at me. Sensing he's upset, I sit down opposite him, wondering if he too is feeling bad about Marielle. Then, as he looks up at me over the coffee pot, I see his badly cut and swollen eye. 'Oh, Ethan. My goodness ... what happened?'

He pours me a cup of coffee. 'We had a bit of trouble on the beach last night.'

'What? When? I heard nothing? And what about the others – are they okay?'

I know that when I'd said goodnight last night, everything on the beach and in the camp had been absolutely fine. David and George had relieved us at midnight and I'd gone to my room and climbed straight into my hammock. I'm realising now that I must have slept through some kind of commotion and even the noise of the bullfrog.

'Aye, they're okay. I'm just glad they came and got me and didn't try to handle the situation themselves. David woke me at 3 a.m. to say they'd seen a couple of poachers on the beach. A nest was being raided. I managed to tackle one of the men and that's how I got the black eye. They both got away, unfortunately, and with most of the eggs from Pizza's new nest.'

I immediately burst into tears. 'Oh no, poor Pizza. All her babies. The last of her babies!'

Ethan shrugs despondently. 'We do what we can here. Sometimes it's not enough.'

I wipe my tears away with the back of my hand. 'And poor you, getting punched.'

He says nothing and hands me his paper napkin.

I weep some more and then blow my nose on it.

Chapter 11

Koh Phi Tao (iv)

In just a few days, turtle-nesting season here on Koh Phi Tao will be over. I'm reluctantly counting down to our very last day here because I really don't want it to end. Ethan and the lads have been here for almost eight weeks now and the girls and I have only been here for the time it takes to have a holiday – but it somehow feels like I've been here a lifetime.

I'm already starting to fret about missing the group and this island in my life. In such a short time, they have become like another family to me.

I've also learned so much about turtle conservation. Now that my foot has healed, and I'm playing my full part in all the tasks and activities, the days are incredibly full and busy. We do still occasionally have a turtle coming up the beach at night, so we have stepped up our vigils by overlapping our shift rotas, but our efforts are now mainly concentrated on the nests hatching from their secret locations at the top of the beach and also in the hatchery.

Every day now, hundreds of baby turtles are being born and we are overseeing their safe passage into the sea. This has lifted everyone's mood after the terrible loss of poor Pizza's nest a few nights ago. If I'm not on beach patrol with Ethan or taking my turn at kitchen duty, I'm spending my time happily sitting in the middle of the hatchery in my bikini and my oversized sun hat, watching for little rumbles in the sand and waiting for tiny flippers to appear and little heads to emerge and take their first breath of fresh island air. I greet each one as it is born and gather it up and place it very carefully into the collecting bucket with all its brothers or sisters.

Interestingly, each nest will either be all male or all female, depending on the ground temperature in their sixty days or so of incubation time. Warmer temperatures in the nest always produce females. Cooler nests always produce males. Ethan says the easiest way to remember this is to say, 'cool dudes and hot chicks.'

In the evenings, despite our few resources and only a few red lights to illuminate the place after dark, we are also kept busy because Ethan has a great love of games and team-building exercises and he says it's not a good thing for any of us to be left alone with too much time in our own company on an island that can be walked around in fifteen minutes.

He says it brings on island craziness, something he's seen too many times.

I wonder if he is referring to Marielle's now famous temper tantrums?

So, between our evening shifts and lazy afternoons we play board games and card games and beer pong. I'm getting really good at beer pong! We also hold quizzes. We pair up into teams – it's always the lads, the lassies, and Ethan and I, and we take turns to stage the questions.

All of this is taken quite seriously, as the winning team gets a decent prize.

It could be the last packet of cookies or a free pass to get out of washing up duty.

Another popular game involves Ethan on his guitar enthusiastically playing a series of pop intro tunes for us to guess. This is always hilarious, with people humming and singing bits of tunes and holding up the next intro because they claim they know it and 'it's just on the tip of my tongue'. I also love our time sitting around singing while Ethan and George are jamming away on their guitars and we are all belting out iconic songs at the top of our voices whether we can hold a tune or not. We sing songs by The Eagles (*Hotel California, Tequila Sunrise, Lyin' Eyes*) and some of the old classics by Janis Joplin (*Me and Bobby McGee, Mercedes Benz*) and sometimes we even have the howling monkeys in the trees joining in with us. It's so much fun. I'm going to miss those evenings so much.

Our very last evening on the island, after a very beautiful and productive last day, we have an interesting meal together. I say interesting because I manage to successfully combine a jar of peanut butter with noodles and mango with chilli and rice. Ethan provides us with a red snapper that he caught while on his last guard duty on the rocks at the end of the beach. The lads make a fish curry with it and the girls provide our dessert of pineapple pudding.

After dinner, while the others are cleaning up, Ethan and I take our last walk down the beach together to watch the sunset, just as we've been doing here on most evenings since Marielle left. He calls it our 'grown-up time' together.

And there is always something in the air between us. A tension. A frisson.

We are acutely aware of our connection but we don't dare speak of it. So our conversations are deliberately steered away from anything overtly personal in case we inadvertently veer into something sensitive. I'll admit, even though every day is full of wonderful times, this is my very favourite time of the day; when we stroll down to the water's edge to sit and sip our beer and chat together.

Over the past week, we've often played 'where in the world', 'likes and dislikes', 'three favourite things' and 'name three things you'd take to a desert island' as a covert way to get to know each other better. This keeps things between us cordial and safe and polite and also fun.

Where in the world: It seems he's been almost everywhere and from what I can tell, he's also managed to tick off everything on my bucket list.

Likes and dislikes: He doesn't like women who wear too much make-up (he prefers the natural look) or women who have hang-ups about food (so I guess Marielle was just naturally skinny) and he also says he doesn't like pineapples, which is weird, as he has at least two shirts with a pineapple pattern and he eats pineapple pudding.

Three favourite things: Name three of your favourite artist/bands, songs, animals, colours, books, foods, drinks, movies. *Me:* Jack Johnson. Anything sung by Jack Johnson. Dogs. Green. *Him:* Morrissey. Every Day is like Sunday (says it reminds him of Scotland for some reason). Orangutans. Blue.

Three things you'd take to a desert island: *Me:* a box of books, a bag of sunscreen, and a crate of wine (he said that's cheating). *Him:* a machete, a flint, his guitar.

But tonight. Well, tonight has a whole different feel to it.

There are no gaming questions. No teasing or even any tentative flirting.

Tonight, there is a feeling of sadness in the tropical sultry air between us.

This time tomorrow, I will be on Langkawi island and Ethan will be in Kuala Lumpur.

So, when we reach the water's edge, we sit on the sand next to each other, close enough to feel each other's body heat but not quite touching and we sip our beer and we watch the sun go down and we are silent. We both know there are things to be said but neither of us feels the need to say anything just yet. I suppose it's our way of honouring the incredible beauty of our last sunset together on this beautiful island and respecting nature's nightly spectacular lightshow of pastel pinks and violets deepening into magenta and amber as the sun dips down over the horizon. It certainly warrants us being speechless for this grand finale.

Although, I see it's also dark and stormy in the far-off distance.

It's reflective of my mood. It's just perfect right now but it could be gloomy later.

The fluorescent green lights of the squid boats on the far horizon are brighter than usual against the inky blackness of those tumbling clouds. I can hear the warning sounds of faraway rumbles of thunder. We continue to sit as the light fades and then we turn our faces to the night sky. Directly above us, stars are starting to pop out like faraway flashbulbs, planets and universes and cosmoses too, are all being reflected in the still lagoon in front of us and creating a miracle of tiny lights with no up or down or end in sight.

I take a deep breath, filling my lungs with the warm and salted air and after holding it for a moment, I let it go as one long and heavy sigh, breaking our mutual time of silence.

'So, Lori. Tell me, have you decided where you're going after Langkawi yet?'

'Yes. I'm thinking of going to Borneo to help out at an orangutan orphanage.'

He smiles and nods. 'You are a lovely lady, Lori. Gosh that sounds just like a song lyric. I must write that down. *Lovely lady Lori...*'

He starts to sing it. I laugh. 'What, you'll write a song ... about me?'

'Aye. A love song...' he says, finding my fingers and lightly kissing the back of my hand.

My heart is melting and his words and his lips are like an aphrodisiac to my love-starved body. My wanton lust for him is off the Richter scale. When I lift up my eyes to meet his, it actually terrifies me how much I want him. But I remember the words whispered to me

227

by the young monk of Chiang Mai about 'want'. *There was once a lady who said to Lord Buddha, 'I want happiness' and Lord Buddha told her that she must remove 'want' because that was her greed. And then, she would be left with 'happiness'.*

In another time and place – somewhere real – I know I could easily fall in love with him.

But right now, it's a bit like Marielle's spirit is sitting between us, a ghostly chaperone.

'I see another opportunity for you. If you're interested?'

I gaze at him curiously. 'Really? What is it?'

'You could come with me. I'll be in Kuala Lumpur for a couple of days before I head over to another small island just like this one. This time it's a re-established coral garden. I need another diver to work with me. It's mostly shallow diving, so you're already qualified for the job. It would be the perfect place for you to increase your logged dives and even get your advanced diver certification. How am I doing? Have I talked you into it yet?'

I stare at him. I think I might have even left my mouth open. I don't know what to say.

Was this perhaps our other time and other place?

'So where exactly is this island with its coral garden?' I ask him.

He sits closer to me, leaning in, as if he's telling me a secret.

'It's in the Sulu Sea, just off northern Malaysia, in the national marine park there. It'll just be for a month, maybe less, all depending on the arrival of the seasonal tides.'

I'm tempted. Diving. Spending more time with Ethan. It sounds heavenly.

It sounds perfect but then perfect is not always real, is it?

He reaches out to touch my face and his voice is now low and gentle.

'I really want us to be together, Lori. Please say you'll come?'

And, as much as I want to say yes, I really don't think either of us is ready for that big a commitment. Not yet. He's not offering me a job. He's offering me a relationship. It's true we have made a connection here but, whether it is real or imaginary, we are also both still connected to other people. He might be separated but he is still married to Marielle.

Just as I'm still married to Charles. And it's not past history – its current news.

I'm starting to feel guilty about something but I'm not sure what. Maybe it's just being so far away and out of touch. My kids are still my kids even if they are also grown men. I still have accountability to them if not responsibility. Being off grid has certainly been conducive to my state of mind – it has helped me think

more clearly – but seeing things clearly often comes
with mind-blowing guilt trips as a consequence.

Ethan is waiting for my answer.

He continues to hold onto my hand but I think he
realises I'm about to turn him down.

I take a deep breath. 'Ethan, these past two weeks
have been very special to me.' I pause, trying to keep
my voice steady and to deliver my thoughts coherently,
even though I'm trembling inside and I don't trust that
what I want to say will come out right. 'But, we are
both actively dealing with the end of our current relationships, so I feel the timing is wrong for us.'

I chew on my lower lip anxiously and wonder how
he'll respond.

'Timing...?' he reiterates, as if he can't quite believe
my reasoning.

I nod. 'Yes. Ethan, the truth is, I wish you and I had
met six months from now.'

'But I was going to say that the timing is perfect,'
he argues. 'We have both realised our current relationships – only I'd much prefer to call them past
relationships – aren't working and that we are both
free to move on.'

'Ethan, I disagree,' I counter immediately. 'We are not
free to move on and that is why our timing is truly
terrible. Please, believe me, when I tell you that I wish
things were different and that I will really miss you.

I've loved being with you here and having this time together.'

He kisses my hand again. 'Okay. I get it. You need more time.'

We walk back up to the camp. The lads and lassies are nowhere to be seen.

Ethan and I stand facing each other in the dull red light from the camp and he wraps his strong arms around me and hugs me tightly. I hear him sigh and feel his warm breath on my hair and the softness of his lips as they graze past my earlobe and across my cheek.

I know he wants to kiss me.

With all my heart, I want to say *yes, yes, yes.*

But I bury my face in his palm tree-patterned shirt and I swallow back a sob while holding onto him. I know that in the morning, when we part company, there will be no time for sentiment or tears or anything other than a firm shake of hands and cursory kisses to the side of the face. I want to kiss him properly now but I know if I start then I won't want to stop.

I inhale his scent – an intoxicating mix of manliness and coconut oil and sea salt – and I whisper into his ear. 'So, I guess this is goodbye.'

As he looks down at me, I see his sea green eyes are sparkling with sad glossy tears.

And my heart aches all the more.

'Lori, if this really is goodbye, then do you fancy a little nightcap?'

'Do you mean a beer?' I actually can't face another beer this late in the evening.

He smirks at me. His boyish grin has returned. 'Do you like whisky?'

'Well, that rather depends on whether you mean Scotch or Thai?' I reply quite honestly.

He disappears to his bungalow and soon reappears with a bottle of Scotch.

He pours two good measures into a couple of clean jam jars that doubled as glassware.

We sit down next to each other on the wooden steps in front of Turtle HQ.

'What are we drinking to?' I ask him, raising my glass.

'How about better timing?' he suggests, looking me squarely in the eye.

'Sure. To better timing!' I knock my glass against his.

When I get back to my bungalow, my heart is heavy and my body is tingling from the after-effects of the whisky and the after-shock of Ethan's farewell embrace. I wanted to kiss him. I ached to kiss him. But what good would it do either of us to taste forbidden fruit?

I shower and treat my foot, smearing it with a little antibiotic cream.

There is an indented patch of new white skin forming

over where the infected graze had been but it's healing nicely. Ethan says I'm likely to always have a scar there now as a reminder of him. But I think the scar that will remind me of him is on my heart, not my foot.

I chase the bellowing bullfrog around the bathroom for a while before I give up and go to lie in my hammock. My mind is full of thoughts about Ethan. I try to imagine the small tropical island he is going to and what it might be like to go diving there on the coral garden reef.

Then I try not to think about us spending all our time together on the beach, in the sea, and what it would be like sharing his bed and to make love with him every single night as the sun sets on our very own paradise. Oh, how my heart aches. How my poor body aches for him!

And all this while, Barry the bullfrog White is doing a duet with a fuck-you lizard.

A couple of hours later, there's a tap on the door.

I answer it in my shorts and vest to find Ethan standing outside my door.

'Have you come to catch my bullfrog?' I ask him, hopefully.

'Come on, I want to show you something,' he says, holding out his hand to me.

I follow him outside into the darkness and he guides me along the path to the beach.

When we reach the point where our feet touch the sand, we stop and I gasp in wonder and astonishment. What is happening here? What is this?

The night sky is filled with thousands of stars. Tiny, twinkling, sapphire blue and white lights all being reflected in the flat calm liquid mirror of the lagoon. But now, in addition to the night sky, the sand on the beach is full of stars too. I've never seen anything like it.

A sparkling Disney-esque fairy-tale or something out of the movie Avatar?

Am I still asleep in my hammock and dreaming this?

The whole beach is glowing with tiny individually luminescent sand particles.

'It's bioluminescence,' Ethan explains. 'A natural light-show from phytoplankton.'

'I'm completely bowled over – it's like nothing I've ever seen before,' I breathe.

'It's been washed up on the beach, and now the tide's going out, it's leaving behind these tiny light-producing organisms in the sand. It's so beautiful, isn't it?'

This truly is a spectacular phenomenon. Ethan scoops up a handful of sand and he pours it into my cupped palm. I'm left with a handful of sparkling electric blue particles running through my fingers. It looks like stardust. We run into the middle of the beach to be enveloped in the magic of it all. Once again, I'm amazed by the natural wonders of this world of ours.

Ethan still has hold of my hand. He pulls me slowly and purposefully towards him and he looks deeply into my eyes. 'I felt the very same way, the first time I saw you, Lori. Completely bowled over.' His voice is gentle, soulful, and sincere. 'Would you mind if I kissed you?'

I tip my face up to his and say to him softly, 'I think your timing is perfect.'

Chapter 12

Koh Lipe

The speedboat arrives the following morning, on time at 10 a.m. Onboard are the new team members taking over our responsibilities for the remaining nests and for their own assignment.

There are two girls and two guys, who seem to me to be overly enthusiastic to meet Ethan. There are also half a dozen passengers onboard who are heading down to the border with us and who are all agog with amazement at stopping off at an island none of them had known existed and that looks so out-of-this-world perfect.

There isn't much time for a handover, but we've cleaned up the camp and packed up our personal belongings and now Ethan and Jodie and Laura and George and David and I are all stood on the beach with our backpacks, ready to climb aboard the boat headed for the last vestige of Thailand where it meets Malaysia.

As we speed along the Andaman Sea in the fast-moving speedboat, with the wind whipping our hair and snatching away our voices, conversation isn't easy, so we are left alone in our thoughts about the time we have shared together and our adventures still to come.

At breakfast this morning, everyone had spoken enthusiastically about travelling to their new destinations, even though there was a tangible feeling of sadness that our mutual time together on Koh Phi Tao had come to an end. David and George still have each other's company to look forward to and so do Laura and Jodie, as they're moving onto new teams and new adventures with the Goldman Global Foundation in the Philippines and Indonesia respectively. Ethan is sat across from me on the boat. He is wearing dark sunglasses and he has his Indiana Jones style hat pulled down over his face. I guess he may or may not be sleeping. Either way, despite the heat of the day, I feel a cold tangible distance between us now.

When we get to Koh Lipe, the beach is busy. It could have been idyllic, but it's teeming with people and the waterline is packed with long-tail boats all anchored in lines and on ropes and with their extended bows bedecked with colourful garlands and flowers. We join the masses of people and their luggage in the line to clear border control and the customs office checkpoint, which is of course, in a small hut under a palm tree on the beach.

The heat on the beach is stifling and shade is non-existent. I'm so glad to have remembered my sunhat this time or I don't think I could survive standing in line for the time it takes to get to the front of the queue. When it eventually comes to my turn, I find myself at a small window where a uniformed Thai official is sitting. He demands to see my tickets, my departure card and my passport and then he waves his hand dismissively, flicking his cigarette ash at me. 'Go. Wait. Go!' he yells. I guess someone is having a bad day.

I step aside and Ethan takes my place at the window and goes through the same procedure. Then we both shuffle aside to wait as we're told, with another group of people.

I feel so nervous at having to give up my passport. I mean, it was after all my most precious possession, and there are so many people here and so many pass-ports being handed over that I'm determined not to let this official out of my sight while he has it.

This means waiting in the scorching sun until my precious passport is back in my hand.

Ethan says he'll go and find us some water and then he disappears into the melting madness and reappears over a dehydrated hour later, by which time I'm sure I have sunstroke, with two bottles of water for us. He says the queue for refreshments was unbelievable madness.

Just as I am thinking how awful all this all is, there is suddenly a commotion.

Something is happening. A border official has appeared and is calling out names.

I listen carefully for 'Lorraine Anderson' and then step forward when my name is called. I am given a label for my backpack and sticker for my shirt that says *ferry* on it but still no passport. 'Can I have my passport back please?' I ask him politely but I am ignored and more names are read out, Ethan's included, and he steps forward too.

'But when do we get our passports back?' I want to know.

Another passenger tells me our passports would now be given to the ferry boat captain, who would keep them until we were physically out of Thailand. I do not find this at all reassuring and so follow the official carrying a box of passports right down to the beach where all the long-tail boats are lined up and where I can see a large ferry waiting out at sea.

'No. Not yet! Wait up there, not on beach!' I am told by the officially rude man.

I pretend I don't understand him. Ethan has joined me on the beach now and this tactic at least has us first in line for boarding the long-tails that would transport us to the waiting ferry. Then, after being packed into one of the long-tails, gripping my backpack and gritting my teeth, I manage to head the scramble to get aboard the ferry and secure us two seats on the upper premium deck where I think I'm less likely to get seasick.

The seats upstairs cost just one hundred baht extra – around a measly two UK pounds – but they are larger, more comfortable, in an air-conditioned cabin and also include a bottle of cold drinking water each. An absolute bargain.

As soon as we are out in the open sea, I see an official on deck with the box of passports.

There is immediately a crowd around him and again, we have to wait for our names to be called out. I keep thinking that if they've somehow missed putting my passport onboard – and with all the passengers and confusion and waiting around it's a distinct and very real possibility – then I'm screwed for getting into or out of Malaysia.

But after just a short time my name is called and I step forward. The official looks first at me and then my passport picture. My passport is five years old and I'm suddenly embarrassed because I know it's not a good likeness of me.

I'd had the photo done in a hurry in one of those photobooths in the supermarket while out shopping. It had been cold and raining and blustery that day, but

Charles had said he was taking me to Tenerife for our twentieth anniversary (a trip that didn't actually happen for reasons I won't bore you with) and I'd been so busy thinking about how I was soon to be basking in warmer climes, that I'd been blissfully unaware of how I'd live to regret looking rain-splattered and wind-blown in my passport for the next ten years.

The official takes his time looking me over. 'You not look like this anymore...' he points out. He hands back my passport. Feeling embarrassed, I gratefully scuttle back to my seat to realise that I'm now starting to feel queasy. The boat is lurching and pitching in the water.

It's clear to me that others are starting to feel queasy too.

I see a few people with their eyes closed, looking decidedly green. Except for Ethan. He's pulled down his hat again and appears to be sleeping. I check my watch and wonder if the staff will be issuing sick bags any time soon. I then overhear some people in the seats behind me talking about a one-hour time zone change. Apparently, the island of Langkawi is one hour ahead in time which, to my great relief, means that by my new calculations we'll all be on this ferry boat for an hour less than I'd previously thought.

But I'm still looking around in acute distress. The woman sitting across from me smiles, catching my eye, and I attempt to smile back. She asks me something, but I think she is Russian, and of course I don't understand. She takes something out of her bag – it's a packet of seasickness tablets – and offers me one. Gratefully, I take one and wash it down with my no-longer-cold bottled water. Another half an hour later and I'm starting to feel better.

What a miracle! What an amazing invention – who knew seasick tablets actually worked?

When we arrive at the ferry port on Langkawi, Ethan wakes up and we disembark. He and I are some of the first in line to get through customs. It doesn't take long. I made sure to check my passport to see that I have been given a full ninety-day entry stamp into Malaysia.

Then Ethan and I look at each other and we both know this is the final goodbye.

I try not to cry. Suddenly Lorna and Jodie and David and George appear and there are hugs and kisses and thanks and goodbyes expressed with great gusto and lots of laughter and we all promise to keep in touch with each other. Everyone adds me to their Facebook.

They ask me if I have Instagram and Twitter but I say that I don't have either of those.

I immediately feel like an old dinosaur but when I find out Ethan doesn't have any social media at all – not even Facebook – I feel slightly better but then worry how I might keep in touch with him in the future. To my relief he pulls out his phone and asks me for my number.

I tell him it and he types it into his phone and calls me so I now have his number too.

'Call me when you're ready. I'll be waiting,' he says to me, but his tone of voice is low and flat as if he doesn't ever believe I will call.

I'm clutching my phone to my chest protectively, while he kisses my cheek one last time and then suddenly everyone has gone – including Ethan – and I'm alone with hundreds of strangers. I start to search the heaving masses for him, desperate for one last glimpse of his broad back and his muscular frame and his brightly coloured crazy shirt, but he has disappeared without a trace. I'm now feeling bereft and asking myself if I've made a terrible and stupid mistake.

Malaysia is just as hot and humid as Thailand. I have nowhere to stay, so I find a café in the shopping mall outside the terminal and buy a cup of coffee, so I can connect to the internet for free. From what I can see on my hotel booking app, most of the hotels and restaurants are in the lively Cenang Beach area of Langkawi. I resist the temptation to stay at a fancy five star with a huge swimming pool, even though my spine is screaming for a big soft bed after spending every night for the past couple of weeks in a hammock suspended from the ceiling.

But I really do need to start watching my spending. With no income, if I want the money in my bank account to last me for any considerable length of time, I must start to cut back on unnecessary luxuries. So I book a budget hotel for a couple of nights and grab an Uber to take me there. On the way, I gaze out of the window at the sights of Langkawi and I distract myself from thinking about Ethan by keeping my eyes peeled for somewhere interesting to eat.

I haven't exactly been starved on Koh Phi Tao but perhaps surprisingly, fish was in short supply there and seafood is a firm favourite of mine, so as we drive along past restaurants specialising in fish and lobster and shrimp and every other type of seafood, I ask my driver for a recommendation. 'Madam, I will show you the best seafood restaurant in Langkawi!' he tells me with great enthusiasm. 'Tell them Sami sent you. Yes! Please! Thank you!'

Between the ferry point and the Cenang Beach, Sami also points out many places of interest and where to get the very best of everything cheaply because he tells me Langkawi is a duty-free island. And he yells *yes, please, thank you!* after everything he says, which covers all bases in polite English.

The seafood restaurant he recommends is on the main street behind the beach.

It doesn't look like much. I think I might have just

walked passed it if it hadn't come recommended. There are tables inside and outside – plastic chairs and plastic tablecloths – but I can see it's busy and the seafood being displayed is alive and in a huge glass tank right next to the pavement and in full view of passers-by.

I practically squash my nose on the taxi window just trying to see what's swimming around in it. When we reach my hotel, the fare is such a pittance, that I tip Sami generously and he gives me his business card in delight.

'Call me directly next time, madam. Yes! Please! Thank you!'

I check into my hotel. It's a clean and modern two-story building.

My room's fine – in a basic travel lodge kind of way; clean and comfortable with a small bathroom and the usual flat screen TV opposite the bed. As soon as I throw down my backpack, I plug in my phone and charger and excitedly call each of my boys as promised. Disappointingly, Lucas doesn't pick up but Josh answers straightaway.

'Mum! I've been worried sick about you!' he tells me anxiously.

'But I told you not to worry and I was going off grid for a while.'

The fact that this sounds like parent-son role reversal isn't lost on me.

'Anyway, I'm fine. How are you, darling? And how is Lucas?'

'We just need to know you're safe, Mum. I mean, one minute you're in Thailand. Then you message us to say you'll speak to us next from Malaysia, for heaven's sake!'

'Yes. That's right. I'm in Malaysia now. I'm on the island of Langkawi. It's lovely here.'

'I've no doubt it is!' Josh exclaims. 'But when are you coming home, Mum?'

There is a silence while I think about how to tell him I'm not coming back yet.

'Mum ... are you still there?'

'Yes. I'm here, Josh. But I'm not exactly sure when I'll be back. I want to travel for a while longer. Do you understand, darling?'

'But Mum, you're all on your own at the other side of the world. It might be dangerous!'

'Darling, I'm a grown woman. I can look after myself. It's not like I'm being reckless.'

'Dad said he wants to see you too. I spoke to him yesterday.'

'Oh, does he? Well, I don't want to see or speak to him.'

'He says there are things that you two have to sort out.'

'Like the terms of the divorce?' I say, sourly.

'Yeah. He said he wants to keep the house. He wants to buy you out of your fifty per cent.'

'For cash?' I say, suddenly a lot brighter. 'Tell him I accept. I want fifty per cent of the current market value. If he agrees, I'll sign the house over to him and give him his divorce.'

'Don't sound so cheerful about it, Mum! I thought you'd be gutted?'

'No. I was gutted a month ago. Now I'm over it. I'll admit, it has taken a lot less time than I expected to get over twenty-five years of marriage,' I say, with a little sigh of acceptance.

'Mum, are you sure you're okay. Are you ... drunk?'

I laugh. 'No! I'm certainly not drunk. I'm perfectly sober and absolutely fine.'

'Mum, Lucas and I have been talking. We think all this business about Dad and his affair and the divorce might have given you some kind of breakdown, so if you're not coming home, we're going to have to come out to see you. I'm looking at flights online right now.'

'Oh, Josh. Really? You'd come out here? Both of you? That would be fantastic!' I squeal.

I know they want reassurance that I haven't completely lost my mind, but once they get here they'll clearly see I haven't. I need to see them so much. 'When will you come?'

'We can fly directly from London to Kuala Lumpur and arrive on Saturday morning.'

'This weekend coming, you mean?' I clarify, sounding as though I'm checking my diary.

'Yes. We can only stay two nights. We'll get Monday off work. I'll say it's a family emergency. I can't get any longer off work this close to Christmas. I'm sure Lucas is the same.'

It's only then that I realise it's already December.

Just one week to Christmas. When it's so hot and sunny it's hard to contemplate it.

'Would you mind bringing me over a few things?' I ask him tentatively. 'I don't need much but I'd love to have my little laptop with me and my camera and just a few bits and bobs.'

'Okay. But I'm only bringing one bag. Message me with what you need.'

So we agree to meet up in Kuala Lumpur. The boys say they'll send me their flight times and I agree to meet them at arrivals on Saturday. I'm so excited. Seeing my boys again is just the tonic I need right now. All my anxiety over Ethan and whether I'd done the right thing by not going with him has been brushed from my mind because my boys are coming all this way to see me. Josh is right, we do need to talk. It has to be hard on them, knowing their parents have separated. And I can understand how worried they are about me. If it had been either one of them who'd experienced such a terrible shock and then taken off around the world, then I'd be worried sick too.

At least this way, I can reassure them both face to face.

And, if Charles wants to buy me out of my share of our home, that's a perfect solution for me. With my bank account topped up with such a lot of money, I will be able to keep travelling for far longer than I originally thought possible. In fact, I might never have to go back ever again. I imagine myself as an old woman living in a little hut on a tropical beach.

Smiling happily to myself, I pick up my phone and log into a local air travel website and I book myself a one-way flight for Friday afternoon from here to Kuala Lumpur. I then book us into one of the finest hotels in the city, right opposite the fabulous and famous twin Petronas Towers. A Christmas present to myself and to my boys. I'm so very excited!

Chapter 13

Langkawi, Malaysia

Feeling far more upbeat than when I first arrived here on Langkawi, I go out exploring and shopping. With Langkawi being a duty-free island, and with a decent exchange rate for the local ringgit plus the low cost of living, it makes for a very happy and guilt-free shopping location. I buy myself a good moisturising face cream (I'm a little worried about the sun aging my face even though I feel ten years younger with a tan), a bottle of perfume (my favourite Chanel *Mademoiselle*), several new light cotton dresses, lots more tops, a couple of (flattering) bikinis and a nice bottle of wine to drink in my room later while watching my big flat screen TV. Low cost luxury after basic island living.

But I really have to eat. I want seafood and lots of it.

So I go along to the recommended street restaurant to discover I'm lucky to even get a seat. The place is packed out and obviously very popular with locals as well as tourists. I am seated only because right at the same moment I arrive, someone else just happens to be leaving. I am given a small plastic bowl – exactly the kind I used to use at home for washing up dishes – and in it I'm asked to put my chosen seafood.

I choose a small lobster. To my horror, it's black and shiny and moving about. Its claws have elastic bands around them to stop him nipping at me. It looks at me with its beady little eyes and I admit that I start to feel horribly guilty for wanting to eat him.

'How you want it cooked, madam?' I'm asked by the chef standing by the barbeque grill.

I look unsure. I'm not used to seeing my meal at this early stage.

Normally, I would expect to choose a lobster from a menu and only actually see it once he was dressed and ready to eat. 'Ermmmm...'

'With garlic and butter is the most popular choice, madam?'

'Yes! Please! Thank you!' I say quickly, adding a huge tiger prawn and a big scoop of mussels and clams to my bowl.

When it all come to me on a smoking hot platter, and dripping with butter and garlic from the barbecue grill a short time later, it looks so amazing and fantastic, that I take a photo of it before I got stuck in. I always wondered why people did that but now I know. It's food porn.

Groaning from the amount I've eaten, but vowing to do it again before I left Langkawi, I call for my tab while I finish my glass of local beer. I see the poor waitress is rushed off her feet. When she brings me my bill, I can hardly believe how little such an extravagant meal had cost. I gush praise about the deliciousness of the food and get chatting to my waitress. 'How long you here on Langkawi, madam?' she asks me.

'Oh, just a couple of days,' I reply.

'If you would like a tour of the island tomorrow, I can take you to all the best places.'

I am just about to decline when she gets her phone out and starts to show me photos of her car. 'Look, I have a very nice car. It has air-conditioning. I can take you to the cable car and the sky bridge and the waterfalls. All very beautiful. You can hire me and my car for the whole day. Very good price.'

'That is a very nice car,' I agree, feeling a little under pressure.

She flicks through her photo gallery and shows me photos of her whole family.

'Look, this is my daughter,' she continues, pushing the phone screen under my nose.

She smiles at me with such dark and pleading eyes,

that as a mother myself, I can see, despite the very nice car, that she is desperate to earn some money and that waiting tables isn't covering all she needed. 'Okay. Yes. I would like to take the tour,' I tell her.

'Very good. My name is Zara. I'll pick you up at your hotel at 8.30 a.m. promptly.'

I tell her my name and where I am staying and I pay my bill.

Then, as I head back to my hotel – just a five-minute walk – I realise I hadn't asked her for the price of the tour. Oh, I'm such a mug, I think to myself. I go back to my room, undress, showered and open my bottle of wine.

I plug in my phone to charge up and flick to my contacts to look at Ethan's number.

I stare at it and then repeat it to myself. I really don't know why.

My mind flashes back to the first time I saw him, when he introduced himself to me on the beach. To his concern when he was attending to my cut foot. His cheeky grin and sexy wink as he handed me a cold beer for 'pain relief' and how handsome his silhouette looked against the night sky as we'd sat together on the beach guarding the turtle nests.

I switch on the TV to find one of my favourite movies just starting and so I settle down to watch it. With a full tummy, a glass of wine and a movie, I know this is going to be an okay evening. I will get over Ethan. It just might take a little time, that's all.

The next morning, at eight-thirty on the dot, I'm at reception when Zara arrives.

She gives me a huge smile and escorts me out to her car. It is indeed the same one she had shown me in the photos and it's spotlessly clean and polished inside and out. Once we're inside, seatbelts on, she presents me with a bottle of water and a packet of shrimp flavour crisps. 'Drink and snacks for you, madam.'

I insist she calls me Lori and then we're off into the morning traffic.

She drives carefully and confidently, so I do feel I'm in safe hands.

Zara tells me she's taking me first to the very popular cable car and to the very famous sky bridge and that we have to be there early to beat the queues and she'll wait while I go up the mountain and have a lovely time.

'But don't worry. I will have you first in the line, Miss Lori.'

'Don't you want to come too?' I ask her in surprise, as she's supposed to be my guide.

'No, no, Miss Lori. You go and I will wait here for you. Take your time.'

When we get there, I wander off to the ticket office and take the cable car to the top of the mountain, where the views are literally breath-taking. It is possible to look out from this great vantage point and see all the green islets and rocky islands around Langkawi's coast and the breeze is refreshingly cool and a relief from the humidity at lower levels.

From the top of the viewing station on one mountain peak, I walk across the curved skybridge, an incredible feat of engineering, to another mountain peak and the views from there too are spectacular. It's also incredible to look down from the bridge into the dense jungle below. Being a little afraid of heights, I cling to the handrail. It's too high to see anything below in any detail, except the tops of the trees. But as this is one of the oldest jungles in the world, I can easily imagine it's populated with the most diverse wildlife and of course, plenty of snakes.

I probably spend about another half an hour just enjoying the views and the breeze.

Then I make my way back down the mountain in the cable car to meet with Zara.

She's waiting for me at the bottom, all smiles and pleasantries, with the news that she's taking me to lunch and then onto one of the most beautiful water-falls on the island. Lunch is a café next to the cable car station but again she insists I have a 'lovely meal' while she waits for me outside. I worry that she doesn't have the money for cable car fees or café lunches, so I make it clear that I would be paying for her, but absolutely nothing I can say will persuade her to join me.

I bolted down a much needed iced-coffee and we're soon on our way again.

This involves driving along narrow winding roads through the jungle and taking steep roads up into the mountains. Here, there are monkeys everywhere. The side of the road is lined with monkeys of all sizes and lots of the females have babies clinging to their bellies or riding on their backs. They're playing run and dare with the traffic or congregating like teenage gangs on laybys or sunning themselves right in the middle of the road and making all the cars go around them.

Every time I yell, 'oh, wow, look – a monkey!' Zara stops the car while I get out to take photos and she shakes her head and laughs. I suppose that's because she's so used to seeing them herself and they hold no novelty for her.

'Be careful, Miss Lori. Keep tight hold of your bag and phone!' she warns me.

Holding onto my possessions and with no free hand, I shove a bottle of water in the crook of my arm while I take a photo of a cheeky looking monkey and the bottle is snatched right off me by another in the troop. Then, I watch in astonishment, as it cleverly unscrews the top and drinks it all before throwing the empty bottle back at me. What a cheeky monkey!

I'm just so grateful it hadn't taken my phone, simply because it has Ethan's number in it, and despite trying to memorise the number last night I can't recall it again now.

Further down the road, we drive past a man standing at the roadside. I notice in passing that he's very tall and incredibly thin with a bare concave chest and dirty wild straggly hair and he's wearing Indian-style pantaloons and some kind of long scarf around his neck.

Zara pulls the car over into the kerbside.

I assumed it's because she thinks I should give the poor man a few ringgits.

'Would you like to see a snake?' she asks me, with a bright smile.

I look at her in horror. 'A what? Did you just say snake?'

'You like monkey. So I think you also like snake, yes?'

I turn and look out the window and quickly realise that the stick thin beggar man doesn't have a long scarf wrapped around his neck – that's a snake hanging from his shoulders.

'Oh my g-g-goodness!' I say, covering my mouth in case the f-word pops out.

'He's blind and very poor, so he waits here with his snake for tourists to come. You can hold the snake for just a few ringgits.' She explains this to me with a look of sympathy on her face that leaves me in no doubt that I have to get out of this car and give this man some money, then get back in again unscathed and as quickly as possible.

Zara sees me hesitating. 'He would appreciate your charity, Miss Lori.'

'Okay, I will give him some money, but please tell him that I don't want to hold the snake.'

'I will take your photo!' Zara enthuses, totally ignoring my last comment.

We get out of the car and the beggar man hears me approach and holds out his arms expectantly. He looks straight ahead, unseeing, but the snake is watching me from where its great head is resting on his shoulder. It's huge and its scaly body is a golden yellow colour. Its tongue is flicking in and out of its mouth. It's the biggest snake I've ever seen.

In a panic, I reason over when I'd actually last seen a snake of any size?

In the zoo, I think, when the boys were little. They'd loved seeing them in the reptile house where they were at least behind glass. But not like this – a big thick heavy looking monster coiled around this man's neck and body. I look down to rummage in my purse for some cash and the next thing I know, the snake is suddenly around my neck and wrapping itself into a tight coil. I can't believe how heavy it is. 'Noooooo! Get it off me!' I squeal.

Then Zara is beside me, grabbing my phone and snapping away.

'Smile! Say slippery snake!' she insists, laughing.

I grit my teeth and pose just to get the whole ordeal over with so I can get back in the car.

After the terrifying snake episode, we drive on along winding roads until eventually, we pull over into a monkey-filled carpark area. This is apparently the start of the trail to what is the most beautiful waterfall on the island. It all looks like virgin jungle terrain to me.

Zara insists it's just a ten-minute walk to the waterfall, but we spend the next hour or so hiking along a narrow uphill stony and muddy path, picking our way through slimy green mud and ankle-deep water. Flip flops are not ideal for this but then any other type of footwear would have been totally ruined. It's hot and steamy and slippery as we cling to and practically swing from overhanging branches and thick hanging vines just to make our way forward in the absence of any handrail and to prevent sliding to our deaths in the jungle and raging river far below us.

We could have been walking for hours – it's hard to tell while covered in sweat mud and mosquito bites – when eventually I hear the thunderous sound of water falling from a great height not too far ahead of us and we pick up the pace.

Then suddenly, we're at the lagoon below the falls. A

blue-green oasis of calm water and plunge pools. The falls are impressive, tall and narrow, the thunderous water gushing through a misty rainbow at the top of the towering rock face and hurling down into the steaming lagoon below. This really is the stuff of dreams and so breathtakingly beautiful.

Now that we have finally made it here, I'm glad we didn't turn back, as I'd certainly considered doing so at least a dozen times during the journey. I slip out of my shorts and shirt (I'd come prepared and was wearing my swimsuit) and I slide carefully off the slippery rocks and into the cool water. I'm surprised to find myself immediately surrounded by lots of large friendly fish that are only visible when I look very carefully, as they're completely transparent in the water. They swim around me, nipping at me curiously but painlessly with their beaky lips. They don't seem to mind people at all and so I don't mind them either.

Zara sits happily on the rocks with her feet in the water as I lie in the lagoon on my back, floating bliss-fully in the deliciously cool and refreshing water and looking up at the sparkling rainbow above us. Another big tick off the bucket list, I tell myself, happily.

When Zara drops me off at my hotel in the late afternoon, after a full day tour that had been all and more that she had promised me, I ask her how much I owe her. At this point, having enjoyed my day so much,

I really don't care what she asks me for because I've had such an amazing time. But the amount turns out to be completely unrealistic and utterly ridiculous. I am completely taken aback – because it's so little.

In the UK, I've paid as much just to take a fifteen-minute taxi ride into town.

'No, Zara. That is not enough. You have put fuel in your car and driven me around all day.'

'No, Miss Lori, that is my price and I have really enjoyed the time we have shared together.'

I give her a hug. She's such a lovely and honest and kind person. I feel humbled.

'Me too, Zara. I've had a day to remember for always. But I must pay you this much instead.'

I give her a note from my purse that's around three times what she asked for and yet I still feel like I'm taking advantage of her somehow. 'Will I see you later, at the restaurant?

Zara says that yes, she's working this evening and that she will reserve my table.

I think hungrily of all the delicious seafood I'm going to eat there tonight.

Indeed, that evening, the food is superb and the restaurant is a little less busy.

We get to chat a little more, and I tell her that I'm off to Kuala Lumpur in the morning to meet with my two sons. I also show her some of the photos on my phone and she shows me some more of hers. And, before I bid her a fond farewell, I make sure to tip her well.

I walk back to my hotel feeling happy. This is what a life of travel is all about. Getting to spend a wonderful day exploring a new country is fantastic but it really is all about the people you meet. I fondly think of all the people I've met so far during my travels – Summer and the lads travelling with us to Railay Beach. George and David and Laura and Jodie – and of course Ethan. And Zara ... having the good fortune to spontaneously meet someone local and honest and hardworking like her and to spend some quality time with her today.

Yes, that's what makes the journey so worthwhile.

Chapter 14

Kuala Lumpur

Kuala Lumpur, or KL as it is known, is a modern shiny high-rise metropolis and the capital city of Malaysia. I arrive after a short flight from Langkawi and I take a fast train from the airport straight into the city centre or KLCC, as it is known. It's from the window of the train, as we speed into the city in twilight, that I get my first exciting glimpses of the fabulous Petronas Towers and the famous KL Tower, all lit up and twinkling in white lights and dominating the KL skyline. Just seeing these iconic sights fills me with tingling excitement.

I'm in Kuala Lumpur – and just the sound of its exotic name gives me a thrill.

It also thrills me – and disconcerts me in equal measure – that Ethan is also in KL.

I don't know where he's staying. But I know from what he'd told me on Koh Phi Tao, that he's staying here for a few days before he flies to Northern Malaysia. He might, of course, be staying with friends rather than in a hotel. He might even be on the train that's passing mine right now at high-speed heading back to the airport for all I know.

I have my phone in my hand from taking photos.

The same phone that has his number programmed into it.

I wonder, if I call him right now, if he'd answer it.

But I know that I'm not going to call him.

I'm still too afraid of the awful imaginary worst-case scenario of my heart being broken again. Besides, I remind myself, I haven't come halfway around the world looking for a new man in my life. I've come out here looking for a sustainable lifetime of happiness and purpose and I'm still waiting for the sign I've been promised.

However, even this self-pep-talk doesn't stop me from searching for him in the crowds once I reach the city centre, or my heart from skipping a beat at spotting a tall and handsome man in an extravagant shirt, who for a moment looks just like him.

I check into the Intercontinental, where I've reserved a room for Josh and Lucas too.

I've found, in Malaysia, with such a favourable exchange rate and a lower cost of living, that my money goes a long way here so I splash out on an upgrade.

As I'm expecting to be cash-rich soon anyway, from Charles buying me out of my share of the house, I check us into two suites at club level. My suite is a luxurious dream. Its centrepiece is a humongously downy soft bed with whiter than white top-quality bedding, set amidst classy furniture and gorgeous thick carpets. My bathroom is even dreamier in marble with gold accessories, and with every luxury imaginable included – a huge bathtub, a very fancy separate rainfall shower, a vast double-vanity with huge mirrors and soft lighting and a complete array of quality complimentary toiletries. There's even a welcome basket of fruit and chocolates.

I leap onto the bed and am immediately so comfortable I take a much-needed power nap.

I wake at 7 p.m. and liven myself up with an espresso coffee from the posh-looking coffee making machine on the refreshments counter and then spend a lot longer than entirely necessary soaking in the tub with my complimentary aromatics.

Then, in a soft fluffy bathrobe, I stand at the wall-to-ceiling windows admiring the twinkling lights of the city of Kuala Lumpur beneath me and indeed all around me and it all looks so amazing that I have to pinch myself to prove I'm not dreaming.

I wouldn't want to leave my room at all, if it wasn't for the temptation of complimentary canapes and cocktails in the executive club lounge, that I've been told is included in my stay. The club lounge is one floor up in the elevator. I'm greeted warmly and offered champagne, which I sip while marvelling at the uninterrupted views of the shiny white sparkling lights of the twin Petronas Towers opposite.

They look like tall and magnificent twin Christmas trees.

Of course, now we're so close to Christmas, I can see a tiny Christmas tree at the base of the towers and in front of a lake with its multi-coloured dancing water fountains. It's probably a gigantic tree at ground level, all lit up and decorated with colourful baubles, but from here it looks dwarfed by everything around it, that's even taller and more majestic.

The following morning, I go shopping. There are two vast shopping malls filled with all the top designer names just opposite each other and very near to my hotel. I buy a couple of new city outfits. My floaty beach dresses and cut off shorts and flip flops look rather out of place here even though we're still basking in around thirty-six Celsius.

I have my hair and nails done too and later that afternoon, I take the train back to the airport to meet my sons. I can hardly wait or suppress my excitement at seeing them again.

They messaged me twelve hours ago, just as they were boarding the plane at Gatwick to say their flight was on schedule. I wait at the barrier in the arrivals hall. When I see them walking towards me, looking a little tired and dishevelled and jetlagged, I can hardly believe they're real and I throw myself at them, hugging them both at the same time.

It's a messy scene. I can't help but shriek and weep buckets.

'Oh, Mum, look at you!' Josh exclaims, looking shocked and holding me at arm's length once I've finally released him. 'You look ... amazing. I didn't know it was possible to get so suntanned. I hardly recognised you!'

Lucas looks equally taken aback by my new look.

'Gosh, you've lost an awful lot of weight, Mum. But Josh's right, you look totally amazing.'

I must admit, I've also been rather surprised at seeing myself in a new light and in a full-length mirror in my bathroom at the Intercon. There's been quite the transformation in me.

As a housewife, I invariably wore my hair tied back and never wore any make-up on my face unless I was going somewhere special. So my complexion has always looked pale and insipid. In the cold weather, I covered my nondescript lumpy figure with an unvarying routine of warm clothing, usually several layers of vests and sweats, and on even colder days, a big baggy sweater over the top of those layers, with jeans or stretchy black leggings that didn't do me any favours either.

I couldn't look more different now. After a whole month of Asian food and a mostly vegetarian diet, I'm a lot slimmer. I now wear light clothing to fit and skim my body and I can get away with it because, thanks to all the sunshine and so much walking and swimming and even a little yoga, my new figure not only looks slimmer, but also firmer and toned and tanned.

Of course, I wear my hair differently now too, I leave it long and free and tousled and it is a far more flattering shade of natural sun kissed blonde than could ever have been achieved in a salon. Today, I've had it washed, deep-conditioned and curled with a styling wand at the salon in the mall. It looks soft and shiny and natural.

Knowing I look so much better than before has given me a new confidence.

I've never been one of those super-confident and self-assured women who can walk into a room and turn heads – but I have always envied those qualities in other women.

I appreciate my boys noticing.

We take the fast train from the airport. The boys are a little jet-lagged but still impressed by the views as we speed into the city. I am buzzing with excitement. 'Wait until you see our hotel. It's fabulous,' I tell them. 'You'll be able to freshen up in your suite and then we can have a couple of drinks and a light meal before you both get some much-needed sleep. Then tomorrow we can explore KL together!'

The staff at the hotel are so kind and welcoming. I chatted to them earlier and told them that my sons were joining me from London, so they make sure to check the boys in quickly and go straight onto offering us cocktails and wines and even champagne in the club lounge, while also serving us a fantastic selection of nibbles from the cold platters or hot appetisers from the chef on hand at his cooking station.

We lounge on big comfortable squashy sofas, me in the middle of my two sons, in full view of the sparkling steel and glass Petronas Towers, as we eat and drink and chat. The boys tell me they've brought the few personal items I asked them for, and there's also some paperwork from their father. I glance through the papers and note that they're divorce proceedings. He's cited an irrecoverable breakdown of marriage rather than his infidelity as the reason for our divorce. But I'm really past caring. I've surprised myself (and, admittedly, shocked my boys) by how indifferent I now feel about the whole affair and the separation and divorce.

'And what did he say about me being willing to sell him my half of the house?'

'Are you sure you want to do this right now, Mum? We could always do this tomorrow?'

'Yes, I want it all out of the way, so we don't have to talk about legalities again.'

'Okay, then these are the deeds of transfer Dad wants you to sign for the house,' Josh explains. I take a good look. And, just as I'd asked, the house had been assessed and revalued.

'Well, I see that's all been executed with your father's usual efficiency,' I say, taking a pen and signing the deed with a flourish. 'Although I do wonder how he can afford to buy me out, as I doubt Sally keeps anything but a pair of overnight knickers in her designer handbag.'

'I believe he's secured a mortgage loan, Mum.' Lucas explains, ignoring my snarky comment about Sally. I ask our hostess for some champagne with which to celebrate.

I see a look of cautious exchange between Josh and Lucas.

It suggests they can't quite believe how absolutely fine I am about all of this.

Three foaming flutes are brought over and once they're in hand, we raise them.

'So what are we drinking to exactly?' Josh asks me.

'Let's drink to your father,' I say, feeling generous. 'I think he's got far more than he bargained with Sally.

But if it wasn't for them both, we wouldn't be sitting here in Kuala Lumpur drinking champagne today.'

We clink our glasses and Lucas frowns while Josh laughs uneasily.

With the champagne sipped, I see Josh is now looking a little anxious.

Ever since he was a little boy, he's had a tell – if he has something bothering him, there's a little raised vein pulsating in his forehead. Not many would notice it, but I am his mother.

'What is it, Josh? Come on, you can tell me.'

'I was worried about telling you this, Mum, but as you do seem fine about all of this, Sally's already moved in with Dad. When her husband found out about the affair, he kicked her out.'

'So what's happened to all my personal things?' I ask, suddenly sitting bolt upright and changing my amicable tune. 'I don't want that bitch rooting through my wardrobes!'

'Don't worry. Lucas and I packed up all your clothes and everything we thought was yours and we put it all into rented storage in town. It will be safe until you get back and find yourself somewhere new to live.'

'But you can always stay with one of us, in the meantime, Mum. Not that you'd consider either of our apartments to be ideal, but you are very welcome,' Lucas adds.

I hug them both again. I had no idea they'd done this for me and I'm really touched.

'Thank you, boys. I really appreciate it. That gives me piece of mind while I'm travelling.'

'Mum, what do you mean? You've been travelling. You been away for ages and perhaps you don't realise it, but Lucas and I are here to escort you home,' Josh informs me.

'It's Christmas next week, Mum. We were sure you'd want to come home for Christmas.' Lucas rallies in support of his elder brother. 'We miss you. Gran misses you too. We want you to come home. We've already booked you at seat on our return flight.'

I must look quite horrified. 'Look, boys, I really appreciate all you have done for me but I don't want to go back yet. I want to travel. I've caught the wanderlust. Gran has her network of friends and clubs and I miss you too but you both have busy lives. Come on, let's be honest. We have all lived in the same town since you both came back from university. Yet, I hardly see either of you without prior arrangements. So, I'm sure we can manage being in different countries for a while and seeing each other on Facetime or Skype!'

Josh and Lucas look completely stunned by my tirade.

'I'll admit it. I was shocked and angry. I was running away at first. But, now that I'm travelling, I feel free. I'm just starting to appreciate a different way of living my life and I want you to understand and support me and not worry about me so much.'

'But you're our mum. You're hardly a backpacker!' Lucas exclaims.

'I am now!' I laugh. 'But I promise you this … I will always let you know where I am in the world and, if either of you or your Gran ever needs me, then I'll be on the first flight back.'

'Well, I suppose you don't look like you're having a nervous breakdown.' Josh says sulkily.

'Yeah. You do seem to be handling it all quite well,' Lucas agrees.

I throw my arms around them both again. 'Then can you just let me have this … please?'

Josh gives out a heavy sigh of defeat. 'Just as long as you also promise us that you'll be really careful. No wandering into a war zone or a crazy druggie commune or somewhere dangerous where you'll get kidnapped.'

I laugh. 'Okay. I promise that too.'

The following day, the three of us have breakfast at the hotel and then ask our concierge for his top three tourist hotspot recommendations for KL. First off, he recommends to us that we take the tour at the Petronas Towers and see the city from the observation deck on the 86th Floor, and then follow this with a walk over the famous skybridge that links the two towers together at the 42nd

Floor. Josh and Lucas really like this idea as both the towers and the bridge have been used in so many famous action movies. Then there's the KL Tower, with its revolving restaurant at the top. We're told this is an excellent choice for lunch. The third recommendation for our afternoon's sightseeing is to head just outside the city to the Batu Caves. 'The caves are a big attraction. They're home to a Hindu shrine and a temple and the tallest statue in Malaysia as well as lots of monkeys.'

My eyes light up at the mention of monkeys, shrines, and temples.

But the boys look a little reticent until our concierge also mentions the Dark Cave.

'The Dark Cave at Batu is very famous too...' he explains. 'For bats and rare spiders.'

And, of course, boys of any age love the idea of bat caves and creepy crawlies.

We have a truly amazing day together, exploring the sites and posing for lots of photos.

'So, where are your travel plans taking you next, Mum?' Josh asks me once we're back on the big squashy sofas in the club lounge later that evening.

'Yeah, what will you be doing for Christmas all on your own?' Lucas wants to know.

'I've decided I'm going to stay in Malaysia. Not here in KL but over in Borneo. I'm actually hoping to volunteer at an orangutan orphanage for the next couple of months.'

'You're going to help save orangutans? In Borneo?'

I nod. 'Yes. I loved my time helping to save the endangered turtles. It was fantastic. At first, I just wanted to travel for travel's sake but now I want to travel with a purpose. I want to see if I can make a difference in the world. I want to help endangered animals and people and even plants. I think it will make me happy.'

My boys look at me with a softer look in their eyes. I think it's admiration.

'Well, I think it all sounds pretty cool. We're so proud of you, Mum,' says Josh. 'Not many people can say that their mum's helping endangered animals in Borneo.'

'Yeah, our mum, the backpacking housewife!' Lucas laughs.

Early the next morning, the boys take the train back to the airport. I wave them off knowing there will be an empty seat in their row on the flight back to London, but I'm feeling far less guilty now that we've had a chance to talk. They've both given me their blessing to carry on travelling and they've forgiven me for being away from them at Christmas.

As long as I promise to stay safe and out of trouble.

And I'm sure I can do that quite easily, can't I?

Chapter 15

Kuala Lumpur (ii)

I'm back at my luxurious hotel, taking full advantage of club lounge facilities by enjoying a glass of champagne and some very tasty nibbles while I'm busy on my phone flicking through my photos from yesterday. There are some fun shots of the boys and I in the Petronas Towers and on its skybridge and at the Batu Caves, with its hundreds of steps and shrines and giant gold statues and all the friendly and photogenic monkeys.

Happy times and wonderful memories.

I post my favourites to my Facebook page and make sure to tag Josh and Lucas too.

I check the time. They'll be in the air by now and well on their way home.

On my laptop, I look up the orangutan orphanage website and how to get there tomorrow and I'm just about to go ahead and book my flight over to Borneo, when I see an incoming message. It's from Summer. She's just seen my Facebook post and realised I'm in KL.

I'm in KL right now too! Let's meet up!

I immediately invite her to join me here. I have a double capacity suite and knowing she's sure to be staying in a cheap hostel somewhere in town, I want to invite her to stay over with me and to join me for complimentary drinks and canapes. I can't wait to see her again.

Half an hour later, Summer arrives, looking lovely as usual and she gives me a big hug.

'Oh Lori, I could hardly believe it when I saw your post on Facebook. I got into KL earlier today myself and wanted to hit the city for a few hours before I fly out to Bali tonight.'

'Bali? Oh, how wonderful. Are you going there for yoga?'

I see her blush. 'No actually, I'm going there with someone. Remember Nate? One of the lads we met at Railay last month?'

I nod. 'Yes, of course. The one that looked like Prince Harry?'

She giggles. 'Yeah. Well, we kept in touch and I'm meeting him later. He's flying in from Bangkok in a couple of hours and we are heading over to Bali together for Christmas.'

'It sounds so romantic!' I enthuse, feeling so happy for her.

She shrugs and laughs and tosses back her long shiny dark hair from her shoulders.

'Well, so far it's all been jokey texts and silly photos,' she says, 'but I really like him a lot.'

The hostess comes over to ask Summer what she'd like to drink.

'I'm on the champagne. It's very nice,' I tell Summer.

'Ooh yes please!' she breathes. 'And how awesome is this hotel?'

'I know...' I whisper. 'Only in Malaysia could I afford such an extravagance.'

'I was reading an article in an airline magazine. It said that KL has the most affordable five-star hotels *on the planet*,' Summer tells me, emphasising her words while accepting her glass of bubbly from our hostess.

'Well, I was going to offer you a bed in my suite, but if you're leaving tonight then you'll just have to wallow in free champagne instead.' I laugh, raising my glass to hers.

We chink glasses and chorus 'cheers!'

'Tell me more about you and Nate?' I say, as she seems so full of bubbles herself.

'Well, we do have an amazing connection and he is such fun. I love his accent, so much that I can't wait to meet up with him again to hear him talk. Basically, we are just going to take things slow and get to know each other a little better in Bali!'

'It sounds very ... sensible, as well as very romantic?' I say.

'Well, I've been in love before and that's the problem...' she says with a heavy sigh.

I sip my champagne and realise her words have touched a nerve.

'Anyway, I saw from your Facebook post that you've just had your sons to visit. I loved the photos and your sons are very handsome. You must have had them so young!'

I smile, appreciating the flattery. 'It was great to see them again, even for just a short time.'

I start to laugh. 'You won't believe it, but they'd actually come over to take me back to the UK with them. They thought I was having some kind of mid-life crisis or even a nervous breakdown and needed rescuing!'

Summer looks at me thoughtfully. 'But you're still here. So did they understand that you wanted to stay?'

'Yes. I managed to talk them round in the end.'

'I think it's kinda cute for them to worry. I guess they just needed to know that their mom's gonna be okay travelling on her own. But why did they think you were having a breakdown?'

'Well, it's a long story,' I say.

'I have both time and champagne.' Summer tells me

with a shrug. 'Tell me why they were so worried about you that they came all the way out here from the UK for the weekend, Lori?'

I sigh. I realise that she and I had chatted for hours on the train from Chiang Mai to Bangkok and at Railay, but neither of us had ever broached the subject of our personal lives.

I still know nothing about her home life in America or why she's travelling alone and she knows nothing about my previous life in the UK, simply because it has never been part of our conversation. I've found this typically happens with people I've met on my travels.

It's all about who you are, not what you are.

Topics of conversation are only ever about what you've seen and the adventures you've had.

I find this refreshing. As a traveller, you are only ever judged on face value.

But now, knowing each other a little better and with my tongue loosened by champagne, I start to tell her about walking in on my husband having sex with my best friend. I tell her how, after we had parted on Koh Lanta, I'd got my dive certificate and how I cut my foot in the Emerald Cave and ended up by fate and happenstance at the turtle sanctuary on Koh Phi Tao.

'So now it's your turn. How did you get your heart broken?' I ask her.

'A similar story, except we were engaged to be married.

It happened the night before our wedding. I found him with my chief bridesmaid and he had the gall to tell me he was having a last fling on his last night of being single. I told him to take his time. I left for India the next day.'

I sympathise with her whole-heartedly and we both have another glass of champagne.

'So that's why I'm gonna take things slowly with Nate. He seems so nice but it's hard to trust a man again after being so horribly betrayed.'

I nod. 'I know. I get that completely. I've met someone too but I'm not as brave as you.'

I tell her about the people I met on Koh Phi Tao and what happened on the island between Ethan and Marielle and how Ethan and I had felt something special happening between us – but that we never spoke of it or acted on it until our last night together, when he'd kissed me and asked me to travel with him and I'd turned him down.

Summer listens with understanding. 'I get the feeling you really like this guy a lot, Lori.'

'Yes ... I do. But he's married and going through a divorce and so am I.'

Summer reaches over to me and squeezes my hand. 'I'm so sorry, Lori. That kinda sucks.'

'It's really bad timing,' I tell her, getting a bit emotional. 'And that's why, on the island and over the past week or more, I've had to tread extra carefully around Ethan. I loved every minute of being on the island and helping to save the turtles, but spending time with him was, to be honest, exhausting. I was in a constant state of emotional turmoil when I was alone with him – whether we were in Turtle HQ mulling over the computer records together or he was taking my hand in the dark to lead me into the jungle to show me interesting creatures or have me listen to weird mating calls. When he made eye contact. When he laughed. When he sang. And damn it, when he walked around half naked – which was most of the time!'

'Oh wow. You've really got it bad, Lori! So, tell me, why didn't you go with him again?'

I think it's quite obvious, after what I've just told her.

'I mean, it sounds to me like you two had more than just a fling going on?'

I shake my head. 'Because it was like a holiday romance. I fancied him. I kissed him once. We watched sunsets together. That's where the story has to end, unfortunately.'

'Why? And why is it bad timing? I really don't under-stand. He's been separated from his wife for a few years and you are dealing with your separation. Surely your divorces are just a formality?'

'That's exactly what he said, but I don't see that it's as simple as that because...!'

'Ye-es...?' Summer laughs and waits for me to explain myself even more.

'Because it's a relationship built on sand – on a fantasy island. The main point being, it's not real and the last thing Marielle said to me about her and Ethan's relationship was that their love affair hadn't survived leaving the island. She said to me – *nous sommes touts hors d'amour* – we are all out of love for each other.'

'And trust the French to make even that sound romantic!' Summer gasps.

'I was afraid that Ethan and I wouldn't survive leaving the island either,' I confess. 'That's the real truth. I mean, rather than the bullshit I fed Ethan, about bad timings and our separations and our impending divorces.'

'Why? Does Ethan remind you of Charles in some way?'

'No. Not at all. Ethan is nothing like Charles. Ethan's charming and clever and practical and he has such integrity. He spends his life working to make the world a better place for everyone and everything. Those are very attractive qualities in a man.'

'Okay...' Summer says. 'So now we both know the real reason you turned Ethan down and I do understand. But I'm prepared to give love another go and so should you – you should call Ethan right now and tell him you'll give him a chance. You never know, he could be The One. After all, it was fate that brought you two together!'

I run my fingers through my hair in frustration. 'You know, at first, I was so sure that fate was playing a big part in all of this but now I'm not so sure. I was told by a monk in Chiang Mai that I would receive a sure sign that would lead me to my place of happiness and, so far, I've seen nothing. There's been no sure sign. No pointers. And so, I've had to conclude that no sign is indeed a sign in itself and this is not meant for me. That Ethan is not meant for me.'

I decide to change the subject and tell her about the orangutan centre and how I plan to go over there and volunteer. 'I'm planning to fly to Borneo tomorrow,' I explain. 'I'm going to go and apply in person for a position there for the next couple of months.'

Summer looks a little hesitant but then she steels herself to tell me something that she maybe thinks I might not like to hear. 'Look, Lori. I don't wanna rain on your parade or anything, but I really doubt you'll get into the orangutan orphanage programme this year. Those positions are highly sought after and fill up like a year or more in advance. You should give Ethan a chance – just take it slowly with him. I mean, from what you've said, he obviously really cares about you and you absolutely adore him. My mom always says, it's better to do something and regret it than to never do it and to always wonder what might have been.'

She seems so adamant. So sure.

And, when I see things through Summer's eyes I can't help but see things differently too.

I suddenly have a horrible sinking feeling in my belly.

I think I've had too much champagne.

I wave Summer off at the train station. She's giggling from champagne and bubbling with excitement to be seeing Nate again and to be heading off to Bali. Her parting words to me are a reminder to call Ethan and once her train pulls out, and I'm once again alone with my thoughts, I return to my suite and take a long hot bath.

I often find relaxing in the bath is conducive to making important decisions or resolving complicated issues. I think about Summer taking a chance on Nate and how happy she seems. I look down at my wrist and see that my string bracelets are looking a bit ragged and grey. I'd been so determined to wear them until I'd found my place of happiness. Ethan had made me happy but now he's making me miserable.

I'd memorised every word the young monk had spoken to me in Chiang Mai.

Am I missing something? What did he say about opening my heart?

Rest assured, if you are willing to open your heart, then Lord Ganesh will guide you.

Is opening my heart to Ethan the key to finding the sign?

Will I always regret it if I don't at least try?

With my heart racing, I jump out of the bath and grab both my phone and my robe.

I bring up Ethan's number and hold my breath as it rings out.

After just three rings I hear his deep Celtic-sounding voice.

'Hey, Lori! Tell me you're missing me already?'

My heart soars. It's so good to hear him say my name again.

'Yes. I am missing you already, Ethan. I'm in KL. And I was thinking, well, as we're both here in the same city, then maybe we should meet up again, after all?'

My voice is an octave higher than usual and I sound like I'm blabbering.

I take a deep breath and wait quietly for his response.

'You're in KL? Damn it. I arrived in KK an hour ago.'

'KK? You're where?' I stammer.

'Kota Kinabalu.'

My heart drops. I've not even considered that he might not still be in KL.

I'm achingly disappointed. Now he's hundreds of miles away.

'I'm in KK tonight and heading over to the island tomorrow,' he explains.

'Oh, I see. What a shame. It would have been good to see you and have a chat.'

My heart is pounding against my ribs. Am I about to chicken out and say goodbye again?

'Aye, it would. So, what did you want to chat about?' he asks me directly.

Men. They are so bloody direct. Straight to the point.

'Erm, well, I was thinking...'

'Hey, you wanna come to the island? Have you changed your mind, Lori?'

Again. No messing about. I brace myself to answer him.

'Yes. Actually, I've changed my mind. I want to come!'

He starts laughing and then whooping. His enthusiasm is endearing.

I am smiling like an idiot into my phone.

'I'll catch the first flight over to KK in the morning. Will you wait there for me?'

'Aye, of course, I'll wait for you. I'll be here. I can't wait to see you.'

'Then I'll see you tomorrow, Ethan. I'll text you my flight arrival time.'

'Great. See you tomorrow. Goodnight sweetheart!'

Chapter 16

Kota Kinabalu

Two minutes after speaking with Ethan, I've managed to book a seat on an early flight out to Kota Kinabalu, the capital of Malaysia's northern Sabah state in Borneo and a city in the shadow of Malaysia's highest mountain, Mount Kinabalu. The city is on the coast and partly surrounded by one of the world's oldest rainforests. An apt place to be meeting up with my own real-life hero again.

I throw all my stuff into my backpack, hang a white cotton shift dress on a hanger to wear to travel in and climb into bed with my alarm set for 4 a.m. My dreams are wonderful ones of islands and beaches and diving in warm seas and of being kissed by Ethan *Indiana* Jones. When my alarm goes off, I am up and out despite the early hour.

I feel energised and ready for this new adventure.

On arrival in KK, I immediately see Ethan waiting for me in the arrivals hall.

He waves his panama hat in the air enthusiastically when he sees me and shouts my name.

I hurry over to him and it amuses me to see he's wearing his usual style of baggy shorts and a brightly patterned shirt. This one has little green turtles all over it. He also wears a huge smile and when I reach him, instead of kissing me on both cheeks, he scoops me into his arms and twirls me around and kisses me passionately on the lips.

Any doubts entering my mind this morning about what I was doing are instantly kissed away. 'I'm so happy to see you again Lori. It's fantastic you are here!'

He helps me with my backpack, which is much bulkier now that I've steadily been acquiring things along the way. 'Hey, something has come up and I think you're going to like it,' he tells me. 'While I was waiting here for you, I happened to bump into an old friend and he's offered us a lift across country to Sandakan in his private plane.'

'Oh, wow. That's great,' I enthuse. This sounds very exciting indeed.

I've never known anyone who owned their own plane.

'Sam said to wait over in departures and he'll come and see us through security in about fifteen minutes. So, let's go get a cup of coffee.'

Ethan leads the way to a café where he buys two coffees while I'm busy on my phone messaging my boys.

The airport in KK is a new and modern building, but I'm prepared for the rest of our journey across Borneo and to the remote islands to not be as conducive to reliable digital communication. When Ethan comes back with our drinks, I am still on my phone. 'I'm sorry, I really should have sent this message last night but with all the champagne and excitement, I forgot. I just need to let my boys know about my change of plan.'

Ethan looks amused. 'All the champagne and excitement?' he repeats.

'Does the island we are going to have a name?' I ask, trying to type quickly.

'Aye, it's called Reef Island. It's part of the Tun Mustapha Marine Park in the Sulu Sea.'

Change of plan. I'm with a friend heading to an island called Reef Island off the coast of Borneo. I doubt there will be internet. I'll message when I can. Don't worry if I'm out of touch for a while. Merry Christmas and lots of love, Mum xx

Then I put my phone down on the table top to show him that he now has my full attention.

'So, I've been thinking. While we are here, I've a suggestion for you, but it'll mean a wee detour,' Ethan proposes.

I listen, wondering if this is something I'll also need to let my boys know about.

'I remember you saying you wanted to check out the

orangutan orphanage and, if you'd like to go there today, I can easily arrange it. We can go over to the island tomorrow, instead?'

'Really? We can do that?' I gasp. This will be absolutely amazing.

'No problem. I know a few people there. I'll give them a call.'

I laugh. 'You seem to know people everywhere!'

'It's my job...' he says, with a boyish smirk.

After making the call, he tells me a woman called Jenny is going to come out to the airport at Sandakan to meet us. I wonder if everything in Ethan's life is so easily organised.

I sip my coffee. 'Thank you. I'm excited.'

He looks at me curiously. 'So, are you going to tell what made you change your mind?'

I am just about to answer him when my phone pings.

I blush at the embarrassment of having to put my reading glasses back on and pick it up again. 'Sorry. This will be my boys getting back to me.'

Ethan nods, indicating that of course I should answer it as a priority.

Mum – that part of the world is very remote - please reconsider!

'Is everything okay?' Ethan asks me, seeing my frown.

'My eldest son is under the impression I need looking after.'

'You want me to speak to him? I can assure him you have your bodyguard with you.'

'Thank you. That's very kind but won't be necessary.'

I can just imagine Josh's reaction to another man saying he's going to look after me.

I text back, telling Josh I'll be working on an important project and that I am travelling with a friend and not on my own. Then I switch my phone to silent to answer Ethan's question about why I changed my mind, as it's still hanging in the air unanswered.

I've been preparing to answer this question all morning and want to answer him honestly.

Ethan waits patiently and keeps unnerving me with his ecstatic gaze.

'Well, last night, I realised, that not only was I missing you but I was also missing out on a great opportunity. I want to be honest with you, Ethan. I'd said no to you before, not because of bad timing, but simply because I was afraid. I was scared of it all going wrong between us once we left Koh Phi Tao.'

He smiles. 'So, you decided to live dangerously?'

'No. I decided to live bravely. Like a lion,' I tell him, laughing.

And he reaches out and takes my hand. 'You can trust me, Lori, and you can assure your sons that I'll look after you. You have nothing to be afraid of ... okay?'

'What is it with you men? Why do you all think I

295

need looking after?' I protest, knowing that my eyes are getting all shiny and my chin is starting to wobble. His words touch my heart and I know I do trust him and I'm not afraid. I'm a lioness and he is my lion king.

Just then, a rather untidy looking man approaches us wearing a tatty looking Bob Marley T-shirt and surfing shorts and old flip flops. He's smiling and he holds out his hand to me.

I immediately assume he's begging for a few ringgits and look for my purse.

Ethan gets to his feet and introduces the man. 'Lori, this is Sam, our pilot. Sam, this is Lori.'

Sam shakes my hand. To me, he doesn't look anything like a pilot of any plane.

'Please, Lori and Ethan, excuse me. I need five more minutes and then we will fly.'

Sam is pointing outside while he speaks. I assume the five minutes will be enough time for him to change into smart dark trousers and a starched white shirt with epaulets on his shoulders and a cap on his head, just like a pilot. But no, instead, Sam is just going outside to light up a cigarette.

My initial thrill at being told I'd be flying in a private plane starts to fade a little.

Five minutes later, Sam leads us through security, where he and Ethan seem to know everyone really well. There's lots of laughing and backslapping and appreciative male glances at me, but I'm not asked for my name or my passport and we're ushered through the building and out onto the tarmac without so much as an X-ray, a scan, or a pat down, to where Sam has parked his small plane. When I say small, I mean tiny.

It's a Cessna with one engine and it looks like a relic from another age.

Feeling speechless with nerves, I look to Ethan for reassurance.

He gives me a big grin and holds open the flap of a door that accesses the back seat.

'Ladies first,' he tells me. I climb inside in a rather unladylike way, in my short dress, probably flashing my knickers, as I squeeze myself in between our two backpacks and Ethan's guitar case. Ethan climbs into the co-pilot seat next to Sam and they both put radio headphones on. They're chatting to each other using microphones as we taxi out onto the runway.

I have no headphones to wear so can't hear what they're saying and spend the whole of that time trying to put my seatbelt on. It isn't long enough to go across my lap. I can see the problem. It's partway stuck in the seat. So, I give it a sharp tug, only for the whole thing to come away in my hand. Oh well, no point in complaining now, I decide. We're already lined up for take-off, with wings waggling and the engine tuk-tuk-tuking.

Oh wow – I'm in a tuk tuk with wings!

And if we crash, seatbelts or no seatbelts, I've already decided we'd all die anyway.

As we accelerate down the runway, I watch Sam operating the dials and turning knobs and putting our coordinates into what I guess is a GPS system, while he laughs and chats with Ethan. I really think, at this crucial moment, that he should be concentrating on steering the plane. I quickly decide that I'm better off looking out of the window than watching him and suddenly we're up in the air. The engine is a vibrant bone-shaking constant drone.

I stare down into the vast area of steaming jungle below us, mesmerised.

It looks like a lost world down there. Suddenly, I'm so in awe of what I see that I start to feel privileged for such an incredible view of what is one of the oldest rainforests on earth.

It's suddenly so exhilarating to be part of the exciting world of Ethan Jones, and my body is filled with adrenalin and endorphins. Suddenly I don't mind that I'm risking my life in this tiny precarious plane. In fact, I decide it's worth it. I mean, people die in horrible accidents every day, but not all are so lucky that the last thing they see before they meet their end is a frothing blanket of verdant green virgin equatorial rainforest.

The trees and vegetation below us look so dense and

impenetrable that I can't help but imagine all the wild animals that live there – endangered species and those not yet even discovered – and I do wonder (I'm still thinking about crashing) if our single engine failed and we went down, assuming the trees broke our fall and we survived the crash, if we'd ever find our way out again or if we'd be lost forever?

I'm engrossed in visions of various crash scenarios and even a mini Tarzan and Jane type fantasy about living in the jungle with Ethan for the indeterminable amount of time it takes us to fly from KK to Sandakan on the opposite side of the country.

As we begin our descent, once again I find I'm far more interested than I'm actually worried.

Our decent is slow and our wings are waggling as the landing gear grinds down into position.

Sam lines up the small plane with a tiny strip of faraway runway right ahead of us and in our last moments of flight, I'm gripping the edge of my plastic seat with one hand and holding onto the end of the flapping seatbelt strap with the other, as the wheels touch down.

I have the urge to clap my hands in celebration.

Hats off to Sam, our skilled pilot, for such a soft and graceful landing.

Chapter 17

Sandakan Borneo

We bid our farewells and give our thanks to Sam and then we head over into the arrivals building where an attractive red-headed woman, whom I guess is around my age, wearing khaki shorts and a T-shirt with a cute picture of a baby orangutan on the front of it, is literally jumping up and down with excitement to see us – or at least to see Ethan.

His reaction is to hug and kiss her on both cheeks and, for some strange reason, I feel a little bit jealous of their ecstatic reunion. I do my best to smile as I wait to be introduced.

'Jenny, meet Lori!' Ethan says, and Jenny takes my outstretched hand and we do the double side of the cheek kiss. 'Lovely to meet you, Jenny,' I say.

'Jenny is a surrogate mummy to around eighty baby orangutans,' Ethan says proudly.

'Actually, we have ninety-two right now. Sadly, it has been a bumper year for orphans.'

We follow Jenny outside into the bright sunshine and steamy heat to her big open back truck. I notice that in sharp contrast to all the other vehicles in the car park, it looks quite new.

It's one of those with big tyres for tough terrain driving and it has a logo on the side doors with *Northern Borneo Orangutan Orphanage* and the same cute picture of a baby orangutan that Jenny has on her T-shirt. As I open the passenger door, I also notice a smaller sign with *Goldman Global Foundation* on it and I realise this is the same foundation that is funding the turtle sanctuary on Koh Phi Tao and the reef recovery programme we are assigned to on Reef Island and that Ethan's association with Jenny is through the GGF.

He throws our bags in the back of the truck and then climbs in along with them.

'Lori, why don't you ride shotgun with Jenny? I'm sure you'll want to ask her all sorts of stuff about the orangutans. Jenny, be warned, Lori asks a lot of questions!'

As we drive along, I explain to her how I'd been intending to apply to volunteer at the orphanage, until I accepted Ethan's offer to work as a diver on the reef project instead.

'Ah, I expect he'll have made you an offer you couldn't refuse, right?'

I look at her and wondered what she means by that exactly?

She throws me a genuine smile. 'Our programme is closed right now, but on Ethan's recommendation, I would've made a space for you without hesitation. So maybe next time?'

'Oh, that's so generous. Thank you. I guess Ethan is a great asset to the GGF?'

'Oh yes. Around here what Ethan wants Ethan gets!' she laughs.

I give her a look of surprise.

'Oh, we all love him here. He made me an offer I couldn't refuse too,' Jenny tells me.

'Is that why you came to Borneo?' I ask her.

'Yes. Before here, I was working in a zoo looking after primates. It was pretty ghastly. Conditions were bad and funding was tight and I only stayed because I couldn't leave my animals. Then a miracle happened. Ethan closed it down.'

'Really? He closed down a whole zoo?'

'Yep. He got the GGF involved and closed it down. Just like that. And all the animals went into retirement at various sanctuaries all over the world to live out their lives happily. He recruited me to run the orphanage here. I've been here eight years now and I love it.'

Jenny flashes me another of her wonderful smiles and I see that she looks quite emotional.

Tears of joy? It's no wonder she loves Ethan. He's her real-life hero too.

We leave the main highway and drive through a small town before taking a long straight road heading out into the jungle. The *Northern Borneo Orangutan Orphanage* is well signposted from here as it's a popular visitor centre. Jenny tells me that the aim of the orphanage is to nurture the orphans and to teach them all the skills they need to be rehabilitated back into the protected area of jungle where adult orangutans can now roam freely and safely.

'Orangutans have the longest childhood dependency on the mother of any wild animal in the world.' Jenny explains. 'Typically, a baby will stay with its mother for up to ten years and in that time, will learn from her how to live in the rainforest and how to be independent.'

The afternoon is spent taking a VIP tour of the orphanage with Jenny.

She shows us the visitor centre first and we sit and watch a short, harrowing film, on the plight of orangutans in Borneo. I learn how their habitat has been destroyed by logging and by jungle clearance in favour of palm oil plantations and how they're now in danger of extinction.

I'm left in tears over how many traumatised babies have been brought here, having been found clinging to their starved dead parents, or after being kept as pets by the loggers or plantation workers themselves. Then we're shown a couple of new arrivals in the hospital quarantine facility. It's heart-breaking. In a pen, are two tiny females, both apparently less than a year old, who had been found starving and alone and clinging to each other for support in the jungle.

They have wild patchy red hair and traumatised eyes and have been named Thelma and Louise.

'When they first arrive here at the orphanage, malnourished and dehydrated, they are so distressed that it takes a long time to gain their trust,' Jenny tells us.

It's heart-achingly sad to see them both sitting there, like terrified children who want their mummy, unable to understand what's happening to them. My maternal instinct to love and to care for these darling infants is in overdrive and I'm filled with admiration for the important work that Jenny and her team are doing here.

After spotting an 'adoption plan' offered to visitors as a way of raising important sponsorship and additional funding, I immediately ask if I can adopt Thelma and Louise.

It turns out, 'adoption' really means donating a small regular amount of money and I quickly fill in the paperwork. Jenny then takes us into the 'jungle gym' where we meet lots of other young ones who are all happily strengthening their limbs and learning to climb and swing from ropes.

Then we take a long walk through the jungle to a viewing area and feeding platform.

'It's here that we can observe our success stories...' Jenny tells us proudly.

And it's fabulous to sit and watch these fully-grown, happy and free orangutans, confidently swinging in from high in the ancient forest canopy to enjoy the twice daily offerings of fruit laid out for them. It's heart-warming to know that one day, through the love and care and devotion of the staff and the volunteers here, poor Thelma and Louise will get the chance to recover and to thrive and to live safely in this sanctuary too.

When our tour comes to an end, Jenny drives us back into Sandakan.

We thank her and she gives me a hug. Any jealously I'd initially felt towards her has been been replaced by admiration and respect. 'Lori, if you want to come and work for us anytime, then just give me a call and you're in. No problem. We'd love to have you!'

I can hardly believe my good fortune.

At Sandakan, Ethan and I check into a small hotel near the harbour. He takes the lead at reception, while for a moment, I have to recover from the exhausting and energy-sapping heat and humidity outside by standing next to the cold blowing air-con unit inside the lobby.

By the time I join him, he's taken two rooms for us.

I'm surprised but also relieved. I feel pleased that he hasn't just assumed we would sleep together tonight. But part of me is also disappointed because throughout the day, I've been in heady anticipation over the 'will we or won't we sleep together tonight' scenario – especially after hearing the zoo story from Jenny. If it's even possible, I'm in even more lustful hero worship of Ethan now.

He hands me my key and we go up in the elevator to the second floor without speaking.

I'm now hoping our rooms might be next to each other and therefore interconnecting. I imagine him knocking gently on the door, before sweeping into my room upon my lustful invitation, to take me into his arms and make love to me passionately.

But to my dismay our rooms aren't even close. They're a length of hallway apart.

So, in a bit of a fluster, we go our separate ways to freshen up after arranging to meet up again in the lobby in one hour, so that we can go and watch the sunset together. Ethan says that this part of the world is famous for two things, and one of them is the most incredible sunsets – leaving me to ponder on what might be the other.

My room is clean and comfortable and has wi-fi. I immediately start up my laptop, so that I can view my photos from today and message them to my boys.

I send them a photo of me in the jungle, surrounded by tall grasses and ancient trees. I include one of Thelma and Louise, of course, informing them they now had two cute baby sisters. And also one of Jenny and I surrounded by lots of happy youngsters in the jungle-gym.

It's then that I suddenly realise, to my dismay, that I don't have any at all of Ethan.

Not that I want to send one of him and I together to my boys anyway.

With amusement, I recall how when I tried to include him in a photo, he whisked my camera off me to insist that he took a photo of me instead. I guess he must be a little camera shy.

Before I take a shower, I decide to do a little bit of research.

Ethan's job intrigues me and I want to know more about the Goldman Global Foundation.

An internet search brings up their involvement in projects all over the world. Fiji. The Philippines. Indonesia. Asia. Bahamas. The Caribbean ... just to name a few places.

I read that as well as land-based eco-projects, protecting illegally hunted animals and those in danger of extinction, the GGF also has a fully equipped ocean-going ship able to attend to any conservation crisis or controversial marine concern in any sea or ocean across the world.

There are reports of the ship and its crew shadowing Japanese whaling ships and successfully interfering with illegal slaughter and then deterring poachers in the Galapagos.

It seems to me that Mr Goldman is even more of a real-life hero than Ethan.

Yet, strangely, there are no photos of him in any of his news features.

He is described as an intensely private man and something of a nomadic recluse – yet respected and supported all over the world by green-politicians and eco-warriors and campaigning celebrities alike. The GGF website has a project location map where I find an article on an innovative artificial reef construction project being fully funded by GGF in the Sulu Sea off northern Malaysia. Knowing this is the same project that Ethan and I will be working on together makes me feel incredibly excited and proud.

I take a shower and wash my hair, rubbing some coconut oil through my tresses to control the humidity frizz, and then also use the same oil on my skin. My body is glowing like a nuclear reactor after the heat of the sun today. I slip into an off the shoulder dress with a pretty lace bodice that I bought in KL and realise that I'm tingling all over with fervent anticipation.

As I come out of the lift, I see Ethan waiting for me in the lobby.

My heart skips a beat when I see him smile at me. He looks so handsome and like he could be from a far more exotic place than Scotland, with his dark skin and casual but stylish tropical garb. Tonight, he's wearing long trousers and a blue shirt with a flower pattern.

He looks me up and down in appreciation. 'Lori, you look lovely!'

Then he links my arm through his and escorts me through the door.

'I've been trying to guess the other thing that Sandakan is famous for other than its sunsets – is it orangutans?' I ask him. 'Otherwise I really haven't a clue.'

'No, actually, it's your favourite food. Lobster and shrimp and clams!' he tells me.

And I am both impressed and delighted that he's remembered this from our 'name your favourite food' quizzes on Koh Phi Tao. We stroll along a boardwalk until we come to a restaurant at the end of a long narrow wooden jetty. Despite it being busy, we are seated at a small table for two with an uninterrupted view across the bay. The evening is mellow and the breeze warm and salty and garlic infused.

'It's a beautiful evening and it's been a beautiful day,' I tell him appreciatively.

'And we are just in time for the grand finale.'

Indeed, the sun is just starting to go down as we're given menus and asked what we'd like to drink. We order two beers and a seafood sharing platter.

And then it happens – the sky is suddenly alight with the deepest colours imaginable.

'There are three unique elements that sets apart a sunset in Borneo from anywhere else in the world,' Ethan explains to me knowledgably. 'The warm air, the tropical humidity, and its proximity to the equator.'

Most people are getting up on their feet at this point, meals and drinks temporarily abandoned, so they can point their cameras at the bands of pink and the purple hues and deepening reds and oranges and streaks of violet light.

I take just one carefully focussed photo and then put my phone down so that I can simply sit and experience and appreciate this special show through my own eyes, albeit through my sunglasses, as somehow, the sun looks twice as big and twice as bright as I've ever seen it before. It shimmers, refracting orange and cinnamon rays across the sea towards us and through the tumbling clouds, turning into red and vermilion coloured streaks.

In the foreground, dark silhouettes of small boats against the fiery glow give the whole scene perspective.

Then, when the sun finally dips below the horizon line, the whole sky and the sea light up together in a final explosion of light and a blazing inferno of colour.

It's breath-taking. I can't help but marvel at the incredible beauty of it.

'That was truly the most amazing sunset I have ever seen,' I tell Ethan.

Our food arrives and is enough to feed a small army but we show it no mercy.

'Dessert or coffee?' Our waiter suggests, on clearing away the debris once we're done.

'Oh, not for me,' I protest.

Ethan regards me from across the table with a gleam of approval in his eyes.

And suddenly, I have an acute case of first date nerves, thinking he's keen for the evening to be over and that my refusal of dessert might be taken as a signal to head back to the hotel.

'But as the evening is still young...' I stammer. 'Shall we have a bottle of wine?'

I sit back in my seat and cross my legs, making a deliberate show of how comfortable and keen I am to linger awhile and enjoy the ambiance. Then, as the waiter produces the wine list, I focus on staying in the moment and relaxing while we linger over our wine and enjoy the pleasantly subdued evening temperature. Most of our conversation is about the orphanage and the importance of the work done there by Jenny and her team.

'I can't thank you enough for taking me there today,' I say.

'It was my pleasure. I heard that you impressed Jenny so much she offered you a job?'

'Yes, she did. But I declined. I told her you'd promised to take me diving in a coral garden.'

He smiles. 'Indeed. It's still on your bucket list together with swimming with dolphins in the wild. I'm sure we can check that one off soon, too.'

I am doubly impressed. A man who actually listens and wants to make all my dreams come true. 'So, tell me, what's still left on your bucket list, Ethan? Is there anything special still to do?'

He studies me for a long moment over the top of his wine glass and his eyes shine with warmth in the soft light from the candle between us. My eyes are focussed on the beautiful curve of his mouth that I am now daydreaming about kissing.

'Aye, something very special, but I'm a patient man. I'm waiting for the time to be right.'

I catch my breath and he raises his eyebrows in recognition of his point hitting home.

He is referring to what he'd said on our last night together on Koh Phi Tao.

Okay. I get it. You need more time.

And he had been showing me his patience and his respect by booking us two rooms.

He's making it clear that he isn't rushing me but also that I should be the one to make the first move. It's ridiculous how nervous I feel. I haven't slept with any man other than my (soon-to-be-ex) husband in about thirty years and I'd only had a couple of other boyfriends before I met Charles. But it's crazy how much I want to be with Ethan tonight.

I have palpitations. My whole body aches. I long to be intimate with him.

Although, I'm also scared of being a disappointment to him and to myself.

What if I'm not very good at making love?

Ethan has been separated from Marielle for several years but he has women like Jenny (and I don't blame her) who fawn all over him. With his good looks and his penchant for championing all the world's problems, he's a woman magnet. But then, with his nomadic life-style, he's also someone who might love and leave. I immediately cast that one aside.

If I'm going to dwell on that old chestnut again, I may as well not be here.

We make our way back along the boardwalk to our hotel, holding hands, fingers entwined.

When we walk into the lobby and head towards the elevator, I take a deep breath.

'So, do you still have a drop of Scotch in your bag for a nightcap?' I venture.

He looks both surprised and delighted in equal measure.

'Aye, I do. If you're not too tired. Erm ... for a nightcap, I mean.'

We go up to his room. He busies himself getting two tumblers from the bathroom while I stand waiting. The large double bed immediately becomes the elephant in the room. I don't know where to sit because his guitar case is on the only chair. Seeing my predicament, he moves the guitar to make a point, but I sit on the bed anyway.

I slip off my sandals and make myself comfortable, while he goes outside to the hallway to get some ice from the ice machine. Then, with an ice cube and a generous shot of whisky in each of our glasses, Ethan sits down next to me on the bed.

I lean towards him and a moment later the shots are on the bedside table and I'm in his arms at long last. 'Oh Ethan, wanting to kiss you tonight has been driving me crazy.'

'Did I make a mistake in booking two rooms?' he asks me, gently kissing and nuzzling my neck and nipping my earlobe and making me shiver and tingle with excitement as his hands and fingers trace a line down my back while unzipping my dress.

'Yes. But I appreciated the sentiment,' I gasp.

And as our lips meet and my dress slides to the floor, any doubts or anxieties I might have had are cast aside too.

Chapter 18

Reef Island

We leave the hotel late morning, after being the last people down for breakfast and coffee. Looking happy, tired and a little dishevelled, we haul our backpacks and head over to the pier to find a boat to take us to Reef Island. According to Ethan, we stand a good chance of getting a boat captain willing to take us over to the island at this time of the day, as the fishing boats are returning with their catch and are now looking to make a quick buck transiting travellers and tourists to wherever they need to go.

Indeed, there are lots of boats of all sizes at the docking area and the strong smell of fish in the air. I offer to wait with our bags while he goes to negotiate. The heat today is incredible. I'm stood on a concrete slip next to the sea and I feel like I'm being steamed alive.

My dress is already stuck to my body in the torturous

heat and humidity and I'm physically aching after last night's lovemaking – every part of my body as well as my ardour feels like it's alight as I watch Ethan with a lustful eye, admiring his every move and his athletic physique from my vantage point on the pier. Every little throb and ache and twinge reminds me of the places he's kissed and pleasured.

I sigh deeply with happiness and give myself a little reality check, by averting my gaze down into the water lapping against the jetty, where a shoal of colourful fish move like a team of synchronised swimmers in the crystal clear water. I long to strip off my clothes and join them but I have the responsibility of guarding our bags and also Ethan's precious guitar.

I try lifting his canvas bag but it's too heavy.

I had joked about it being full of colourful shirts but he claims it's full of his dive gear.

At last, I see him shaking hands with a fisherman and counting notes into a weathered hand.

I'm so excited about getting to the island. It sounds idyllic. I'm also excited about diving again and I'm particularly excited about diving with Ethan. To think that I'll be on a tropical island with the man of my dreams over Christmas and New Year.

I'm convinced that life really can't get much better than this.

Ethan waves and gives me the thumbs up sign and

then he comes racing back over to help with the bags. He picks up his guitar, swings the impossibly heavy bag over one shoulder effortlessly and throws mine over his other one. I trot behind him in my melting flip flops.

'He'll take us over to the island for fifty dollars.'

'Each?' I ask, thinking it sounded like quite a bargain.

'No. That's for both of us,' he replies, as if I'm crazy.

Our fifty-dollar ride is a small boat with a wheelhouse and an open deck that is mostly taken up with smelly fishing nets. We hand over our bags into the safe keeping of our boat's captain, whose name is Kiko, and we head over to a large warehouse on the dock to pick up supplies.

Inside the warehouse, it's like a general store on a massive scale.

I browse the shelves while Ethan speaks with the manager. I overhear them discussing stocks of drinking water and canned and dried foods and fresh items and crates of local beer. Ethan is referring to a prepared list he has retrieved from his breast pocket. I hear him arranging for the same items to be delivered to us on a weekly basis – cash on delivery.

It's a similar arrangement to what we'd had on Koh Phi Tao.

I pick up a tube of toothpaste and a tub of sunscreen and a couple of bottles of wine and then spot various items of watersports equipment. I choose a facemask and a snorkel and fins in my size and take everything over to pay. Ethan is still busy organising.

We are taking our first week of supplies with us and they are brought over to the boat in wheelbarrows by three small barefooted men. Ethan tips each of them generously and they wave us off like we are old friends. Then we head off under blue skies and calm seas into the open water to our island paradise.

Only very soon, the sea becomes quite rough, and I realise I forgot to pick up some seasickness tablets. So, within half an hour, I'm 'feeding the fish' over the side. To make me feel worse, Ethan and Kiko are now tucking into a big bag of something that looks and smells like beef jerky. When it's clear I've finished hurling my breakfast, and I'm sitting on my backpack with my head between my knees, Ethan comes over to me with a bottle of water and gives me a compassionate hug. Then he kindly distracts me from my misery by pointing out all the islands on the horizon line along our route.

'This area is known as the Coral Triangle. It's an archipelago of islands and atolls that are part of the Malaysian coastal shelf. In the past, parts of the reef here have been decimated by dynamite fishing. But in the last ten years, it's been designated a conservation area and thanks to the concerted efforts of GGF marine biologists, it's all now starting to recover.'

'I did a bit of research on the Goldman Global Foundation,' I tell him. 'I think the conservation work they do all around the world is incredible. I read that the foundation not only supports this marine park but it fully funds the artificial reef system we will be building at Reef Island. I'm so thrilled to be involved. I really am!'

Ethan seems pleased by my enthusiasm. 'Aye, and the work we'll do will hopefully keep the GGF shareholders allocating funding to this part of the world for another year.'

Ethan suddenly stops talking and stands up to gaze out into the sea.

Something has caught his eye. I catch my breath. Is it dolphins?

Oh, please let it be dolphins!

'Look, out there, at all those birds circling a fish boil. Do you see it?'

I peer through my sunglasses across the watery vista wishing I had invested in polaroid glasses.

'Hey, Kiko, do you see that?' Ethan yells into the wheelhouse.

The next thing I know, our boat is accelerating towards what I can now see is a bubbling commotion in the sea, over which hundreds of seabirds are in a flying frenzy.

'What is it? I don't understand? What is the significance of a fish boil?' I ask.

Ethan is pulling out his snorkel gear. 'Lori, get your mask and snorkel and fins on quickly!'

We soon arrive at the area and 'a fish boil' is a good description.

There are masses of fish leaping up at the surface.

The water quite literally looks like it is boiling.

'It's tuna. They're being driven to the surface by something from beneath and that something, if I'm right, is a whale shark!'

'And we're going to swim with a shark?' I gasp, thinking he's gone completely mad.

'No. It's called a whale shark but it's actually a fish. This is a fantastic and rare opportunity to swim with the biggest fish in the sea – so get ready. When I say go, in we go!'

My heart is banging against my ribs and I'm shaking with nerves and excitement as I pull off my dress and put on my gear. I don't have my swimsuit on under my dress but I'm guessing that my matching bra and knickers are more or less the same thing anyway. The captain steers the boat in a big circle around the boil which is getting bigger and more active by the second – it looks like an active underwater volcano erupting – and I'm sitting on the side ready to jump in on Ethan's signal. He must be crazy and I must be completely mad.

But I'm excited. Then something totally mind-blowing happens.

First there is a glimpse of a giant fin, then a great blue-grey and white-speckled bulk bursts through the middle of the leaping tuna, before disappearing again into the depths.

'Go!' yells Ethan and I take a leap of faith and follow him over the side.

The sea is warm and silky on my skin. I take a deep gulp of air from the surface and swim down beneath the waves. Through my mask, I can clearly see the whale shark just a few metres away from us. I try to dive deeper, kicking my legs and pushing the water aside with my arms to follow the whale shark and Ethan, who is swimming effortlessly alongside this beautiful huge and gentle creature. My head is spinning with excitement.

I'm swimming in the open sea with the biggest fish in the world!

The whale shark glides effortlessly away and disappears into the blue as Ethan and I surface together. We pull off our masks and take out our snorkels and we are laughing.

I realise I'm trembling. Ethan takes my face in his hand and plants kisses on my face.

Is every day with this man going to be one great adventure?

Back on the boat, all thoughts of seasickness are forgotten and I'm chewing beef jerky too, and we are chatting enthusiastically about what just happened and guessing how long the whale shark was. A short while later, it's like we've finally reached the end of the world and we see our island in the distance. A tiny green oasis in a vast blue sea and our home for a while at least. Our captain carefully negotiates the reef until we are in the shallows of the lagoon and we can wade ashore. I see the beach and its white sand and how pristine it all is except for a few driftwood sun-bleached logs that have been washed up there. I'm looking to see who else is there ... but there is no one else. No welcome party. No sign of life.

Well, that's not quite true. I see a huge iguana sitting on one of the logs.

I look to Ethan. He's already hauling our supplies ashore.

He's whistling happily to himself. I pick up a few of the smaller boxes to give him a hand.

'So ... what do you think?' he asks me, putting a box of bottled drinking water down on the sand and opening his arms wide as if he was about to burst into song.

'Well, I think it's stunningly beautiful. But I had thought there might be other people here?'

Really?' He scratches his head. 'I don't remember saying there would be?'

'Well, you didn't say there wouldn't. I suppose, I just thought, if this was an important conservation project being funded by the GGF then there would be a whole team of people here to help with the important conservation work?'

He casts his gaze over the dazzling bright tropical scene. 'Nope, it's just us here.'

I can hardly believe it. I'd purposefully not asked him too many questions about coming here, even though my mind was full of them, as Ethan had quipped to Jenny yesterday about how many questions I asked and I'd felt rather reprimanded. But now my mind is a scramble of thoughts about just the two of us living here like castaways and whether that would be a good or a bad thing?

'So, if I hadn't come along, you'd have been on your own over Christmas and New Year?'

He shrugs. 'Well, I'm sure it would've got a bit lonely after a while.'

With our belongings ashore, we stand together on the beach watching Kiko leave.

Ethan takes my hand firmly in his and gives it a squeeze. 'Don't worry, we do have supplies.'

I start to walk up the beach to where I assume our camp might be – just set back from the trees, in the shade. Ethan follows me carrying our bags and his guitar case.

But the only building I come across is a small dilapidated looking hut.

One, tiny, wreck of a hut with half a roof and holes in the floor and gaps for windows.

'Home sweet home!' Ethan enthuses, putting down the bags.

I stand in the ferocious heat of the day wanting to panic but knowing it's far too late.

As our only way off this island is now just a blip on the horizon.

'Is that it?' I exclaim. 'I mean, where is the kitchen?'

Then, realising I sound like a housewife rather than a scientist, I quickly correct myself.

'I mean, where is the research facility?'

Ethan shrugs and I plop myself down under the shade of a palm tree and almost get killed by a falling coconut. I jump out my skin. It hits the ground a few feet away from me.

'Phew, that was a close one!' Ethan remarks, looking concerned for the first time since we arrived here on castaway cay – which is what I've now decided to call this place.

Ethan picks up the coconut. 'Do you know that one hundred and fifty people a year are killed by falling coconuts. That's fifteen times more than people killed by sharks.'

Then he takes out his machete, which of course he keeps in his canvass bag, and proceeds to chop the top of the coconut. I watch him with interest. It's certainly done with some skill.

With the top off the coconut, he quickly grabs a bottle of rum from a supply box and pours a good glug of it inside. 'There you go. A rum cocktail for the lady!'

I'm so flabbergasted at this surreal scene and this ridiculous situation, and the fact that he has just surreptitiously ticked another box off my bucket list, that I burst out laughing.

'Okay, what's so funny?' he asks, in amusement.

'This! You! You bring me out here to a remote desert island and somehow you manage to rustle up a rum and coconut cocktail. It's amazing.'

I knock my nut against his bottle and I take a sip. It's a little warm but still delicious.

Ethan takes a couple of glugs of straight rum and casts his eyes over the derelict hut.

I wave a casual hand. 'If it's not too much trouble, I'd like running water so I can take a shower before sundown.'

'Oh, we already have running water,' Ethan says glibly, plonking himself down next to me.

'I'm serious,' I tell him. 'The very least I expect is bathroom facilities.'

'There's a waterfall in the middle of the island. It's where all the mermaids hang out.'

He seems to be enjoying himself immensely. I sip on my rum and coconut.

'I have to say, Lori. I'm surprised at how you've suddenly become high maintenance.'

I almost spit out my cocktail, as I splutter, 'What? High maintenance? I have needs and expectations!'

'And I wouldn't dream of disappointing you. So, my darling Lori, you'll be relieved to know this is all a bit of a joke. I remembered this old tool hut being here on this side of the island, so I got Kiko to drop us off here.'

'This is not our house?'

He stands up and offers his hand to help me up to my feet. 'No. Of course not. Our place is on the other side of the island. I think you'll be very happy when you see it.'

'You tricked me?'

He is laughing so hard he has to hold onto his sides. 'And you fell for it hook, line and sinker. I can hardly believe you'd have been willing to share that run-down shack with me and for that I think I love you even more!'

He loves me … even more?

On the opposite side of the island, which is about a ten-minute walk away, is another beach and on it there's a low-lying and sprawling two-story wooden-clad house. It looks like something from a tropical holiday brochure. It has an upper floor balcony with large windows that overlook a wide curve of perfect beach. Adjacent to the house is a fully equipped storeroom with a generator, a compressor to fill air tanks, and a full complement of dive equipment all hung up on tidy racks. The place is fabulous. My relief is palpable.

'Let me give you a tour and you can ask me as many questions as you like,' he laughs.

We explore the store and equipment room first. At the top of a wooden staircase, there's a large meeting room where the walls are filled with charts and posters of fish and photographs identifying all the colourful coral that was to be found on the reef. There's also a small office area with a computer and a radio transmitter.

Ethan fires up the radio equipment and uses it to check us in with GGF and to get a weather forecast. 'Being remote, we don't have internet but we can get a satellite connection,' he explains to me. 'Except, because it's so expensive to use, it really is for emergencies only.'

'This is all incredibly impressive. The only thing missing is other people,' I quip.

He leans against the wall, still looking mightily amused with himself.

'Okay. You are right about us needing a team but they don't arrive for another week. Until then, it's just me and you and we don't even have to wear clothes, if you don't want to.'

I sashay over to him. 'How romantic. We can live here like naked savages.'

'But with supplies...' he adds, taking my hand and leading me back into the house and up the staircase. 'Let me show you to your bedroom.'

Upstairs, a hallway leads to bedrooms. Ethan takes me to a doorway at the far corner of the house. Inside, the space is large and bright with a whole wall of window and glass doors and the outside wraparound balcony. The flooring and furniture are all darkly polished wood but the walls and the fabrics and sheets on the oversized bed are all white. The room is hot and oppressively stuffy, so Ethan goes straight to the doors to throw them open and to let in some air, sending the fine white muslin drapes and the mosquito net over the bed into billowing sails. While the room cools, we walk out onto the balcony to take in the view.

I lean on the wooden handrail and take a deep breath of hot and humid and salty air. It's all so perfect here. I see that a weathered wooden jetty leads straight out from the beach across the shallows of the cobalt blue lagoon and into slightly deeper azure waters where there's an old boathouse. The beach below us is the shape of a crescent moon.

'This place is a paradise!' I breathe, as Ethan comes to stand behind me and wrap his arms around my waist and to playfully nuzzle and kiss the back of my neck.

I sigh with pleasure and turn to him. As I press my body against his and our lips meet, I hear him groan with desire. Then, unwilling to wait any longer to make love again, he scoops me up into his arms and carries me over the threshold and back into the bedroom.

Chapter 19

Reef Island (ii)

The next morning, as the light of a new day filters across our bed and our tangle of limbs, I lie awake quietly watching Ethan's dark eyelashes fluttering on his mahogany tanned cheekbones as he sleeps, tracing the line of his ruggedly handsome profile with my eyes.

He's beautiful. His mouth, forming a slight smile, looks so adorably kissable.

When he eventually stirs and opens his eyes, his smile broadens.

'Good morning, beautiful...' he says to me and I take that as an invitation to snuggle.

We have a tropical breakfast together – fruit and cereal and coffee – sitting outside on our balcony with a view of the beach and the lagoon and then we spend the rest of the morning out of the escalating heat inside the dive equipment room. I make myself useful with the more mundane jobs of cleaning while Ethan is busy checking and servicing the dive gear.

He tells me we'll be diving on the reef this afternoon.

I've been excited about diving again but now I'm sick with nerves. I try hard not to show it. We haven't actually ever dived together before and I feel like this is going to be a test to see how well I perform. I'm sure I've forgotten everything I've been taught and I'm terrified of getting everything wrong and failing him.

I'm not just here on a holiday. I'm here to dive. I'm here to help save the reef.

'Our first job is to collect data and compare our findings with that of a year ago,' Ethan tells me, gathering up some equipment. 'How about I do the measuring and you can take the photos.'

He gives me an encouraging smile and an underwater camera.

As it turns out, what I thought was going to be a nerve-wracking and testing experience, is actually a beautiful and relaxed couple of hours spent swimming about in shallow bathwater-warm clear waters amongst exquisite corals and colourful fish on an area of reef really close to the shore. This goes a long way to settling my nerves.

Over the next few days, we repeat this process of diving on the reef to gather information in the mornings and comparing historical data in the afternoons and we celebrate with a sundowner when it becomes clear to us that the reef is showing fabulous signs of recovery.

Ethan explains that some of the faster growing branch corals have gained around twenty millimetres of new growth over the past twelve months and this points to a healthy and recuperating reef system.

I've only had one truly terrifying moment while we've been out diving. I suppose, having spent the first few days in the shallows just off the shoreline, where there are shoals of tiny pretty and colourful fish of the kind you see in tropical aquariums, I'd been lulled into a false sense of security in thinking there was nothing dangerous out there in the deeper waters.

It was when we ventured a little deeper that we came across a great swarm of sea snakes – the stuff of nightmares – and I was immediately in an absolute panic. I hate snakes of any kind but especially sea snakes. I've seen little banded sea snakes before but these ones were much bigger. These were all around me and in a panic I fled to the surface.

Only to find that when I reached the surface they were *still* all around me.

Ethan followed me up – seeing my bubbles coming out in one long scream as I surfaced.

He took me back to the beach to calm me down and to educate me about sea snakes.

He told me that yes, they were highly venomous, but they were very placid creatures who would rather avoid humans than bite them. He also explained how they had to come up for air to breathe. Who knew sea snakes had to breathe air on the surface?

Ethan has such a calm and reassuring manner and he promised me I'd be completely safe.

So, trusting him, I bravely agreed to go back in the water and take another look at the snakes if only from a comfortable distance. He encouraged me to take some photos of a large black and white striped snake curled up sleeping on the sandy bottom, which I later identify as the belcher sea snake, which just happens to hold the title of the world's most venomous snake. 'One hundred times deadlier than any land snake!' I tell Ethan in horror.

And he laughs, while casually insisting that it's good exercise for 'the old ticker' to do something scary every now and again. I tell him that I've had a boa constrictor around my neck in Langkawi. I remind him that I've swam with a whale shark – the biggest fish in the sea – and now I've had the world's deadliest snake within a few feet of me, so my old ticker is getting quite enough exercise, thank you very much.

Interestingly, when I ask what scares him, he quickly changes the subject.

Out in the deeper parts of the sea beyond the reef

there are also scary looking giant fish. They seem to appear from the blue quite suddenly and the first time you see them you can't help but think you might be eaten alive. It's quite terrifying to suddenly see a long silvery barracuda swimming alongside you and to realise that, at six feet long and with a mouth full of razor sharp teeth, he's looking at you as if he might be weighing you up for lunch.

Then there's the enormous bumphead parrotfish with their wide eyes and sharp toothy overbites. Underwater, everything is magnified, but these creatures look big enough to be a fleet of submarines moving through the water. We come across several of these on our dive today.

With great enthusiasm, Ethan tells me he'll take me diving with sharks before we leave here.

He says there are lots of placid, indeed playful, nurse sharks but at deeper depths.

To dive deeper, I'll need my advanced diver qualification.

But I really want to do it and Ethan says he will teach me.

Well, look at me now. One year ago, I might have agreed to playing a game of snakes and ladders. There's no way I'd have considered diving with snakes and sharks!

It's Christmas Eve and I'm lying stretched out on the sundeck of the dive boat in my bikini. My now darkly tanned body is glistening with perspiration and sunscreen. Temperatures are high today and the sky is clear and blue. There isn't one single cloud or even any lines from airplane trails. I've noticed that here, where the Sulu Sea meets the South China Sea, we are simply too far from anywhere to be on anyone's direct route to anywhere.

I can't help but wonder and imagine what everyone back home is doing today?

I can imagine my two sons and their girlfriends, swathed in coats and scarfs and hats and gloves, battling through icy rain or snow on the high street to get the last of their Christmas shopping done. I can picture my mum sitting in her armchair by the fire watching TV with the lights of her little Christmas tree on. I feel distant and my own situation seems surreal.

We're tied to a buoy just outside the reef. The boat is rocking gently from side to side in a sleep-inducing sort of way and I'm humming along to the music play-list coming from a speaker in the wheelhouse. Right now, it's playing Bing Crosby's *White Christmas*.

From my horizontal position, lying on my front while tanning my back, I can see down into the water and Ethan's air bubbles rising to the surface. The water here is so clean on the edge of the reef that I can clearly see him kneeling on the sand below photographing a free-swimming octopus. Soon, he comes to the surface and from the ladder he passes me his camera and his fins and he climbs aboard to remove his heavy air tank. Once he is free of it he unzips his wetsuit and plants a salty kiss on my mouth and wishes me happy Christmas for about the sixth time today. Then with *Jingle Bell Rock* blasting out over the air waves we are riding the sea waves back to the island. Suddenly there is a yell from the wheelhouse and Ethan is pointing ahead of us. The next thing, he kills the boat's engine and we come to a silent stop in the water.

I'm looking ahead. I'm looking all around. What has he seen?

A fish boil? A whale shark?

And then I see what he sees – I see dolphins!

Lots and lots of wild dolphins!

They are swimming at high speed straight towards us, leaping and diving, their shiny grey bodies arcing and twisting and moving like quicksilver through the water. I've already grabbed my snorkel gear and I'm quickly over the side. I let my body sink down and when I open my eyes and look through my mask I find I'm eye to eye with a dolphin and I have around a dozen more heading my way on a crash collision course. With a quick flick of a tail they divert around me, just inches away, and I can see their faces so closely – they really do look like they are smiling at me! Although they are all clearly all en route to somewhere, they circle around us and the boat and come back again to play.

Suddenly, I'm swimming in a pod of at least two dozen dolphins.

Underwater I can hear their – and my own – high-pitched squeals of delight.

Then they regroup, and they leave us as fast as they arrived, and I watch them go, feeling so happy and so elated that I'm weeping with joy. What a truly special moment in time.

And yet another big tick off the bucket list.

What a wonderful Christmas present!

I'm not only in paradise – I'm in heaven!

'Last Christmas, I gave you my heart...' I sing, chopping the ingredients for our Christmas meal. I'm preparing a vegetable salad and a mango pudding while Ethan has gone out to catch our main course. From my spot in the kitchen, through the breezy open window, I can see the tropical beach and the blue lagoon and the palm trees swaying and I'm all too aware that one year ago this very day, through a steamed-up window, I'd have been standing at the kitchen sink peeling carrots and preparing sprouts and the Christmas day turkey would have been in the oven. I'd have been looking out at my small, cold and winter-ravaged garden and

I'd be expecting our boys and my mum to arrive for dinner.

And I'd have had no clue whatsoever that just one year later my life would be so different.

It feels terribly ungrateful to let my mind wander back in time and over so many miles.

I know I really should be fully focussed on being here in this paradise and on my new life, but I'm being haunted by the Ghosts of Christmas Past. I'm missing my family and I'm wondering how they will spend their day without me? I wonder what gifts everyone's bought each other this year? Is it snowing there, I wonder?

It's hard to imagine cold and ice and snow when I'm boiling hot and wearing a sarong.

I expect they're all thinking about me too. Not right now obviously, because I think it's probably the middle of the night there. But later in the day, I'm sure they'll be missing me just as much as I'm missing them. Not Charles though, of course. Not missing him will be mutual. I pause my chopping to imagine him lying in our marital bed next to Sally.

A moment later that ugly dark image is replaced with a sunnier, far sexier one.

I can see Ethan coming back up the beach in his dive gear.

No man has ever looked more handsome than Ethan

Jones in a wetsuit carrying a huge lobster. Okay, enough is enough, I tell myself sharply. I've reminisced and I've wallowed in how much I miss my kids and my mum and my dog and I've given myself an unhealthy dose of heartache, but right here and right now, there is a gorgeous man lighting my barbecue and there is a bottle of chilled champagne that needs opening.

Christmas present and Christmas future cannot be ignored any longer.

And of the future? Well, Ethan and I haven't discussed what happens next or where we will go from here when the time comes to move on. We've simply been focussed on living in the moment and enjoying each day and getting to know each other better, especially as, in just a couple of days, we'll have company. We are making the most of every moment in the here and now. And I've never had such an easy and amicable lifestyle. I've never had it so good.

I ponder once again on the words of the young monk in Chiang Mai.

And I wonder if along the way I've somehow missed the sign he promised?

Had it been far too discreet for me?

Because here I am. I'm in my place of happiness with Ethan.

My only complaint would be that I was hoping for somewhere more enduring.

Somewhere to settle down in everlasting happiness. Like a fairy-tale. Like a happy-ever-after.

Maybe Lord Ganesha thought that I was asking for far too much?

Maybe I was ... and if that's the case then I'm grateful for what I have right here, right now.

We cook the lobster wrapped in banana leaves on the barbeque grill and we eat our Christmas meal under the shade of a palm tree on the beach. We drink champagne from coconut shells and we spend our afternoon lounging on a sheet laid out on the sand, chatting and laughing and making love, with another bottle of bubbly chilling in an ice bucket and with the sun on our skin. I'll admit it feels a bit strange to be on an island with no other people.

'Come on, let's go skinny dipping?' Ethan enthuses, as the hot afternoon sunlight creeps across our previously shady napping spot. I'm a little reticent at first about walking along the beach or swimming in the lagoon completely naked, but once I get used to it and accept that no one else can possibly see me, then it feels truly amazing and entirely natural.

We swim in the lagoon and we laze long into the evening when, after dark, we walk by torchlight out onto the jetty to lay together side by side on the smooth old wooden planks.

Janice Horton

Looking up, holding hands, counting shooting stars, and making wishes.

It's very special and very romantic to be living here on this island like castaways.

Except, of course, with supplies.

Chapter 20

Destination Unknown

Just before noon, on the 27th of December, Kiko's boat reappears and four more people step ashore. Ethan and I have been busy preparing for their arrival all morning and we rush down to the beach to welcome them. I am introduced to Jamie, an American, and Tom, a Brit. Both are highly experienced marine biologists who have worked with Ethan on many previous occasions, here on Reef Island and on several other marine projects around the world. The two girls, Immi and Kara, are younger, in their mid-twenties, and both South African. They studied Marine Ecology at a top university there and, like me, they're both Open Water divers. I'm impressed to hear from Ethan that the girls are part of this venture because they won a hotly contested international environmental conservation competition run by GGF for their innovative ideas on artificial reef development.

345

All four of them are obviously very excited to be here.

'It's such a great pleasure to finally meet you, Mr Goldman,' Kara starts to say.

She and Immi both look a little wide-eyed and shell-shocked.

'Oh, call me Ethan, please. We're all on first name terms here,' he insists.

I feel quite taken aback. *Mr Goldman?*

But Ethan's last name is Jones?

Why has she confused him with the billionaire philanthropist?

Well, I suppose she is jet-lagged and she seems a little nervous. Maybe, she thinks because Ethan is the boss here that he must be Mr Goldman? Yes, that's the simplest explanation.

'Let me help with your bags and show you to your rooms,' Ethan offers.

'And then lunch will be ready,' I say, as I've been cooking all morning.

'And let me tell you, Lori is an amazing cook!' Ethan enthuses.

They follow us up the beach, the guys chatting together and the girls stunned into silence and awe at the absolute beauty of the place. We let them get settled into their rooms and then we all meet up for lunch, which is a great opportunity for everyone to get to know each other a bit better. After we finish eating, Ethan gives a short welcome briefing.

'I also just want to explain our schedule. We have a lot to achieve in a short time here.'

He outlines the nature of the work and explains how we'll all be working on a shift system in our buddy teams. 'This means there will only ever be two teams in the water at any one time. One team will provide diver back up, boat, or land support. Safety is paramount.'

Looking around, it's clear that everyone understands. Immi and Kara, in particular, are hanging onto Ethan's every word.

Ethan also explains about the shift system to cover the more mundane jobs of cooking and dishwashing and housekeeping, so we're all treated as equals and nothing is ever left to just one person. For this, I'm grateful. I'd hate to be stuck in the kitchen just because I'm not a scientist.

Happily, now the team is here, things are going to run in much the same way as they had on Koh Phi Tao, except here there are no night-time shifts and our dives have to be properly spaced out to allow for surface intervals – meaning we all have lots more time to relax and to socialise. We even get a couple of hours extra off after lunch for 'siesta' time.

Although, I find myself blushing every time Ethan mentions this word with such great gusto.

'Siesta' has become our secret code for a couple of hours of afternoon delight, now that being naked and frolicking on the beach has become unavailable to us.

The days go by in the blink of an eye. We've all been so incredibly busy. Under Ethan's guidance, we've fallen into a productive routine of sleep, breakfast, briefing, diving – *siesta* – more diving and dinner and then a few hours of socialising.

Just like on Koh Phi Tao, we chat, hold quizzes, play games and cards and listen to music.

Being amongst marine experts, our topics of conversation tend to be a tad scientific and I'm learning so much and finding it all very interesting. Tom and Jamie have reported excellent results in biodiversity – which is their specialist subject. Essentially this means they are finding growth in the numbers of fish and new species of sea creatures making the areas of restored reef their home. Immi and Kara initially gave us an interesting presentation on how their modular artificial reef system works and now we're all involved in building it into a strong but flexible structure onto which we can transplant coral cuttings and restock the parts of the reef that had previously been wiped out by either natural bleaching or dynamite fishing.

I'm diving with Ethan every day and he's a great instructor.

He's also wonderful at pointing out to me all the little sea creatures hiding in the coral and in rocks, so cleverly camouflaged, I might not have spotted them for myself. He gives me such confidence. And together, I know we are just as strong a team as the others.

Yesterday, Immi, Kara and I started our advanced diver training with Ethan.

Last night, as part of our course, we all did a night dive, which was truly amazing.

It was dark, of course, but in the beam of a torch you can see so much life and colour around you and the water itself becomes strangely invisible so that you almost become unaware of it.

I can only liken the experience to what it must feel like to be an astronaut floating around in space. It felt wonderful. I wasn't afraid at all – even when I finally found out what freaks Ethan out.

It's jellyfish, which are often translucent and so much harder to spot in the water at night.

When we came into close proximity with one, I heard him squeal in an explosion of bubbles underwater. I thought he'd been stung but it turned out he hadn't. I delighted in teasing him about it mercilessly afterwards. Reminding him that it's good exercise for 'the old ticker' to do something scary every now and again. What I hadn't realised at the time of course, was that the object of his terror was a Box Jellyfish. It's quite deadly. And, unlike sea snakes or sharks, it can and does cause many fatalities every year!

After enjoying perfect weather and idyllic diving conditions, today we get some bad news. This part of the world is known for its quickly changing weather situations and volatile storms that can quickly become tropical depressions and even typhoons. For this very reason, Ethan has been checking in with the meteorological department as a matter of routine on the radio every morning. Today, he hears that the stronger seasonal sea currents that don't normally affect this area for another month or so are predicted to arrive sooner than expected. Experts in weather patterns say it's due to global warming.

Sadly, this means that our time here on the island has been cut short.

In his briefing today, Ethan explains to us that while we still have calm seas and good weather over the next few days, we should work to complete all our tasks before we leave.

We've all managed to pull together really well over the past few days to complete all our projects ahead of schedule. All the data has been collected. The award winning artificial modular reef is now in place. And finally, we are confronted with the question of what happens next? Ethan tells me he's waiting for a call back to confirm his next assignment.

I guess we'll have to be patient.

Especially when today is not only our last day on the island, it's also the last day of the year.

It's New Year's Eve.

We've all had a chilled-out kind of morning – a lazy lie in, a late breakfast and a dive on the reef for pure pleasure, and an afternoon preparing for our 'Hogmanay' party.

The guys have all gone off to catch fish and to find shellfish to barbecue later.

The girls and I have been prepping party food in the kitchen.

Fresh supplies have been delivered from the mainland – a whole week's worth, so we have more than enough to eat and drink, including champagne for the stroke of midnight.

With the food prepped, I've come down to the water's edge to cool off.

I can't seem to help it but, rather like Christmas Day, I'm suddenly struck with melancholy.

But then, New Year's Eve is always a time of reflection, isn't it?

It's hard not to take stock of your life, to look back on the past twelve months and to think on the year ahead and wonder what it will bring. I feel optimistic because I've realised I'm in love. I haven't told Ethan yet that I love him. Neither has he spoken those exact same words to me – not sincerely anyway, as I don't count it said while joking or being flippant or cursory. But I know what I feel in my heart. So why the sadness?

Right now, it's because I'm thinking about my boys, my mum, and my friends back home.

It seems that happiness always comes with a price tag.

I'm sitting in the lagoon when Ethan came back with his haul of fish.

I guess he knows from the look on my face that something is wrong.

'Lori, what is it? Sweetheart, what's happened?'

'I miss my kids,' I confess to him straightaway. 'Here I am, in paradise, but I miss them so very much. I missed them at Christmas too and now it's almost New Year. I've never been away from them in the holidays before. It all seems so strange and ... well ... it hurts!'

I don't really expect him to understand because he doesn't have any children.

But he holds out his hand to me in support.

The way he's always done from the first moment I met him.

I take his hand and he pulls me to my feet and into his strong arms.

'I'm sorry, my darling,' he says to me tenderly, holding me and kissing me and wiping my salty tears away from my sweaty face with his big fishy fingers.

'No, I'm sorry,' I insist. 'I have no right to spoil a lovely party with my silly tears. I'll be absolutely fine in a minute, honestly.'

And I do recover quickly. Soon, I'm swept up with the vibrant mood of our camp.

Ethan and I are in charge of the cooking station. We have music playing. On the barbeque we have snapper and lobster and shrimps. The girls are keeping the beers cold and mixing mimosa's and the lads are building a driftwood bonfire for later on the beach.

The party fun, the food and drink, and the dancing on the sand, take us happily into the evening. After dark, we all sat around the bonfire, hoping the fire might deter the usual night time armies of hermit crabs from invading our area of the beach.

We play Ethan's 'guess that pop tune' game to great frivolity and then we all join in with him on the guitar singing along to those old classics. I notice Ethan is wearing his watch tonight, keeping a keen eye on the time for what he called 'the bells'.

When it's almost midnight, we wade into the lagoon with our cups charged with champagne and count down the seconds to midnight under a sky filled with stars.

'Three, two, one. Happy Hogmanay!' Ethan yells.

We all cheer and sing *Auld Lang Syne* and of course, Ethan, being a Scot, actually knows all the words. What a fabulous but totally surreal way to see in the New Year.

Tropical heat and a gorgeous beach to ourselves; except for the hermit crabs.

'Hey, Lori. I have a surprise for you.' Ethan tells me, as he takes my hand and leads me up the beach. 'What is it?' I ask him. 'Does it involve going into the jungle in the dark?'

He shakes his head. 'No. It's something to make you feel better, I hope.'

'But I do feel better,' I insist. 'It's been such a lovely party.'

He leads me up to the meeting room and offers me a chair in front of the computer screen.

'We might have already celebrated New Year, but it's still only 4 p.m. yesterday in the UK,' he tells me. 'So, I've arranged for you to Skype your family via the satellite link.'

I'm completely blown away, not only by his kindness and thoughtfulness, but also because I know it costs an absolute fortune for him to secure a satellite link across the world from this location.

'But you'll have to bear with me for a moment and I just hope it works!'

I sit and wait while he secures the link.

Then, suddenly, there in front of me on the computer screen, are my mum and my boys.

'Hi Lorraine!' says my mum. 'Isn't this wonderful of Mr Goldman to set this up for us?'

Ethan affords the same treat to everyone. Jamie gets to chat to his family in New York and Immie and Kara connect with their families in Johannesburg. Tom connects with his parents in London and everyone is happy and excited and delighted.

Except, I notice that Ethan hasn't yet connected with his family.

He explains that he'll arranged to chat with them later.

I wonder if he'll be chatting to the Jones family or the Goldman family?

But I hold my tongue and pick up a bottle of water and head to the stairs.

I'm tired and a little tipsy and feeling ready to retire for the night.

Suddenly, Tom bursts out of the meeting room and urgently shouts out to Ethan.

'Hey, Sir Ethan. My father said to pass on his congratulations to you!'

Ethan, who is keenly striding up the staircase after me, turns to Tom in astonishment.

'Why? Congratulations? What for?'

Tom is laughing. 'You've been awarded a knighthood in the New Year's Honours list. For your services to conservation!'

Ethan's face drains of colour. His usual bronze was now grey.

'Really? No ... that can't be true. It must be fake news,' he insists.

'Oh, it's true. The list has been leaked. It's apparently on the front page of today's London Telegraph.'

'Oh Ethan...!' I gasp. 'That's such fantastic news and so well deserved!'

But the very moment we're alone in our bedroom together, I turn to face him.

'Sir Ethan Jones has a real ring to it, doesn't it?' I quip.

For the first time since I've known him, he looks nervous and uncertain.

'Or should that be Sir Ethan Goldman?' I question.

I watch as his brow furrows at my waspish tone. I notice how he busies himself in a fumbled attempt to undo the buttons on his orange-yellow-and green frangipani patterned shirt.

'On Koh Phi Tao, I'll admit that I held back on you, Ethan,' I confess. 'I didn't tell you everything about me or how I really felt about you. Or the effect talking to Marielle had had on me at the time. I didn't talk much about my family – not the really personal stuff anyway. But here on this island and in our bed I've told you everything about me. I've opened my heart to you. I've told you all my hopes, my dreams, my fears!'

I realise I'm yelling now. 'And yet, despite our intimacy and my honesty, you have been holding out on me. Worse – you've been lying to me all along!'

'I'm sorry Lori...' he starts to say. 'I might not have been totally honest with you...'

I continue to rant. 'Am I the only person on this island who thought you *worked* for the Goldman Foundation – not that you *were* the foundation? Why didn't you tell me that *you* are Ethan Goldman? Why the charade?'

'It's not that I meant to deceive you – not purposely. It just that—'

'It's just that you didn't trust me enough to tell me who you really are!' I conclude for him.

I pace the room wringing my hands. 'So where does that leave me now? How do you think that makes me feel? Well, I'll tell you. It makes me feel dreadful!'

He laughs and shakes his head.

I raise my eyebrows at him in disbelief. 'Do you think this is funny?'

I end my tirade on more of a shriek than a high note. 'I've been sleeping with you every night for weeks and I didn't even know your real name. Right now, I can think of another few names I'd like to call you, and one of them is lying bastard!'

'Ouch, that's a bit harsh!' he retaliates. 'Okay. Let me explain. I use an alias with people at first, because if I don't then I find they treat me differently. It's awkward for me and they feel intimidated somehow. And, just to be clear, I've never actually lied to you, Lori. I've never directly told you any name except for my first name. You must have heard it from others.'

That much is true. It was Laura and Jodie that told me Ethan's name was Jones.

I remember because they'd called him 'Indiana Jones'.

'And besides...' Ethan continues in his own defence. 'I honestly thought you knew who I was from the time we left Koh Lipe together. Because on the ferry, when we had our passports returned to us, my real name was called out right in front of you – twice, in fact.'

'Oh, I don't recall. I suppose my attention was set on hearing my own name at the time.'

He steps towards me and reaches out to stroke my hair while his eyes are fixed on mine.

'And you're a billionaire...' I tell him, quite unnecessarily, while I sulk.

'Well, I hope you are not going to hold that against me?'

And I see his expression is sincere as he holds me in his love-locked gaze.

He cups my face in his big warm hands and his voice is soft and gentle.

'I love you Lori Anderson, also sometimes known as Lorraine Anderson, and if I've hurt you, I'm truly sorry and I hope you'll forgive me and that you'll still want to be with me?'

I try to look hesitant but who am I kidding?

I nod. 'There's a romantic cliché that says, "I'll follow you to the ends of the earth" and I'm saying it to you right now because I really would. I love you too, Ethan Whatever-Your-Name-Is – and I really would go anywhere to be with you.'

He laughs with relief and delight and pulls me into his arms to squeeze me tightly.

'Then that's all settled. The ends of the earth it is - and we set sail tomorrow!'

I lean into his bare chest and wrap my arms around his waist and squeeze him back with all the love in my open heart. 'Set sail? I reply out of curiosity. 'You mean we're travelling all that way by boat?'

'No, not by boat, by ship. I have one coming to pick us up tomorrow to take us to a beautiful island in the eastern Caribbean Sea. It's an equal distance between the Cayman Islands and mainland Honduras. It's almost a secret because hardly anyone knows about it. It's exactly how you might imagine the Caribbean used to be before any tourism commercialised it. It's special because it's surrounded by the second largest barrier reef in the world after the Great Barrier Reef of Australia. Except, this one is in pristine condition and our job will be to keep it that way. Not to save it this time but to preserve it. And the diving is incredible. I'll promise you whale sharks and dolphins and turtles...'

I listen to him describing this place and I'm captivated not only by his words but the passion in his voice. It's like he's describing the Lost City of Atlantis to me.

'Your description of this island sounds familiar somehow...' I reason.

And I cast my mind back to when I was on the boat to Railay Beach with Summer and the lads and they were all talking about an island in the Caribbean with the best diving in the world.

It sounded exactly like this one.

Summer said she'd learned to dive there and I'd written down the name of it in my notebook.

Could they be one and the same place?

'Is this island called Geluk by any chance?' I ask him, as soon as I recall the name.

Ethan looks at me in amazement and nods. 'Aye, so, you've heard of it?'

'Yes,' I say. 'It's a strange name, isn't it? I believe it's pronounced *Gluck*.'

'Aye. It's derived from an old Buddhist word. It means "place of happiness".'

Acknowledgements

My real-life backpacking hero and I are now into our fifth fabulous year of travelling the world.

To date we have explored over fifty countries after selling up everything we owned once our children had grown up and flown the nest. Selling our home, cars, and almost all our possessions has not been the hardest thing in the world to do but saying goodbye to our loved ones for long periods of time has been both difficult and heart-wrenching at times. I love my family and friends very much and so my first big THANK YOU is to modern-day communications and the social media technologies that make our world a smaller place and keep us connected to those we love wherever we or they happen to be in the world.

My next big THANK YOU is to my darling Trav, for being my best friend and my soul mate and my back-packing husband. Not only is he a great travelling companion, I'm proud of him for working so hard to achieve his dreams and personal ambitions of becoming a PADI IDC Staff Instructor, a PADI Elite Instructor, as well as a ITYW qualified boat captain during the time we have been travelling. Scuba diving has always been his passion. Over the many years we have been married, bringing up our three sons together, the diving has often been put on hold. I'm sure he's enjoying it all the more now and deservedly so.

I'm also quite proud of myself, in that I too have been able to realise my own dreams and ambitions of being a published author both before and during our travels and more recently in signing a contract with Harper Impulse for this novel - *The Backpacking Housewife* - a romantic adventure story loosely based on my own travel experiences. I need to say a huge THANK YOU to my lovely writing friend Linn B Halton, who encouraged me to submit to Harper Impulse and an equally huge THANK YOU to lovely editorial director Charlotte Ledger and her wonderful editors and staff at HarperImpulse with a special mention to Eloisa and Sahina and Claire.

I'm often asked if it's hard not having a home base? Is it difficult living out of a backpack? Do I regret anything? My answer is no, sometimes, and absolutely not. The years my husband and I have been travelling and exploring this beautiful world of ours have brought us great joy and happiness and fulfilment and it's all been a fantastic adventure. I'm very thankful that we took the decision to do it now, while we're still reasonably young and healthy, and I really hope we can continue to travel for as long as possible.

The most special thing I've found about travelling? Without doubt it's the new friends we've made all over the world who have now become lifelong friends. To facilitate the writing of this novel, we settled down in south west France for six months on a housesitting assignment, which was fantastic. THANK YOU to homeowners Frances and Piers, who trusted us to look after their gorgeous five-hundred-year-old chateau and their handsome cat, Mr Smudge.

Most of the places and islands that Lori, the heroine of *The Backpacking Housewife*, visits in Thailand and Malaysia are real places that I have travelled to myself but a couple of the locations mentioned - Koh Phi Tao in Thailand and Reef Island in Malaysia - are fictional locations. At the real locations, there are people I'd like to thank for inspiring my story and for educating me on the aspects that dealt with the conservation of endangered species. In the story, our heroine Lori finds new purpose in her life by helping at a turtle sanctuary and she also visits an Orangutan orphanage. I did these things for both the experience and for research purposes.

So, I would like to say a sincere THANK YOU to the staff and volunteers at The Sepilok Orangutan

Rehabilitation Centre for all the important work they do in saving threatened and endangered and orphaned Orangutans in North Borneo. Seeing these beautiful animals being so lovingly cared for and rehabilitated by such dedicated people was heart-warming.

A huge THANK YOU also goes to Bubbles Turtle and Reef Conservation on Perhentian Besar in Malaysia, for the important work they do on turtle conservation on the island and for the truly unforgettable week I spent there learning about Green Turtles. Holly Fletcher and James Fowler and Jorge Palomo kindly and patiently answered all my turtle questions and allowed me to see for myself the nesting turtles coming up the beach at night to lay their eggs. I also loved being part of the excitement of nests erupting and baby turtles being born and released into the sea. It's an experience I'll remember and treasure all my life.

Finally, I'd like to THANK YOU dear reader for buying and reading this book. This novel has been an adventure and a joy to write and I hope you enjoy reading it. If you do enjoy this novel, please do consider leaving me a favourable review on Amazon. This helps other readers to find my books amongst the millions of others available and plus, I will be ever so grateful. If you'd like to contact me or keep up with my travels and adventures or find out what I'm writing about next please do follow me on social media – Facebook and Twitter and Instagram and on my Website at www.thebackpackinghousewife.com Don't feel shy about messaging or asking me anything about travel or my books. I promise to reply from wherever I am in the world as soon as I have an internet connection.

Happy backpacking!
Love, Janice xx

Q and A with

JANICE HORTON

THE BACKPACKING HOUSEWIFE

What was your inspiration for the book?

When housewife and homemaker Lorraine Anderson's ordinary life is turned upside down by the discovery of her husband's affair with her best friend, I really wanted to help her to not only recover from her terrible shock and ordeal, but to send her on an epic adventure to find happiness and purpose in her life once again. So, inspired by my own profound experience in a temple in Thailand, I decided to send her off to Chiang Mai in Thailand to be blessed by a monk. I thought this would be the perfect way for Lori to start her adventure – not just as a journey in a physical sense, but in a spiritual sense too. Other inspirations for the book came from my own experience of taking a train from Northern Thailand to Bangkok and from island-hopping along the Andaman Sea from Railay Beach all the way down to Malaysia. Lori's involvement at a remote island turtle sanctuary, at an orangutan orphanage in the jungle of Borneo and her experiences swimming with a whale shark and dolphins are all inspired by my own personal experiences and have been used in telling Lori's story.

Have you always wanted to be a writer?

From an early age I was an avid reader with an overactive imagination. As a girl, I adored classic children's stories like *The Chronicles of Narnia*, *The Secret Garden*, and *Heidi* before becoming obsessed with the *Jill* series of pony books by Ruby

Ferguson. After finishing a book (and feeling totally bereft at having to leave the fictional world it had created for me), I would often sit down and write my own sequel to the story. I think it was these early reads that impressed on me the want to be a writer.

Are any of the characters based on you or people you know? If so, which ones?

This makes me smile because, as a writer, I'm often asked this question. I think it must be because readers want fictional characters to be tangible or at least based on someone real. None of my characters are wholly based on any one person in any of my books and none of my characters are me. In creating characters, I might occasionally use a blended combination of real people's character traits and even one or two of my own to create a rounded and believable fictional person. I will often use a photo prompt (often someone famous) for helping to bring to mind my invented character's physical attributes. But for me, the fun of writing fiction is in making it all up. So – the answer is no – I have never based any character wholly on myself or on one single person I know.

It's amazing that you get to travel so much, but how do you find time to write? And where do you write when you do?

For me, it's not so much finding the time, but rather in finding the right place to write. Travelling might inspire my stories but it is hardly conducive to finding the peace and the solitude to focus on writing. I spend a lot of time in airports and in airplanes but it's really tiring and hard to concentrate while you are in transit. So, when I was asked by HarperImpulse to write *The Backpacking Housewife*, I suggested to my husband that we stopped travelling for a while (we were exploring Vietnam) and settle down somewhere for the time it would take me to complete the book. We decided that the solution to our homeless situation at that time was to either find somewhere to rent or to secure a house-sitting assignment somewhere in the world. We'd never tried housesitting before – an arrangement that sounded attractive because it meant living rent free for a while – so we signed up to a housesitting website. We applied to be the guardians of a 500-year-old chateau just outside Bordeaux, France. And, after a few email exchanges and a Skype interview with the homeowners, we were delighted to be offered the job. We flew from Asia to France and found that living in France for six months was the perfect respite between our travel adventures and the perfect writing retreat for me.

What has been your favourite place to visit?

This is a difficult one. There are so many amazing places in the world for so many different reasons. But, if I had to pick just one place as my favourite, then it would be the laid-back island of Utila in the eastern Caribbean. Utila is the smaller of the Bay Islands just off the coast of Honduras. It sits on a beautiful coral reef and is known as a scuba diving paradise. There are no hotel chains or burger franchises or first-world conveniences on Utila – just one main street, friendly people, local traders, dive centres, fresh fish, hammocks strung up between palm trees, white-sand tropical beaches and rum cocktails. I've heard Utila described as the Key West of the 1950's and that is certainly part of its charm. It has been a couple of years since I've been on Utila but I'm heading back there this summer – so while you're reading this book it's probably where I'll be, in a hammock sipping a rum cocktail!

Have you got any funny travel disasters you can share with us?

I have lots – and most are only funny in hindsight! I've been covered in thousands of angry red sand-fly bites in the Caribbean. I've slipped (while totally sober) in Thailand and cut my foot – which then got horribly infected (this also happened to Lori in *The Backpacking Housewife*) proving that no experience for a writer is ever wasted. I used to think I had a strong constitution but while travelling I've had lots of stomach upsets (usually from suspect water or food poisoning) which has led me to me extra careful and vigilant about bug repellent, slippery surfaces while wearing flip flops, and standards of food preparation in tropical places. Is it worth all that to travel the world? Of course!

Do you have any advice for readers who want to follow in your's and Lorraine's footsteps?

There is nothing quite like travelling the world. Experiencing other countries and meeting new people and finding alternative ways to live is a great way to gain worldly perspective. My advice for undertaking a longer length trip is to not plan in too much detail beforehand. This might take you out of your comfort zone. But by remaining flexible with both your outlook and your plans and in having faith that things will work out (in the same way that Lori does in *The Backpacking Housewife*), you will ultimately have a richer and more organic travel experience.

What would you like readers to take away from Lorraine's story?

In *The Backpacking Housewife*, Lorraine realises that happiness and purpose are the two things that she wants and needs in her life and so she sets out on a journey to find them. Despite feeling pain and despair and anger over being betrayed by those closest to her, she overcomes a lack of confidence and shows great strength, dignity and fortitude by walking away from all the negativity in her life. If there is a message in Lori's story for readers, it is to be brave and take positive steps into the world to find their own happiness and purpose.

Who are your favourite authors and have they influenced your writing in any way?

My favourite authors and books constantly change as I discover new ones but Jilly Cooper has always been a firm favourite. Jilly creates fictional worlds and characters that feel real to me, and her wit and unique author voice shines through her writing and her fabulously entertaining books. At first, as a new writer, I used to try and emulate Jilly's writing style – but of course – I couldn't. I had to find my own style and voice.

If you could run away to a paradise island, what or who would you take with you and why?

An easy question at last! I actually do often run away to a paradise island and the only person I want to take with me is my own real-life hero, my wonderful husband, Trav. He is always resourceful and fun to be with and if I ever get stressed he is a calming influence. He's also a Mr Fix-It and if things go wrong he can always be relied upon to make things right. I dedicated *The Backpacking Housewife* to him.